FOR LOVE OF SAPPHIRES

i

5 Star (*****) "Love of Sapphires" Reviews

Roland Cheek's new book, Yogo, is vintage Cheek. He does his homework in a way that allows the reader to experience authentic history in a "Micheneresque" manner - accurate, detailed history balanced with the evolution of predictable and not-so predictable characters, conflicts, and imagery that is spun from the carefully selected words of a master storyteller. Discovering a mother lode of gems goes hand-in-hand with greed, but what happens when the discoverer has the strength of character and wisdom to follow his heart? Can't wait for the sequel!

- Cheri C. Johnson

Very well written and shows evidence of good research. Author does have a gift of period authenticity.

- Anon

Roland Cheek's novel, Yogo, is the first of a planned trilogy telling the story of Yogo sapphires. The story starts with Jake Hoover, a prospector and rugged outdoorsman, who first finds the sparkling, blue gemstones by accident.

Alas, Jake's story is all too typical of western mining, as other people, starting with a local banker, and progressing to English financiers, get in the act.

Other characters drift in and out of the story, such as itinerant cowboy Kid Russell, who is just beginning to realize the artistic talent that would make Charley Russell famous. Another is Jake's love interest, Millie Ringgold, a beautiful African-American woman with a mysterious past, who clings to the anchor of her isolated homestead.

This first story ends with shenanigans of bankers and financiers who scheme to control the development of Yogo Gulch and its blue gems.

Now I'm looking forward to more of the story of the Yogo sapphires and what happened in the years leading up to my wife's earrings.

- Paul F. Vang

This book is hard to put down and contains many interesting historical facts and characters. I am ready for the next book!

- Jack Collins

Additional titles by Roland Cheek

Nonfiction

Learning To Talk Bear
Learn About Elk
Dance On the Wild Side
My Best Work Is Done At the Office
Chocolate Legs
(about the life of a single Glacier Park grizzly bear)
Montana's Bob Marshall Wilderness
(coffee table book about an American wilderness)

Fiction

(six titles from the "Valediction For Revenge" series)
Echoes of Vengeance
Bloody Merchants War
Lincoln County Crucible
Gunnar's Mine
Crisis On the Stinkingwater
The Silver Yoke

The Dogged and the Damned
(World War II New Guinea and the effects of PTSD)

Published in e-book version 2014

For information about permission to reproduce selections from
this book, write To Permissions, Skyline Publishing, P.O. Box
1118, Columbia Falls, MT 59912

Publisher's Cataloging in Publication

Cheek, Roland, 1935---

For Love of Sapphires

1. USA—Montana sapphire mining—Fiction. 2. Jake Hoover
(historical character) --Fiction. 3. Gold Miner. 4. Gemstone
Discovery.I. Title

2014 Library of Congress Number (pending)

ISBN: 0-918981-17-4

Skyline Publishing, P.O. Box 1118, Columbia Falls, MT 59912
http://www.rolandcheek.com
email: roland@rolandcheek.com

Acknowledgments

There's a little guilt-trip taking place here as I put this first title in a four book *Sapphires of Yogo Series* to bed with my name on it alone.

Dick Walsh, former Sheriff of Flathead County started me tracking a *very* interesting story about a bunch of Yogo sapphires that made it from the heart of Montana to an English jewelry firm, to the Crown Jewels of a German principality, into the voracious maw of Hitler's Gestapo, to ... but that's giving away the story, isn't it?

I'm indebted, too, to Don Pfau, the dynamic, well-connected owner of a jewelry store who made it possible to visit the barricaded Yogo Mine site, then put me on to several key publications that I found in Lewistown Montana's Carnegie Library.

Thanks, too, to the kind people in that library who enabled me to copy pages from old books and journals.

The people at Royal American Sapphires, who presently own the Yogo Mine, should receive a gentle nod for information their publicity staff provided relative to both history and future plans for the gemstone lode.

And finally there's Jane, who's been at my side for most of two lifetimes—what a partner she is!

Prologue

In the beginning the earth was without form and void and darkness was upon the face of the deep....

Which may not have been entirely true, for somewhere between those eons of eternal darkness and the start of our story, there came a "big bang" (or at the very least, a series of little bangs) bringing forth our own personal star to rectify the burden of eternal gloom. With daylight replacing darkness part-time, our earth took on more form and less void. Life developed below the face of the deep, taking more and more form until, around 300 million years ago, the Master Builder decided what He had wasn't what He wanted and hit the "delete" button to began anew.

But in the interim, while He was making His first stab at creating life, say during the 300 million years or so before our 300 million, residue from all those dead organic failures—their bones and shells and scales—built up beneath the deep to depths of hundreds or thousands of feet, gradually compressing into deposits of solid rock that today we call limestone. During those first experimental millenniums, much of the North America we know was covered by shallow seas and thus is presently overlain with limestone beneath its soil layer.

Master Builders can apparently become disenchanted with a tedious landform development employing sedimentation alone, and therefore utilize volcanism to more rapidly add building blocks. The volcanisms we're most familiar with, of course, are spectacular ones: Vesuvius, St. Helens, Popocatepetl. But the most prevalent forms of our Master Builder's volcanism sometimes fail to reach the surface until thousands—or hundreds of thousands—of years after its initial movement has ceased, as witness the vast array of igneous "dikes" left standing throughout much of the

West, exposed like medieval walls as surrounding softer rock and soils erode.

Much of the time, however, those churning molten bellyaches from the deep strain against sturdy limestone caprock to succeed only in pushing it up into a dome. Sometimes, though, as one might expect, cracks (known as "fissures") develop in that limestone caprock permitting volcanic magma to squeeze up into them like toothpaste from a cracked squeeze tube.

One such dome and fissure combination (called laccolith) occurs in the northeastern foothills of the Little Belt Mountains, very close to the geographic center of the land division we call Montana. Unlike most other igneous dikes within the region, the particular one occurring in a five-mile-long fissure east of Yogo Creek originated at an intermediate depth and is geologically classified as a lamprophyre. Lamprophyres consist of fine crystals that are iron-rich, but silica-poor. Interspersed within the Yogo dike's composition are light-colored feldspathoids which lightens what would otherwise be a very dark igneous rock.

A unique expression of this particular intrusion is that as it is exposed, its mineral composition weathers more rapidly than the surrounding limestone, breaking down quickly under the onset of rain and snow.

Another, even more unique expression of this particular igneous deposit is that throughout the dike's length, width, and known depth the light-colored, granular lava is shot through and through with randomly scattered sapphires. Hundreds of thousands of sapphires. Perhaps millions. Certainly, millions of dollars worth of sapphires. In fact, more sapphires have been discovered in this single five-mile-long dike than has ever previously been discovered in the history of the world. And thus far, man has merely scratched the Yogo dike's surface. The Yogo Mine is the "mother lode" of the earth's sapphires!

Our story then, presented eventually through a multi-book series—each a stand-alone tale with a dynamite beginning, a riveting middle, and a surprise ending will keep you on your seat-edge. But those tales, each utilizing Yogo sapphires as the warp and woof of their stories weaves together Discovery, Development, Royalty, and Nazi Intrigue to bring to pass a largely unknown end to a surprising tale.

My promise to you is that each of the stories begins—and ends—with those sapphires.

Now, FOR LOVE OF SAPPHIRES....

x

Chapter One

He crouched miserably, with his black handlebar moustache tucked as far into the hollow between the dapple-gray's left foreleg and his barrel chest as the big horse would allow. A worn and tarnished yellow slicker draped over the man's shoulders, and the new hat—the wide-brimmed Pine Ridge Scout he'd just yesterday plunked down two dollars and fifty-seven cents for in Utica—was so soaked that he pulled the brim down on three sides, then shrugged and continued to wait out the storm as the deluge sluiced down the horse's sides and down the wretched man's blocky back.

It was the second cloudburst he'd been caught in during his years in the West, and he muttered beneath his moustache that he should've known better this time around.

The first was down on Gold Creek, where he'd made his initial big strike. Then, at least, he'd been camped along the creek bottom, surrounded by huge cottonwoods and doghair lodgepole pines to blunt the cloudburst's brunt. That storm had hit at night, and was accompanied—as was this one—by flashing lightning that brought the short hairs standing aloft along his arms and legs and neck, and by ear-splitting thunder that caused him to whimper and wonder why, as a youth, he'd left the coast of Maine for Montana's mountains.

Despite his present misery the man grinned. Back then, in order to escape the surging stream, he'd had to snatch his goods and grub amid the hammering downpour and flee up the steep hillside behind his camp. At least, the man thought, this time I don't have to worry about getting caught by a wall of water that turns tiny trickles to a terrifying torrent.

1

After twenty years tromping the Northern Rockies he should've had enough sense to pay attention to the sky. Had he done that, he could've rode off this godforsaken plateau while the getting was good. Instead, like a new-borne babe, he'd blundered on, seemingly without a care in the world.

It'd been dead calm when he'd kicked from his soogan at daybreak, and warm—especially for early May at this elevation. He stood there for a few moments in his bare feet, listening to the two forks of the Judith murmur, one left, one right, and to birds singing their hearts out among the cottonwoods. Overhead, a squirrel chattered and goose music rang from a flight of honkers winging north. "Ahh," the man thought, "a beautiful day! A good traveling day." He scratched at the crotch of his gray and grimy longhandles, exploring a hole on the inside of his left thigh. The back flap of the underwear hung at half mast—a result of two missing buttons—and he sighed and scratched there, too.

Dawn! The best time of day! The man's moustache lifted in a broad grin as he recollected what Kid Russell said when he'd first mentioned the crack of dawn to the youngster: "I didn't hear nothin'."

Sunlight kissed the tops of mountains to the West. The man yawned, then strode barefoot to where his blackened coffee pot squatted among the ashes of last night's fire. Within a few seconds he'd kindled another fire, dipped water from the Middle Fork and hung the pot over it. Then, still yawning, the man unbuttoned the long underwear and waded, underwear and all, into the frigid Middle Fork.

After sputtering and rubbing at his hair, face, and privates (in that order) the man slipped from his longhandles, wrung them out and, bare-assed-naked, pulled on his boots to amble into the meadow where his horse grazed at the end of a picketrope. He said nothing to the pony while tugging the pin loose, nor while

2

pounding it in with a rock in another place. But he did stroke the big dapple's shoulder for a few seconds before again yawning and returning to the fire and his coffee.

Now, face tucked against the gray's shoulder pit, clutching the animal's reins in his fist, he cursed again.

The first thing that should've provided a clue to what was coming was the air's utter stillness. And the warmth. Hell, there's always a chill in the air at dawn in these mountains! Still, he'd blindly ridden onto this open plateau at peace with his world. Even after the little puffs of wind began, and the first small clouds billowed over Yogo Peak, he still had plenty of time to head down off the plateau and take shelter in the pine and fir forest below. But he didn't.

Then the angry, billowing clouds in the west swelled even more and churned gray and black and boiled his way. It was when those clouds gathered the anvils and their black bottoms overwhelmed every stitch of white and most of their gray that the man decided to look around for shelter. Problem was there was none to be had on this open limestone plateau, not a tree, not a boulder or cliff. And when the first flash of lightning forked down, the man decided a lone tree might not be such a good idea for shelter anyhow.

In what seemed only moments, the rushing, churning black mass swept over his head and lightning forked to the plateau by the half-second, and thunder rolled as if he was inside the boiler of a steam locomotive while a chain gang beat its outside with sledgehammers. So the man dropped from his saddle and started leading the skittish gray along a fracture in the limestone where soil lay, grass sprouted, and flowers bloomed.

Then the day turned as dark as twilight and hailstones struck, marble sized and stinging! In desperation, he took shelter against the horse, wrapping reins around each front fetlock and

3

holding tight the loose ends. The hail turned to rain that splattered like dairy cows pissing on a milking room floor. That was when he leaped from beneath the horse long enough to snatch his slicker from behind his saddle and shrug into it. His final preparation to battle the elements was when he turned down the brim of his soggy Pine Ridge Scout and once more snuggled up against a hobbled horse that was at least as miserable as was his master.

Water ran down the limestone fracture faster than its dirt and crumbling rock could take in, and sheets of cloudburst-driven torrents flashed across the surrounding limestone swell, drowning and scouring the scanty vegetation growing there. The mans boots filled within seconds, the insides sloshing from water streaming down his trousers and slicker, the outsides from the freshet he could in no way avoid.

An hour of misery inched past, then the lightning moved on and the roiling black clouds turned to roiling gray ones; the day lightened. The man turned, still crouching beneath the horse, and stared out across the plateau, too dejected to move until at last a summer sun broke through to beat down, bringing steam rising from horse, and man, and the barren plateau.

Duck-walking from beneath the gray, he murmured, "God, horse! We took a beating! Every blade of grass flattened, every flower gone! Hell," he croaked, "even the rock chuck mounds are flat." And he wondered what destruction he'd find waiting for him down in Yogo Gulch?

The man shrugged from his slicker, then pulled off his Pine Ridge Scout and re-shaped the brim. Eventually he jammed the hat back atop his mop of wet, black hair, pulled off his boots, poured out their water, and propped them in the sun. Next came his overalls and the red flannel shirt, followed by his soaked and ragged long underwear. Two washings in one day, he thought. Them drawers won't last long with that kind of abuse. Soon, the

4

only thing the man wore was his hat. Pausing to consider the consequences, he donned the boots from fear they, too, might shrink if left to dry on their own.

It was while the tipping the Pine Ridge Scout to his own preferred tilt that the man's eye caught a sunbeam glistening from a tiny translucent blue stone lying amid a flattened marmot mound. He stooped to pick it up and noticed another blue stone nearby. Hmm, there's another. And another.

The man wandered to a second flattened mound and found more of the translucent stones. He held one to the sunlight, delighting in the way light danced from within.

All in all, while Jake Hoover's underwear and overalls and shirt dried, he collected a couple dozen of the little blue stones, dropping them eventually into his shirt pocket. Then, duds in place, he swung into the saddle for the ride on to Yogo Gulch and the placer claim he'd staked there.

Chapter Two

It was bad in the Gulch, but not as bad as he'd expected. Perhaps only the edge of the storm had struck in the bottoms. Still, the packtrail down had been washed out in three places, and a mudslide overran it in another. And though the man led his single saddlehorse over, around, or through the bad spots, he was glad he wasn't trailing a loaded string of packhorses.

Etienne's shack wasn't there, of course. But the gray's rider expected that. After all, he'd shaken his head when the little Metis had built one corner of his pole-and-shake cabin out over the creek so its owner wouldn't have to pack water or dig an outhouse hole.

Etienne was nowhere to be seen, either, though there were boot tracks in the mud where the cabin had been.

The first humans he actually spotted were Logan and his towheaded boy. Logan had a rope around his tiny log cabin, and a block and tackle roped to a gnarled, old fir tree behind. The father was reefing for all he was worth on the block as the boy levered with a stout pole. "Be damned!" Logan cried. "Hoover! 'Bout time you come back."

Jake Hoover checked the gray, then leaned forward and crossed forearms atop his saddlehorn. "'Lo Willie," he said to the grinning boy. "'Lo Bill. Looks to me like she's off kilter."

"Just a little. Little mud inside, too. Netty Mae said she wouldn't muck it out, though, lessen Willie and me put it back to rights."

"Maybe I'd ought to get down and help," Jake said.

"Maybe you'd ought."

Jake swung down and ground-hitched the dapple. Then he walked over to the towheaded lad and, making like he first

6

plucked it from the boy's ear, handed him a piece of hard candy from the Utica store.

Logan shuffled over to watch as Jake took Willie's pole and used it as a lever to pry up the little cabin's corner. It lifted a little, but that's all. Even a cabin as small as this had weight to it, especially when constructed of logs.

"Etienne's cabin's gone," Jake said as he heaved on a boulder he planned to roll into place as a better fulcrum. "So's Etienne. Seen him?"

"Nope," Logan grunted as he shoved on the boulder.

Soon, both men threw their weight on the lever pole. The pole broke. The towheaded boy laughed. Chuckling, too, Jake helped Logan up. "Looks like we might need a stouter pole, Bill."

"Looks like." Logan scratched his head.

"Then how about you trotting off to find one while Willie and I talk about old times."

With the disappearance of his father, the towheaded boy crept closer to the broad-shouldered newcomer. Jake dropped his arm over the boy's shoulders and said, "What's it look like upstream, Will?"

"Your woodshed's gone, and a whole bunch of your front yard."

"Cabin still there, though?"

"Yep."

"How about Millie?"

"Her place's okay. But most of the ones who lost their cabins and stuff is stayin' there. Hear tell it's some crowded."

Logan returned with a bigger, longer lever and when the two men threw their weight to it, the cabin corner raised to the original foundation level. Jake eased off and said, "We locate a couple of short poles for skids, we'll have her there pretty quick."

After the skids were in place and the cabin corner raised

and propped, both men and the boy reefed on the block and tackle. Each time they threw their weight into it, the cabin slid about an inch. Jake grunted, "Ain't there a team somewhere in the Gulch?"

"Couple of 'em," Logan muttered. "But they're working for somebody else. This ain't the only claim what got put upon today."

Jake nodded. "I'd try the gray, but he don't work for sour beans off the horn." Then he added, "There was boot tracks in the mud, down to Etienne's place. Maybe he's chased off down into the canyon."

Logan shook his head. "Reckon he's lookin' for his shack? If so, he ain't likely to catch it afore the Gulf of Mexico, way that water looked."

It took a half hour before Logan eyed his cabin's alignment and pronounced it good as new. He placed a hand on Hoover's shoulder, saying, "I'm obliged, Jake." Then he said to the boy, "Run tell your ma that we got her home back in place. Then trot on up the Gulch and tell ever'body you see that the Mayor's comin'."

When the boy disappeared around a creek bend, Jake took a dark-colored pint bottle from his saddlebags and pulled the cork with his teeth. "I reckon everybody'll need a shot o' this when I ride on. But it's all I got. Your luck is that Etienne wasn't home and you're the first one I bumped into."

Hoover met Nettie Mae Logan shortly after he left her husband; he tipped his hat and said, "Afternoon ma'am." And he met the tow-headed Willie coming back as he pulled up in front of the wreckage at Birchbaum's claim. He handed Willie another piece of candy, then went to perch on the pile of washed-up debris where Bedrock's placer rocker once stood. This time, Jake didn't bother to say anything; just handed the pint bottle on to the morose old man squatting there.

8

Bedrock's adam's apple bobbed once, then he wiped his lips with the back of a muddy hand and handed the bottle back. "You're a good man, Jake. An angel of mercy. But this is it for me. Damned if I'm going to stay here and starve through another week."

Jake nodded as he tucked the bottle into an overalls pocket. "You'll stick around long enough to see if this big rain uncovered a passel of yellow on the Golden Lady, won't you."

Birchbaum nodded, his long white beard bouncing between his hands. "I reckon. But by God, no color, no stay."

Dutch George Settler and Silas Crabtree busied themselves propping pine poles against the side of Settler's cabin to keep a leaning wall from collapsing. Jake wondered why they bothered— that same plank wall had been leaning the same way for the last three years.

"Howdy, Mayor!" Settler called. "We need to take up the matter of flood insurance to the next Council meeting." Crabtree guffawed and slapped a leg, and Dutch George looked immensely pleased at his sally.

On up the Gulch, Jake Hoover waved to his friends, pausing to help some, and comfort others—at least as far as his meager whiskey went. At every bend, he took in the destruction wrought by the flood: the piles of upstream debris on the inside of each bend, newly ripped banks on the outside; sagging or flattened buildings; ripped out or missing mining equipment. Men labored dejectedly amid the waning light. Usually Jake was met with a greeting or a wave, sometimes even with a wan smile. But occasionally he'd greet one of his friends and have the man turn to stare at him with blank hollow eyes, then wheel back without uttering a sound or waving a hand, to tug at a plank half-buried in mud.

It was in the last vestiges of daylight that Jake reached his

9

own cabin. Like Willie said, the woodshed was nowhere to be seen, but the cabin looked all right—except for a six-foot cutbank almost up to the front door. He led the dapple horse to the back, unsaddled him, rustled up some grain from an oak barrel inside the cabin, then released the big pony to scrounge during the night.

After lighting a lantern, the man checked for leaks in the roof, found none, started a fire, then laughed at the way nature humbled him and all his friends. He strode outside in the darkness to stumble his way down the new embankment for a bucket of water. Back in the cabin, he slapped a pot of coffee on the stove, took a slab of sidepork from his saddlebags and started it to fry. Then he scooped flour from a sack in the same barrel that contained oats for his horse, added a little water, and began kneading a pan of dough.

After he polished off his pork and biscuits, he rinsed the plate, turned off the lantern, turned back the covers on his bunk, and finally slipped from his boots, shirt and overalls. Before he crawled into the bunk, however, the man decided another smoke wouldn't be amiss. So he stuffed his pipe, tamped the tobacco, lit it, and pulled the cabin's single ladderback chair over by the stove. It was while he sat comfortably ensconced in a darkened room lit only by a dying blaze that flickered through a stove crack, bare feet propped upon an empty powder keg, that the cabin's rear door swung open. Hoover didn't bother with a glance. "Come in if you've a mind to; shut the door if not."

The door softly clicked. "I didn't see you stop by my place," the newcomer said in a melodious murmur.

Jake chuckled, pushing the powder keg toward his visitor. "Aw, Millie, it looked to me to be crowded enough without me barging in. Besides, maybe you can understand why I wanted to see to my own cabin."

If it hadn't been for the white stripes on Millie Ringgold's long dress—as well as the whites of her eyes, he might not have spotted the woman in the darkened room. By looking close and catching an occasional firelight flicker, Jake decided the dress was the mostly red satin one: his favorite. He also could tell by the way she laid her fingers lightly on his shoulder that he'd been away from the Gulch too long. "Mountain won't come to Mahomet," the woman said in a low voice, "Mahomet'll go to the mountain."

He took the pipe from his mouth. "How are you Millie?"

"Fine as frog's hair," she murmured, jerking a pillow from his bunk to use as a powder keg cushion, settling her long and ample frame to it. "Not enough color comin' from my claims, but it don't take much to get me by." She waited for the man to say something. When he only put the pipe to his mouth and puffed, she said, "Truth is, Jake Hoover, the Bessie Johnson and Dolly Madison, each, produce better than most ever' other claim along the Gulch."

He chuckled and lifted his bare feet to her knees. "That's good. It means all the men's got too much class to steal from a woman's sluices."

She joined him with her own throaty chuckle. "What it really means is they know I'll stove their punkin' heads in if I catch 'em anywhere near my boxes."

Jake Hoover didn't doubt the woman for one minute. Millie Ringgold stood five feet, ten inches in her broad and ample bare feet, and she outweighed most men working along Yogo Gulch by at least ten pounds. Besides, it was a time and in a place where men respected women—all women; even a mulatto woman. Not to mention the question: what woman displayed as much range of temperament as the half-black lady perched on his powder keg—the one who beat Carson McDaniels half to death with an axe handle because he abused his horse, yet opened her home in time of distress to neighbors in need?

11

It was a funny thing about Millie Ringgold: she rang true through and through. A man might laugh if he leaned on a plank bar in Lewistown or Utica and heard another man tell how a nigger woman up Yogo way claimed to have once served American Presidents in the White House. But the laugh soon got stomped out of him by every miner along Yogo Creek if he actually tried to laugh about Millie Ringgold while passing through the Gulch. And if that man stayed longer than a day or two, he'd start to wonder if the woman really had served Presidents? After all she didn't just plop down a plate at her serving table like a slattern in most road houses across mining country. Instead, she handled each tin plate as if it was the finest Peking China, and her grace and poise might easily have fit into place in the classiest dining rooms in Saratoga or Saville Row.

Jake wondered, as he had many times, if Millie had been born a slave? But he knew he'd never ask. And he knew she'd never tell. Close, he decided; it was only twenty-six years since Lincoln freed the slaves, and the way he figured, the woman was in her thirties, or at least the late twenties. But, of course, that didn't mean she was born a slave. Lots of babies were born of free negro mothers before the Civil War.

"You goin' to know me when you see me next time, Jake Hoover?" she said, interrupting his thoughts.

"Hell, I can't see you now," he replied, chuckling, "except for the whites of your eyes." He leaned over to pull out the stove's ash grate and tamped out his pipe.

She said, "You staying here tonight."

"I'm staying here tonight. Too many people up at your place to suit me."

She sighed. "It'll make it hard for me to stay and still get up in time to fetch breakfast up there."

He stood. It was the whites of his teeth this time that

12

reflected the flickering light. "I haven't asked you to stay."

"So far as I can recollect, you never have," she said, rising to look down on the stocky man who warmed his butt through a half-mast underwear flap.

Chapter Three

Jake Hoover filed the first placer claim on Yogo Creek in 1878, near the mouth of Skunk Creek. The discovery touched off a rush to the new district, and during the winter of 1879-80, over twelve hundred miners and their families dwelled in Yogo Gulch. As discoverer of the Yogo's gold and the most popular man in the remote settlement, Jake Hoover was elected "Camp Recorder." As such, Hoover's official duty was to put down in black and white the laws enacted at miners' meetings; hence the man's unofficial title as "Mayor" of Yogo Gulch.

Yogo's ore proved scant, however, and the camp's population dwindled as other strikes were made at Maiden and Monarch, Libby and Limestone, Zortmann and Wheeler and the many Elkhorns. A few individuals refused to stop believing that a Yogo bonanza laid just a shovelful away, however—men such as Pete Weatherwax, "Lawless" Harvey Laulis, Eli Shelbey, Henry Sabbington, and the woman Millie Ringgold.

Jake Hoover rode with the outflow of disenchanted prospectors, away from Yogo Gulch. But he didn't ride far. Jake was a man of so many talents that he seldom wanted for things to do or places to go. Popular everywhere, he might pop up anywhere. But he wasn't known to tarry long wherever "anywhere" might be. Industrious and honest, thoughtful and wise, the man's counsel was avidly sought by all of his friends and most of his acquaintances.

He owned a small ranch on the South Fork of the Judith. A superb hunter, he supplied elk quarters and venison haunches to hungry farmers and townfolk throughout much of central Montana. He helped out at roundup and branding on several ranches, then might disappear for months while prospecting remote coulees in

14

far-off places.

But he always came back to Yogo Gulch, for, in truth, Jake Hoover also had trouble swallowing that his second great gold discovery had not proved as successful as that of his Gold Creek first. It wasn't that Jake regretted selling his first "discovery claim" just as it readied to spill out flour gold by the bushel—not at all. Jake wasn't a whiner or sniveler. Neither did he covet money, nor the ease and luxury it could supply. But he did pant after the challenge of discovery, and he did bask in being thought both lucky and shrewd.

It'd been eleven years since Hoover's Yogo "discovery claim," but Pete Weatherwax was still holding. And Millie Ringgold. It made no difference to Jake who hit it big in Yogo Gulch—just that someone did. Sure, he'd like for the lode spilling gold into Yogo Creek to show up on his own claim. But truth tell, Jake Hoover would rather it was Millie who struck it rich. And it wouldn't bother him at all if the big luck came to the feisty Weatherwax, or even the Logans—though Hoover doubted if Bill and Nettie May would hold much longer.

* * *

Jake's lips pursed at thought that Millie Ringgold might soon be the only woman left in Yogo Gulch. He lay in his bunk and stared at his cabin rafters in the dim light filtering through the muslin cloth at the single window. Hell, they're all good people— them as is left. Even Dutch George and Crabtree. They deserve more, every man-jack—and woman—of 'em. The ones left had faith, he'd give 'em that; faith in the Gulch, faith in him as the finder, and faith in him as their keeper.

He wondered when Millie had left his bunk? He'd heard nothing, felt nothing. Of course she'd have to be gone by now. Probably through with cooking and finishing up the breakfast dishes. He grinned. Would he be too late for breakfast? He nodded,

15

still smiling, certain that the only way he'd have gotten breakfast from Millie Ringgold on this morning would've been to beat her back to her own kitchen, no matter how much raw gold he offered to pour into the woman's light-colored palm.

He soon saw it was colder this morning than the one over on the forks of the Judith. He knew it as soon as his bare feet hit the bare floor, long before he could warm his bare bottom at a stove that had been long barren of fire.

After he'd fetched a meal of hardtack and pork rind, washed down with hot coffee that was dark enough to suck black from a well-hole, Jake wandered out to Yogo Creek to cast around, paying special attention to the bedrock uncovered during yesterday's flood. He spotted a couple of limestone cracks that were horizontal with the flow and filled with sediment. He filed them away in his memory to someday dig out and pan. Then he wandered up creek for a distance before returning to amble up Skunk Creek.

Disappointed that no landslides were triggered by the downpour and thus no new rock outcrops brought to light, he nevertheless decided to take some sample pans along the base of the mountainside to the east. Tomorrow, though. Right now, he put all his industry into scratching the dapple gray's ears; he'd found the big horse grazing contentedly up a hillside shoulder where bluebunch wheatgrass sprouted thick and as tall as it ever grew.

Chores done, Jake wandered downstream to help whomever he could find that needed a hand. Millie found him giving comfort to Bedrock Birchbaum, who was putting up a temporary wickiup shelter at his claim. When the woman called his name, Jake turned and spread his hands. "The old fool won't stay at my place. Was he me, I wouldn't stay for one night out on this gravel bar in a wickiup."

16

"You ain't me, though, Mayor," Bedrock growled. "There may be no gold here, but if there be, ain't nobody gonna get it but me."

"I need to talk to you," Millie interrupted.

"Here? Or someplace else?"

"Here'll do," she replied, lowering her already low voice. "We need meat. This camp is about out of food, but meat is what we need the most."

He nodded. "Consider it done."

At dusk, Jake Hoover led the big gray to Millie's cabin, carrying two mule deer does. Then, while Weatherwax and Lawless Laulis skinned and cut up the deer, the Mayor called a camp meeting.

"Millie tells me you're short of supplies," Jake began.

Dud Dichard said, "A bunch of us lost ours to the flood."

Jake nodded. "I know that, you know that. The question is, what are you going to do about it? Millie tells me it'll be another month before you can expect a supply train. Before a month is over, most of you'll have to drill enough notches in your belts to look like a Chinese checker board."

There were a few nods, but no one laughed or said a word, waiting for the Mayor's solution. "You'll have to pool your dust, of course. It'll take me a couple of days to get back to my ranch and round up a packstring. Then it'll take a couple more days for me to get to Utica and back here again. I'm willing to do it. But what I ain't willing to do is try to take a packstring down from the top into Yogo Creek with the trail like it is. So what I want you to do while I'm gone, is a bunch of you chase up there to dig a new trail through the washouts and mudslides. It'll take you the better part of a day, but you'll have four days to do it. Are you game?"

* * *

That night, the livers and hearts and tongues from two deer

17

disappeared into the hungry maws of a dozen miners, along with scrambled brains, diced potatoes, and a green salad of miner's lettuce.

Jake helped Nettie May Logan and Pete Weatherwax with the dishes, then returned to his cabin to find Millie Ringgold already there. In the morning he tanked up with venison steaks and coffee at her place, then poured Millie a handful of translucent blue stones and rode from the camp.

When he returned four days later with eight loaded packhorses, she served him the last of the venison ribs, then poured the blue stones out on her plate. "What are they?" she asked. "They look like pieces of busted whiskey bottles that got rounded in a stream."

"Whiskey! Now that's a thought," he replied. "Down to my cabin there's a fresh private stock."

"Jake, answer the question."

"Hell, I don't know what they are. What's more, I don't care. Right now I'm only interested in the whiskey."

"Well!" she laughed, gathering up the little pebbles. "That's the kind of thing a woman hears that's certain sure to turn her head."

He pushed back his chair and came to his feet. She followed his example, murmuring, "Why don't you trot down to your cabin for the whiskey, and stay here tonight?"

"Too crowded."

"Ain't either. Most of 'em have gone back to their own places, or built new ones. Just Pete and Abe are squatting here, and they're down to Dutch George's swigging spirits you brought in. Even if they wind up here tonight, they'll sleep in the lean-to and won't bother none."

"I'm too tired." She put hands to her broad hips and he grinned. "Okay, I got a headache."

She said, "Go on! Get out." He turned for the door. "But if you ain't back with that whiskey in twenty minutes, you'll wish you had."

* * *

Millie Ringgold first appeared in Yogo Gulch during the mid-summer of 1880. Where she got the money to buy Herb Joiner's Running Rabbit and Steve Frauson's Gold Bug nobody ever knew. Nobody learned where she came from either. Or why she picked Yogo Gulch. One day, about the time word of the strike at Maiden hit and most everybody else was leaving, she walked into the Gulch. When "Miss Ringgold," as the woman-starved miners first called her, made offers on a couple of adjoining claims that were being abandoned, those offers were snatched up by owners who figured Millie an angel sent direct from Heaven.

Millie Ringgold re-named her two mines after U.S. Presidents' wives, and began working them harder than most of the men still left in the gulch worked theirs. In between, she found time to start a cabin. That cabin turned into more than a cabin when the Mayor of Yogo Gulch wandered by and took a hand in its construction.

Millie, like Jake, was handy at lots of things. When her claims yielded less gold than expected, she started serving meals to hungry miners. Then the woman took in laundry for men who were either too tired or too lazy to wash their own. She stayed put in the lean years as the Gulch continued its decline, too. And along the way, Millie Ringgold became Yogo's "Assistant Mayor" when Jake Hoover was gone from the Gulch.

Later, nobody could ever say when Jake and Millie tumbled into the same bed—even the participants themselves. But somehow they seemed right for each other: never demanding, never angry, never shouting; always giving to the other and to

19

their friends and neighbors, always supportive, always content with what the other brought to their union.

Once, in a melancholy mood, Jake said, "You know, Millie, you might like my ranch if I ever got in a mood to take you there."

She chuckled throatily and propped herself on an elbow to stare at him eye to eye. "If you're leading up to a proposal, Jake Hoover, dump it out of your mind. I ain't the marryin' kind, and neither are you." He pulled her close as she added, "Besides, I won't leave the Gulch, and you won't stay."

"I wouldn't have to come back," he whispered into her ear, "if you parked your fat ass in my South Fork kitchen."

She twisted away, and sat up. As he fumbled for tobacco and pipe she ran fingers through her long black hair and said, "I know what works and what don't work, Jake. And a white man and black woman don't work."

"You ain't black."

"Then you ain't looked."

"Not to me, you're not."

She sighed. "Look, Jake, you're a rare good man. One that I'll admit to being fond of. You're tough and strong and honest. And damn me to hell, you're more pure than you have any right to be. I'm lucky to have any part of you, sure proud to have as much as I get." She turned wide eyes on him as he blew out a first cloud of smoke. "Let's keep it that way, huh? Let's be happy with what we got and not shoot the moon trying for something we don't deserve and will never get anyway."

He stared up at her as he pulled another drag on his pipe and held it. Then he puffed and said, "Okay."

And that was it.

The funny thing was, even though the woman was hungry for money and took in clothes and served meals and provided beds,

20

as far as anybody knew she never sold her body to another soul than Jake Hoover. And what all the other folks in Yogo Gulch never learned was, Millie Ringgold never sold her body to Jake Hoover either.

* * *

"Jake, you've got to tell me what those little blue rocks are."

"I do?"

"You really don't know, do you?"

He laughed. And that's as far as Jake Hoover would go until the next time he showed up in Yogo Gulch and dropped another dozen blue stones into her palm.

One evening, Millie and Jake sat at her dining table, each regarding the other in a strange way. When he winked, she said, "Headache." He laughed, but sat back in his chair, waiting for whatever it was she was going to say. Finally, "Jake, those little blue rocks are jewels. I know they are. I don't know what kind, or if they're worth anything. But as sure as my black kinfolk came out of Africa, those stones are jewels. You've found a source of jewels and I doubt if you even know it.

The man stroked his chin, but said nothing. "Have you tried to find out what they are?" she asked. When he shook his head, she frowned. "Don't you think you should?"

He picked up one of the stones she'd scattered on the table, and held it to the lantern light. At last he dropped it with the others and said, "Maybe I should."

21

Chapter Four

"Pon my soul!" the bronc stomper exclaimed as he dusted off his britches. "Jake Hoover! You ain't made a show here since who flung the chunk."

"Howdy Ben," Jake said, leaning on his saddlehorn and extending an arm over the corral fence to the lanky, shaggy-haired man beyond. "You losing your touch, or is that bald-face needing special work from a bronc peeler who knows how?"

The cowboy turned to fling an angry glance at a sweaty dun horse standing spraddle-legged in the corral. When he wheeled back, Ben Munger wore a gap-toothed grin so wide a hound dog could've shuffled through. "Should you want to stay and play, Jake, you're always welcome. But that dun is off-limits. Him and me, we're still tryin' to come to an understandin'."

"That I can see," Jake chuckled, swinging his head to look at the main house. "Hobson up there?"

"Left this morning early. Driving his buggy. Prob'ly, what with drivin' the town rig, he was headin' for his bank. Had a bag with him, too. Dunno how long he'll be gone."

Jake shook the dapple-gray's reins and wheeled him away. As the horse spun, Hoover raised an arm in salute. "Next time hang with him, Ben."

Munger grinned even wider. "Just a problem of figgerin' where he's goin' next so's I can come down there."

* * *

"Want to see Hobson," Jake said to the teller.

"Yes sir, I'll see if he's in."

"Hell, I can see him through the glass! Tell him Jake Hoover desires a couple of minutes of his valuable time."

"One moment, Mr. Hoover."

22

Jake watched the clerk knock on the bank president's office door, then open it far enough to stick his slick-haired head inside. The man said something, pointing behind him at the same time. But when S.S. Hobson looked up to see Jake, the Mayor of Yogo Gulch was admiring a watercolor painting hanging on a wall of the Fergus County Bank.

"It's been awhile, Jake," Hobson said, striding to his visitor, holding out his hand. "What brings the mountain man to town?"

"This picture, Hob. Got any idea who it is?"

"Certainly. It's by that youngster—Russell. My night herd."

"Shucks, I know that. But do you know who's in it?"

The bank president peered at the painting, then exclaimed, "That's you!" He glanced at Jake. "It is you, isn't it?"

Hoover nodded. "I even remember where it is and when me'n Charlie was there."

Hobson motioned Jake toward his office, then led the way. After the bank officer closed the door, he said, "And what can I do for you? Looking for more grubstake money?"

Hoover shook his head while dumping the contents of a small drawstring sack on Hobson's desk. "You can start by telling me what these are."

Hobson strode around his desk, picked up one of the blue stones, and held it to sunlight streaming through the window behind. "Where did you get these?"

Hoover laughed. The banker reddened, then said, "That was stupid of me wasn't it?"

"Right now I'm just looking to find out what they are."

Hobson shook his head. "I have no idea. Can you get more?"

"I can," the visitor said. "But what good would that do?"

Hobson stared down at the translucent blue stones

23

scattered atop his desk. "Well, if they prove to be some sort of precious stones, knowing there are more where these came from might prove of interest to somebody with money."

"Like you?" Jake said.

Hobson glanced up. "I wouldn't rule it out, Jake. After all, I am your grubstake partner."

* * *

Jake Hoover spent most of the middle months of 1890, wandering the high limestone plateau between Yogo Creek and where the combined branches of the Judith churned. Over a couple of months, digging through marmot mounds, Jake filled a cigar box with little blue stones. But his real purpose was to chart the course of the dike that produced the stones.

As might be expected, by being within easy riding distance of Yogo Gulch, Jake spent much of that mid-summer period at his Yogo claim. His purpose was two-fold: to provide an excuse to suspicious people for spending so much time in the vicinity, and to take shelter from the elements while enjoying Millie Ringgold's company. At his Yogo Gulch gold claim, Jake dug out the cracks exposed during the previous year's flood, washing the contents through his sluice box. He also panned along the mountain face of his claim for any exposed surface gold. In both cases, he raised only four-bits for every dollar's worth of effort. But his activities down in Yogo Gulch provided excellent cover for explorations above it.

On the plateau, Jake surreptitiously dug test holes along the serpentine dike, doing so at night when there was little chance of discovery, then filling in the holes before daylight. He took ore samples of the crumbling rock excavated from below the dike's soil level and was delighted to find that several rocks actually contained more of the blue stones.

Jake's rough survey was that the dike was five miles long

from where it first surfaced on the east to where it disappeared in the rocky jumble of Yogo Canyon. The dike varied in width from as narrow in some places as eighteen inches, to as much as eighteen feet in others. His mean estimate was that the dike averaged about eight feet in width.

Throughout its length and width, Jake found the blue stones.

* * *

"This enough to tickle your fancy?" Jake Hoover asked, sliding a loaded cigar box across Simeon Hobson's desk.

The banker's green eyes never left Jake's black ones as he untied the string holding the cigar box closed. Only when he lifted the lid did Hobson glance down. He closed the lid and slid the box to a desk corner. "Yes, I should think so."

A silence fell as the two men stared, perhaps lost in their own thoughts. "Okay, what now?" Jake asked. "How are we going to find out if there's any worth there?"

Hobson picked up a pencil and tapped it on his desktop. "I have an assayer friend in Helena—Slocum. Do you know him?"

Hoover nodded. "I never had him do any work for me, but I know him. At least I know of him."

"I'll send the box out on tomorrow's stage. We should have some answers back in a two or three weeks."

Again, Hoover nodded.

Hobson said, "Now, let's talk about your discovery."

"Aren't we getting the cart before the horse, Hob? How do we know it's a discovery until we know if it's worth anything?"

Undeterred, Hobson said, "Is it big? Are there lots?"

"Enough."

"Enough for what?"

"Enough for me ... and maybe even enough for you."

Rat-a-tat-a-tat went the banker's pencil. "The stones

25

you've shown me so far are pretty small. Are they all that way? Or are some larger?"

Jake mulled over the question. He shook his head and said, "What you see is what I've got."

Hobson peered at his grubstake partner. "Obviously you're getting them from a placer deposit. Aren't you worried someone else will find it, too? What steps have you taken to protect our interest from someone else's discovery?"

"Come off of it, Hob. I'm not exactly new to the business." Rat-a-tat-tat went the pencil. Hoover shoved his chair back and strolled to the window.

"All right, Jake, how can I get word to you when results of Slocum's analysis comes through?"

Hoover jerked his much abused Pine Ridge Scout from the corner coatrack and said, "I'll either be at my ranch, or else in Yogo Gulch."

* * *

July slipped into August, then August turned to September and September to October. When the aspens yellowed and bared, and the cottonwoods began shedding, Jake Hoover decided he'd better bring in the two dozen cow/calf pairs he'd put out on summer pasture five months before. It was while chousing a cow out of a hawthorn thicket that Charlie Russell popped up alongside.

"You wasn't at Yogo, so I go to your cabin on the South Fork. You wasn't there neither, so I started lookin' for you. Been at it for at least a week. Best time I had all summer." Hoover grinned as the newcomer added, "Why can't you stay better hid?"

"If me staying better hid is desirable, Charlie, then we'll have to spend a little time training these cow brutes to stick tighter to the brush."

"This all of 'em?"

"Far as I know. The brindle ain't here, but she was getting

pretty far along on her span. Anyway, she knows where the barn is, and how to get there. She likes company, too, so either she'll come in or she won't. If she don't come in, no matter how much riding is done won't help."

Jake glanced over at the young man jogging stirrup to stirrup. How old would he be now? Mid-twenties? He remembered when he first bumped into the kid down in Chalmer's Meadows, back in the days when the lad was pure spunk and all of seventeen. Or maybe sixteen....

* * *

He tugged gently on the tiger-stripe buckskin's reins as soon as he spotted the kid. He knew it was a kid even then, sitting on a boulder sprouting on the meadow's far side. Even from here, he could tell that whoever it was, he was dejected as hell.

Jake wrapped his reins around the saddlehorn and fumbled for his pipe. The buckskin tugged on the reins, found them loose enough to slip, and began to graze, joining the three laden, free ranging packhorses who already had their heads thrust deep into the knee-high meadow grass.

Jake wore a beard in those days, and he'd been out prospecting for a month, so it was possible he appeared more fearsome than normal, what with the pistol belt around his middle, and the .44 rifle slung across his lap from a saddlehorn sling. Not to mention the handle of a big butcher knife sprouting from where it was tucked into its dungaree scabbard.

He stuffed the pipe with long-cut Carolina leaf, then lit it with a match scratched across his teeth—a tactic he sometimes used to jelly strangers' spines. Meanwhile, his horses raised their heads from time to time to gaze at the two ponies hitched across the meadow. Occasionally, the buckskin or his black or gray or palomino would switch at a particularly pesky fly, or maybe wildly shake its mane.

27

Jake took in the two horses, the pinto gelding and the bay mare, followed to the blankets spread on the grass at the kid's feet, the California saddle and the old sawbuck packsaddle stacked nearby. He looked for the makings of a fire, saw none; looked for a camp outfit, saw none.

One of his packhorses started to graze between the black bearded man and the scene across the meadow and Jake growled, "Get back, Morg!" and the palomino turned obediently to the side.

Across the meadow, the kid took a last drag from a cigarette, dropped it into the grass at his feet, ground it out with a bootheel, then considered his options. That flight was one of 'em was clear by the way the kid glanced around for the best escape route. Finally, however, Jake saw him shake his head and pull off a battered gray felt hat, exposing untrimmed sandy hair, that was parted in the middle and hanging unbrushed to either side of his forehead. Finally the kid put both hands on his knees and stared back at the black bearded newcomer. Jake could almost swear the kid swallowed.

So the man clucked at his saddlehorse and as the buckskin strode directly toward the figure perched on the boulder, he saw that the youth wore a patched, checkered flannel shirt and leather trousers that had seen the last of their second-best days. One trouser leg was tucked into a worn-out high-topped boot, the other hung outside its boot, to the ankle. The kid had no weapon in sight. He saw no spurs, no neckerchief, no gloves. Jake glanced again at the other's horses; he clucked appreciatively at the pinto and dismissed the bay.

His buckskin was now only ten feet from the kid and coming on fast. "Whoa, Guts." When the buckskin stopped abruptly, Jake and the youth regarded each other for a moment more, then Jake said, "Where you headed, kid?"

"I don't know."

"You don't know? You sure as hell are a long way from anywhere not to know where you're goin'." The buckskin stretched his nose out to a blanket corner and blew softly into it. "All right," Jake tried again, "what are you doing here?"

"Camping."

"Camping? Where's your camp?"

"You're looking at it."

The bearded man leaned forward. "You short on rations."

The kid's wide eyes never wavered. "Little short all right."

"Uh-huh. Where you headed from here?"

"Goddammit, I'm looking for a job!"

The kid's anger didn't faze the newcomer. Instead, he asked, "You ate?"

"Not lately."

Jake swung from his saddle in one fluid motion. In a moment, he stripped the buckskin's saddle and blanket and dropped his headstall. "Go away Guts," he murmured. The big horse side-stepped away, then lay down to roll as the bearded man stacked the saddle and bridle by the youth's saddle.

"Hey Morg," the man called, and the palomino packhorse moved near. The man deftly released the diamond hitchrope and pulled the canvas cover from the animals packs. The youth's eyes widened when he saw the heavy elk quarters beneath.

"Name's Jake Hoover," the bearded man grunted as he dropped the quarters atop the canvas cover. He stripped Morg's packsaddle, then called, "Hey Sherman, come here."

The gray horse stepped forward to have his ears scratched and his packs of elk meat off-loaded. "I'm a hunter," Jake said as he called the last packhorse, the black, who turned out to be hard of hearing. "A market hunter. Goddamn you Charcoal! Get over here!"

Charcoal ignored him, so Jake stomped after him. The

29

black pony came placidly enough when Hoover, play-acting like he was mad, led him back. As Jake unpacked the black, he added, "I got a place up the South Fork and I keep valley folks who're too busy to hunt supplied with meat." When he finished, Jake turned to the still-seated, wide-eyed youth who yet—it was plain to see— feared the stocky, black-bearded hunter-killer. The man chuckled. "Tell you what let's do, kid. Let's get a fire going and we'll carve off a chunk or two of backstrap and have us some supper. Elk meat, now, goes real good on an empty belly. And I never once seen a kid who didn't have an empty belly."

The youth leaped to his feet and grabbed a coffee pot that had materialized from one of Hoover's packs, then trotted to the creek. Later, while Hoover carved on an elk quarter with his big knife, the kid carried in firewood. Then he stood by entranced while watching Jake cut green willow shoots, impale the elk steaks on sharpened ends, and propped them around the blaze.

While the meat cooked, Jake motioned to the youth's two horses. "They hungry?" The lad turned them loose to graze.

The man watched with amusement as the kid gorged on piece after piece of roasted elk meat. At last the sandy-haired lad sighed, shook his head, licked his fingers, and leaned back against the boulder. The bearded man said, "You ain't much on idle talk are you, kid?"

"I guess I never thought much about it."

"How old are you?"

Again a tinge of resentment. "Old enough."

"Likely," Jake murmured. "You're prob'ly as old as I was when I first came out to Montana."

When the youth added nothing, the man asked, "How'd you happen to pick this spot to camp in, kid?"

"Everybody's got to be somewhere."

"True. But you'll have to admit, it looks a little strange. A

30

still wet-behind-the-ears kid, squattin' in a meadow way up the Judith River, clear in the middle of Montana, no camp, no food. It ain't the way things are generally done."

Both the youth and the bearded man wheeled at a commotion in the meadow. The bay mare had just made an ears-back lunge at Hoover's big gray. Sherman ponderously turned his hind-end toward the mare and began backing his lethal hind feet toward her. He wasn't fooling and the mare was. All again grew quiet except for munching horses. It was growing dusk. Hoover murmured, "Like I said, kid, you're not real talky. The only reason I stopped here was for company. I could've made it on into Utica plumb easy, and slept in a bed tonight."

"I didn't ask you to stop! And ..."

"Hey! Hey! You ain't old enough, big enough, nor armed enough to go carrying a chip around for Jake Hoover to knock off. So do me a favor, huh? Quit the bullshit."

The anger slowly faded and at last, the lad grinned. "You're right, Mr. Hoover. I'm grateful for supper. You don't owe me nothing, and I owe you a lot. What do you want to know?"

"Well, for starters I told you my name is Jake Hoover. You might return the favor, whether it's a name you was born with or not."

"Name's Russell. Charlie Russell." The boy held out a hand; a big smile went with it. "And it's real good to make your acquaintance, Mr. Hoover."

Later, the youth fashioned a charcoal drawing on a piece of Jake's worn-out tent canvas. The drawing was of Charlie's mare in an ears-laid-back lunge at Jake's Sherman horse. Jake held the tattered canvas as gingerly as if it was filigreed gold. "By damn, Kid, this is *good*."

* * *

That's been ten, twelve years ago, give or take, Jake

thought. Now the kid had grown up; enough so, that he was selling a few of his paintings, working for Hobson on one of the banker's two ranches.

They brought the cows and calves into the home pasture, turned horses loose, then stretched their legs in Jake's kitchen, a glass of whiskey in each man's fist. Jake said, "You still getting along with Hobson?"

Russell said, "He's okay. Actually he's not around enough to bother ..." Russell snapped his fingers and said, "That's why I'm up here in the first place—old S.S. sent me after you."

Chapter Five

Jake Hoover mulled over what Charlie Russell said about the Lewistown banker wanting to see him. There was no doubt in Jake's mind that Hobson had word on the blue stones he'd picked up on his way to Yogo Gulch. But almost three months had passed since his grubstake partner had told Jake he'd have word in three weeks. As a result, Jake had wasted the better part of three prospecting months. The least the sonofabitch could have done was let him know there was a delay. And why.

"Take the top of off your head and a body could see wheels grinding," Russell said.

"Sounds like a summons, don't it Charlie?"

The younger man pulled out a sack of Bull Durham and a packet of papers. "Maybe," he mumbled, concentrating so intently on pouring the cigarette tobacco into a single paper laid in the crease between his thumb and forefinger that his tongue was clenched between his teeth. "What difference does it make," he said at last, folding the paper over, rolling it, and licking the edge, "he's got all the money."

"I don't like summonses."

Russell scratched a match on the stove and lit his cigarette. "I don't like summonses either, so maybe I ought to take the message back and you can go on about your business and I can spend another couple of weeks trying to catch up to you."

Jake laughed. When he quit chuckling, Russell took another drag and murmured, "Like I said, he's got all the money. What can a man do?"

"Sometimes he can stand up on his two hind legs and throw his own shadow."

"Like you showed me how with Pike Miller?"

Hoover chuckled again and fumbled for his pipe. "Those were the good old days...."

* * *

The kid was already up, had a fire crackling and coffee pot burbling when Jake rolled from his soogan that first morning they met up. "Conscience botherin' you so's you can't sleep?" the black bearded man asked.

"Had my nap out."

Jake threw his bedroll down near the fire and said, "You ready for some more elk steaks?"

"Yes sir. If you're willing."

It was during breakfast that the boy told Jake about why he was in this meadow at this particular time. "My folks sent me out here from St. Louis with Pike Miller to herd sheep. I didn't like it, so one day I quit. Thought I had a job with the stage line until Pike told a bunch of lies about me. When I found out I didn't have a job, I just started riding. Thought this road would take me somewhere."

Jake chuckled. "Well you weren't all that far from the end of it at my ranch."

Later, breakfast wolfed and meat re-slung on the three packhorses, Hoover, saddle in hand, turned from his horse to say, "You don't get a shake on, I'll leave you here."

"Where we goin'?" Charlie asked as he threw his saddle on the pinto.

"That ain't much of a question, kid. We don't get this meat into the hands of them as can use it, it'll spoil for sure. Then we couldn't buy beans or tobacco at the Utica store."

"Where do I fit in?"

The black bearded man scowled as he turned from cinching up the tiger-stripe buckskin. "Well, now that you turned into better company, could be I could use a partner." Embarrassed at the youth's happy smile, Hoover added, "Likely you'll not

34

amount to much. And you'll certain sure take a lot of training, wet behind the ears as you are. But if you're willing to risk it, I'm willing to take a chance on you."

They'd not gone far when Jake led his little string off the wagon road, down to a sprawl of shacks in a river bend.

"Hey, Jake!" came a shout from the barn. "Maw was sayin' just last night that it was near time for you to show."

Jake introduced Charlie to Bill Givens. Givens said, "You'll stay the night?"

"Can't, Bill," Jake said. "Got other meat to drop. Besides, I know you, if we set to bejabberin' you'll out with your corn liquor and the rest of the meat'll spoil hanging on the ponies' backs."

"Okay, Jake, me'n Maw's got enough meat to take us through supper. Don't dump ours off 'til you get through with your other drops, then come on back with ours. Maw'll hold vittles for you."

Hoover grinned as he swung from his horse and began unlashing a quarter from the palomino. "Can't do that either, Bill. Promised Toad and Lucy I'd stay with them next time I was down."

"Well, hell, stay an extra day. That way you can stay with them and with us."

Jake laughed as he hefted a quarter. "Then I won't get my hunting done and you'll be short on backstraps next time around."

Givens snorted. "The day'll never come when Jake Hoover don't get his huntin' done."

After the quarter was hung, the two men sauntered back to Charlie and the horses. While Jake reset the palomino's remaining quarter atop the sawbuck, Bill Givens said, "Business must be good if you're putting on help."

Hoover chuckled. "Don't know yet if he'll amount to much, but he learns quick. Already he learned to talk and I ain't had him for but part of a day, and one night."

35

"Russell, huh? You the one Pike Miller was talking about? When the youth turned red and his mouth pinched into a fine line, Givens turned to Jake. "Are you right sure he can talk?"

From behind: "What did Pike Miller say about me?"

Givens replied over his shoulder, "Don't rightly know, son. But it don't make no difference. If you're a friend o' Jake Hoover's, that's all I need to know."

It was the same everywhere. Young Russell thought Jake Hoover easily the most popular man in the entire country. Young children would dash from isolated cabins at sight of the fearsome-looking hunter. Hoover might reach down from his saddle and pluck a youngster from the ground to place in front him. Once he rode into a farm yard with one in front, one behind, and one clinging from each stirrup.

It was at that farm that Alvie Pedersen said, "Elk ribs ve vould like, Jake. But no money ve have."

Hoover, still leaning from the saddle and grasping the man's hand, glanced around the farmstead and at the kids and said, "Stuart ain't paid for the roundup yet has he, Alvie? Likely he's not been paid himself. Anyway, you'll get it by and by; you can pay me then." And he swung from his buckskin and unloaded an elk quarter.

Later, packhorses empty, Hoover and his new partner stopped at the Utica Store to pick up a few supplies, then ambled next door to the bar. As soon as they pushed through the batwings, someone cried, "Jake Hoover!" A lanky, cadaverous man detached himself from the bar. The man's hair was shaggy and he had maybe the longest, pointedest, blackest moustache anybody ever saw. "Millie was just sayin' the other day that we ain't seen you in a month of Sundays."

"Howdy, Pete. You down from the Yogo?"

"Where else can I be down from? Not heaven, that's for

36

sure. And hell won't let me stay, neither."

"Well, it's good to see you. You thirsty?"

"Hell of a question. Who's the whelp?"

"Name's Charlie Russell, Pete. He's my partner. Step up here kid and shake hands with Pete Weatherwax. Pete's the pride and joy of Yogo Gulch. Only man ever to take in more gold from the Gulch than he spent trying to find it."

"Pleasure, lad," the cadaverous one said, folding Russell's long sensitive fingers into an enormous paw, then pumping vigorously. "Any friend of Jake's is a friend of mine."

When the boy retrieved his hand, he asked, "You have a gold claim, sir?"

"Sure do, boy. Up Yogo Creek. So does a lot of other folks, including Jake, here. Only reason he ain't got a paying claim is that he never works it."

Hoover pushed Weatherwax toward the bar, leaving young Russell standing at the door. He saw other men lined up in the gloom, with their feet on the rail; all were smiling and nodding at Jake. The youth listened to their greetings, then turned and pushed out the batwings, heading for afternoon sunlight ... and collided with Pike Miller on his way in.

"What the hell are you doing still hanging around this country?" Miller snarled.

"You got a patent on the whole shebang, Pike?" the kid shot back. "Way I figure it I got a right to be here much much as any sheepherder."

Miller backed off a step, the better to look Russell over, from head to toe. He rubbed his chin thoughtfully. "Must've took to stealin' else you couldn't make a living after I spread the word about you."

Charlie clenched his fists until the knuckles and face showed white. But he smiled and said, "Matter of fact, Pike, I got me an honest job where the stink of sheep and sheepherders ain't so overpowering."

"Haw!" Miller said. "Ain't a rancher or farmer worth a shit would have a tinker's farthing to do with a pile of mud like you."

"Aww, Pike," Jake Hoover said, shoving wide the batwings. "I wish you hadn't said that about me."

Miller took another step backwards, then another, until he was off the low porch and out in the street. "Said what?"

"That I ain't worth a shit."

"What in the hell are you talking about, Jake? You know me for a friend."

"I always figured that way. Leastways until you said I ain't worth a shit."

Miller licked his lips. "I said no such a thing."

"So now I am worth a shit. First I ain't, then I am. What is it, Pike?" Again Miller licked his lips. The sheepman, like most ranchers of the day, carried a revolver in a holster belted around his middle. But he had no taste for a confrontation with the dark-bearded, fearsome-scowling man standing before him. Hoover, too, packed a weapon at his waist and a thumb was hooked into the belt only inches away from the revolver's butt. Besides that, the handle of a long-bladed knife thrust up near his other hand.

"What in hell's got into you, Jake? Ain't we always been friends? Why you ask if I said ..." Miller's eyes flicked to young Charlie Russell, then back again. "I see," he said. "Looks like I might have spoke out of turn."

"You're talking about my partner, Pike. Speak badly of one and you speak badly of both." The black bearded man turned to look at the youth. "Now look what you've done! When you said Jake Hoover wasn't worth a shit, you made the boy mad. No tellin' what'll happen now."

Miller's eyes followed Hoover's to the puzzled youth.

38

"Look at him, Pike. You ever seen anybody any madder? Why likely I wouldn't give you a snowball's chance in hell of wiggling out of this without a noggin' rap or two."

Miller spun on his heel and stumbled to his horse.

"Now what do you suppose come over him?" Jake asked as Miller kicked his horse into a trot.

"I don't like to be called kid, Mr. Hoover."

"So what?" Hoover absently replied. "Likely that's something you'll have to outgrow."

"I figure I'm growed enough."

"For what?" Jake asked, staring after Pike Miller's retreating pony.

"To whip the next man who calls me kid, and that includes you, Mr. Hoover."

Jake's eyes widened and he swung back to stare at the red-faced youth. Tufts of sandy hair thrust out from beneath the youth's battered felt hat. For the first time, Hoover saw the outthrust jaw and the snapping gray-blue eyes. Russell's fists were clinched, too.

"I don't overly like the moniker 'Mister Hoover' neither," Jake murmured.

Russell's features relaxed. "I'd look on it as a favor, Jake, if the next round was on me." Then he added, "Only thing is, you'll have to give me an advance on my wages in order to make it work."

* * *

"So what are you going to do about Hobson?" Charlie asked a decade later. "Will you answer his summons? Or do you want me to deliver a message for you? Say something like, 'My dear sir, it is entirely beyond my intent to make myself available for any summons for the next four weeks'?" Charlie opened the stove door and flipped his cigarette stub inside.

Hoover yawned. "No, I'll answer the summons. After all, it's like you say, he's got the money. But right now, all I can think of is the elk I heard bugling up on Russian Flats, a week ago. I'll see Hobson all right. But first, let's you and me go elk hunting."

"What if I get fired?"

"Elk, Charlie! You've got to get your priorities right."

* * *

"You took your sweet time getting here."

Jake Hoover eyed his grubstake partner across the banker's desk. The man's summons after three months of silence still rankled. But a week of elk hunting up around Russian Flats and on High Mountain put him in a better mood. He shrugged and held out his hands, palms up. "Elk done it to me, Hob. It's the way I am. Love me or leave me."

Hobson frowned. "And that's the way you are, even when we have word on the gemstones you found?"

Hoover grinned. "If it'd been any good, you'd have found me yourself. Besides, it took a long time for you to get around to getting word out."

Hobson spun his chair to stare out his office window, then spun back. "Slocum didn't have the foggiest idea what they were either. So he sent them east to get an appraisal from a New York jewelry company. It took them that long to make their appraisal and get back to Slocum. Then Slocum took a while to get back to me. Then you took forever and a day to get back so I can get back to you.

"Sounds like a long way around."

Hobson smiled for the first time. "Yes, it did. However, the wait might've been worth it. The jewelry firm in New York is called Tiffany's. They sent back this bank draft." The banker slid a check across his desk. As Jake picked it up, Hobson murmured, "It's for thirty-five hundred dollars."

40

The bank draft fluttered from Jake Hoover's fingers. "Thirty-five hundred dollars!" he blurted. "For what?"

Hobson slid a sheet of paper over from the corner of his desk. "There's a letter with the draft. Go ahead and read it." As the dazed Hoover reached for the letter, Hobson blurted its contents: "Tiffany's says the stones are extremely high-quality sapphires that are remarkably uniform in color, and remarkably consistent throughout each stone. They also intimate that they might be interested in obtaining more."

"What in hell," Jake Hoover mumbled, still dazed, "is a sapphire?"

Chapter Six

Sapphires are a crystalline form of the mineral corundum, or aluminum oxide. Next to diamond, corundum is the hardest natural material known. Although corundum is, itself, common, its gem-quality crystalline forms are extremely rare. Pure corundum is colorless, but the presence of trace elements produce a broad range of colors. Red crystalline corundum is called ruby; all other colors—pinks, yellows, greens, blues, and violets—are known as sapphires.

The most sought after sapphire color is cornflower blue. It's also the most costly. Corundum gemstones other than blue are indicated by their color, such as "white sapphire," "yellow sapphire," "green sapphire," etc.

Translucent corundum gemstones can contain tiny inclusions that yield a faint silky sheen or, when fortuitously arranged by the Master Builder, a six-rayed star. Star sapphires have a stellate opalescence when viewed in the direction of the crystallographic axis (i.e. down), hence the word "star" sapphire. Star sapphires are usually considered by professional jewelers as the most precious gems in their jewelry lines, particularly those star sapphires of size.

Sapphires occur in silica-deficient igneous environments forming within the bowels of the earth where, it is speculated, the supply of alumina and oxygen may derive from the previous existence of rock containing these elements. Clay is the prime suspect, and clay shale is in many of the sedimentary formations into which the lamprophyre dike containing the Yogo sapphires was intruded. Supposedly developing at "intermediate" depth, it's possible intense pressure wasn't part of the environment in which these minerals were formed. But heat was. Intense heat. Magma-churning heat. Magma-churning heat capable of swallowing pre-existing rock that included a few clay-shale layers.

But what of the varying colors of sapphires?

Color is introduced into sapphires through tiny amounts of iron and titanium, thus providing the chemical ingredients added to the basic corundum formula. The reason these minerals are found in clay is that the lamprophyre dikes tend to decay easily, as all iron-rich rocks do, particularly if they're contained in any kind of original igneous, watery environment—such as that intruding beneath lake or sea; or post-igneous environment in which acids are present in the weathering zone.

Clay, of course, is the common by-product of weathering, but the tight molecular organization of the sapphires and corundum and rubies, together with their extreme hardness, prevent these going to clay as readily as their containing rock.

Corundum crystalizes in the hexagonal, or six-sided, crystal system, and hence may appear roughly in a six-sided barrel shape, as was remarkably prevalent in the cornflower blue corundum crystals found throughout the Yogo dike.

* * *

Jake Hoover knew nothing of the above. Nor would he have understood if someone had endeavored to explain it to him. Nor would he have even heard someone if that someone was talking to him about sapphires while he sat in Simeon S. Hobson's Fergus County Bank office in Lewistown, Montana that November day in 1893.

All Jake Hoover could see was a check for thirty-five hundred dollars! And cigar boxes lined up like cordwood, each filled with handful after handful of blue pebbles robbed from an endless line of marmot and gopher mounds!

43

Chapter Seven

When Jake Hoover finally blinked, he saw the Fergus County Bank President staring at him over the tops of a pair of narrow-frame glasses. "I should think," Simeon S. Hobson said, "our next order of business is how to secure your discovery."

Hoover nodded.

Hobson picked up a pencil and began tapping it atop his desk. His eyes were piercing. "Jake, where is your discovery?"

A faint smile flashed across the darker man's features. He said, "I'll take you there, Hob. But I won't tell you—yet."

The banker saw that it was a matter of trust and was irritated. Tap-tap-tap went the pencil. "Very well," Hobson said. "I presume you wish to stake your own claim first. I presume, also, that you'll stake mine at the same time." Tap-tap-tap went the pencil. "What are placer claim dimensions?" His visitor looked thoughtful, even pensive. Hobson threw the pencil aside and said, "When can I visit the discovery?"

"When are you going out to your Glendennan Ranch?"

"So it's out that direction; I can be there in three days. How long will it take from there so I'll know how long to tell my people I'll be gone?"

Hoover laughed. "Oh, a day or two should do it, Hob. The sapphires might be closer to the Glendennan than a body'd think."

* * *

"Why are we out here on this barren plateau? Spare me your joy rides, Hoover."

Jake had picked S.S. Hobson up at the Glendennan Ranch at sunrise. The outdoorsman straddled his dapple gray and led Morg, the ancient palomino packhorse. Hobson was ready, swinging atop a fast-pacing Tennessee Walker of aloof disposition.

44

The Lewistown banker had expected his guide to take the trail to Yogo Gulch and, three hours after they began, he was not disappointed. But three hours later, when Hoover turned from the well-worn packtrail to weave his way out onto the open plateau, Hobson grew irritated.

Jake reined his gray to a halt, staring appreciatively across the landscape to the distant Yogo Mountain. "Pretty, huh?"

"Yes. Yes it is. But we're not here to ogle the view. At least I'm not." When his black-moustached sidekick only grinned, Hobson said, "All right, then, I'll beg: how much farther is it, Mr. Guide Man?"

Hoover's grin spread until it matched the width of the hair on his upper lip. He swung from his horse. "Might as well fall off your pony, Hob. You're there."

"Come on, Jake. My butt's sore and my patience just as thin. If you want to rest the horses, that's one thing. But if not, it's something else." He swung from the sorrel. "I know, and you know, and I know you know that we've got to get to water in order to get to placer claims. You did file the claims, did you not?'

"I staked them, yes."

"Then how long before we get there?"

Jake's eyes danced. "Long as you want, Hob. This is Hobson Number One. Hobson Number Two is up yonder where the little white flag is fluttering."

Hobson stumbled in a circle, then searched his partner's face for sign he was being made the fool. "I don't understand. You said it was a placer strike."

"No, it wasn't me who said it was a placer strike. You said that, not me."

"Are you telling me the sapphires are out on this godforsaken plateau? How could that be?"

Jake ground-hitched his gray, then bent to place hobbles

45

on the palomino to keep him from wandering. When the outdoorsman straightened, his black eyes still danced. "That's what I'm saying, Hob. You're standing in 'em." He kicked at the soil of a fresh marmot mound. Hobson watched as Hoover bent to sift through the dirt. Soon the moustached man dropped a tiny blue stone in the banker's palm.

Hobson abruptly plopped to a rock. "You mean ... here?"

"That's what I mean."

"Way up here?"

"Yep. In this depression where the grass is growing—see it? See how it meanders along this crack in the limestone? It's a dike that's crumbling away faster than the limestone around it. Comes up through the crack and...."

* * *

By the time Jake Hoover finished showing S.S. Hobson the extent of the dike, shadows were lengthening. He uncovered a storage cache of the crumbling dike rock that he'd earlier dug and hidden during previous explorations, then held out small pocketwatch-sized chunks containing imbedded sapphires.

During the hours the two men spent on the plateau, a brisk wind came up, driving occasional particles of snow with it. Holding his hat in one hand and the Tennessee Walker's reins in the other, Hobson said, "I see claims staked along this entire dike. Are they all ours?"

Hoover grinned. "Got a little carried away didn't I?" The banker waited as his partner gazed up and down the limestone rift, then off to the Big Snowy Mountains. "They're all lode claims. You and me, we've got two each. As discoverers, we've got that right. At least I do. And I claimed double for you, too, as my discovery partner."

"But there're more claims than four here!"

Hoover nodded. "Hell, Hob, there's maybe four miles of

46

this dike. Lode claims are a thousand by fifteen hundred feet—three and a half to the mile."

"Fourteen claims," the banker quickly calculated. "Have you staked fourteen claims?"

Jake's teeth flashed again. "Sure did. We'll try it, see if we can get away with it. Mining law allows a vein to be patented and followed. I think an argument can be made that we're following a vein here. Anyway, it'll be up to the government boys to tell us we're too greedy. If they do that, we can get some of your cowboys to file on any claims they take away."

Both men turned their backs to the biting wind. "Anyway," Hoover added, "by filing on the entire dike, it'll buy us time to figure out what we got and what we're going to do with it."

Later that evening, crouched around a campfire blazing in a Judith River cottonwood grove, S.S. Hobson, holding a steaming cup of coffee, asked, "Jake, did you pick an entire cigar box full of sapphires out of marmot mounds?'

Hoover lifted the lid on a Dutch oven and peered inside. "Yes and no. I could've, maybe. But I wanted to look at the source rock, see how it crushed and panned out."

"And?"

"Panned fine. Crushed piss-poor."

"The dike rock looked soft enough to me."

"Oh yeah," Jake said, turning a frying pan of bannack bread. "It's soft enough all right. Too soft. Too easy to fracture the sapphires inside by crushing it."

"Then how can we get at the sapphires if ..."

Jake shook his head. "Hell, I don't know, Hob. But I do know there's a way. The rock chucks are doin' it. All we got to do is find out how. That's what I meant by filing on the whole dike, we'll have time to find out a bunch of stuff about sapphires and how to get 'em."

The two men were lost in private thoughts as they tore off chunks of bread to soak in platefuls of stew. Then Hobson asked, "But you were able to pan out sapphires from the crushed rock?" When Hoover nodded, the banker said, "How did you do any panning way up there?"

The moustached man nodded out into the darkness where horse bells tinkled, "Loaded up my pony with sacks of crumbled stuff, then brought 'em down here to pan."

"That seems tedious. Wouldn't it be better to put water up there? Say a flume with enough head to sluice with?"

"Now there's an idea," Jake mused. "But you're talking money, Hob. You got any?"

* * *

The claims, Hobson's One and Two and Hoover's One and Two were staked and filed on the widest part of the discovery's lamprophyre-intruded fissure. The claims that were more questionable as to whether the two could keep were on either end, where the dike tended to narrow.

With the claims staked and winter approaching, Simeon Hobson sent young Charlie Russell out to help Jake bring Hoover's own cows down to winter on the Glendennan, then Jake boarded the stage for Helena to legally file their Yogo sapphire claims. Hobson, meanwhile, engaged a capitol city attorney to provide legal assistance and political advice to Hoover.

The extent of permissible lode claims in a gemstone discovery proved beyond the purview of the federal claims office in Helena, and the matter was referred to Washington. Hobson joined Hoover for the Eastern odyssey, which proved successful. While in the East, the two men traveled on to New York City to talk to buyers at Tiffany & Company Jewelers and to display a pouch of additional sapphires they'd taken from their Yogo mine.

The Tiffany buyers continued their interest, particularly in

48

larger stones.

Riding high, the two men stopped off in Chicago to meet with a wealthy friend of Hobson's, James Bouvet. As Hobson had hoped, Bouvet and Hoover hit it off well and, as a result, Jim Bouvet, by pledging $40,000 dollars in development capital, was taken in as an equal partner in Jake Hoover's great gemstone discovery.

Back in Montana, Hobson began a search for the right mining engineer to offer suggestions on mining and sapphire recovery operations. Jake Hoover, too, busied himself by locating a surveyor to begin ditch surveys in the spring, obtaining commitment for a source of needed flume lumber, and made arrangement for sufficient Chinese laborers to bring water the several miles from Yogo Creek to their planned washing site, located in a fold of hills equidistant from the serpentine sapphire lode to the Middle Fork of the Judith River.

With passing of the Ides of March and the first warming breezes of spring to strip drifted snow from their claims, Jake Hoover led mining engineer Auguste Huebner, expatriate of Switzerland but more recently from Butte, onto the limestone plateau. Huebner, as it turned out despite his birthplace amid the European Alps and his present station on the "richest hill on earth," had no taste for the Yogo plateau's raw March wind. And when a series of minor snow storms struck, the engineer whined so much that Jake took him out to the Glendennan and instructed Charlie Russell to get rid of the sonofabitch "anyway you can."

Hoover returned to their claims and began a series of his own experiments, digging buckets filled with the crumbling dike rock, then spreading the rock in shallow limestone depressions, exposing it to weathering. He was still at it on a mid-April day when Charlie Russell rode in, bringing a second engineer, Richard Lloyd, recently from the Mesabi Range, but formerly Cornwall.

49

Lloyd set immediately to work; he analyzed and sketched the dike, heartily approved Jake's location for their mine headquarters and washing site, found Jake's experiment in "weathering" the dike rock interesting, then proposed a tunnel from the washing site through the limestone caprock into the dike. "A tunnel could let your crew work during winter, as well as save the cost of wagon freighting down a mountain road to the washing site. What d'you think?"

Jake Hoover saw; he saw lots of hand-pushed carts on narrow tracks, delivering ore into huge dumps near the tunnel mouth. But it was S.S. Hobson who saw expense. However, when Richard Lloyd ran cost figures on seasonal surface mining, lifting, and wagon freighting, compared to year-'round mining via tunnel and underground vein access, he demonstrated that the cost of the tunnel could be returned in less than a year.

"You'll not need any shoring in the limestone—well, not many timbers anyway. So there's a big saving there. When you get to the softer dike rock, then you'll need to shore. But in the dike, you can go right or left, or up or down, see?"

Tap-tap-tap went the pencil. "How far below the surface will we strike the dike?" Hobson asked.

"My calculations run to about seven hundred feet."

"What if there are no sapphires down that far?"

The Cornishman laughed. "Mr. Hobson, I can assure you those sapphires will be scattered throughout that dike rock for several hundred feet; perhaps several thousand.

"What will a tunnel like that cost?" Hobson asked.

"My calculations are approximately three thousand feet through Madison limestone. With the proper equipment, good miners, and effective oversight, one should be able to project around twenty feet per day at a cost of around a dollar per foot."

"Two, maybe three months," the banker muttered. "Three

thousand dollars." He asked, "What do you think of rendering the rock? What of Mr. Hoover's idea of weathering the stones from the hardrock?"

"Frankly, I'm intrigued by the idea, Mr. Hobson. Much more economical than acid immersion, with its consequent risk of water contamination and workman injury. Few people know that rainwater itself is a very mild form of carbolic acid. Given enough time, rainwater will do the work of stronger, more dangerous introduced solutions. Of course there's still the question as to whether weathering will work, but my guess is that it will since the dike obviously weathers more quickly than the surrounding limestone."

Tap-tap-tap. "How long will weathering take?"

"Only time will tell," Richard Lloyd said, adding, "The big problem with weathering is that it will require massive storage dumps. Larger storage dumps will require front-loading the operation; probably for an entire year before sluicing actually gets under way. The initial investment is bigger, but eventual cost of operations is lower."

Tap-tap-tap. "So, with a tunnel and front loading the ore recovery, we're talking about substantial up-front costs, right?"

"Yes sir. That's true. And we have yet to discuss ore storage platforms to control gemstone wastage as the rock deteriorates." Then the engineer shook his head and chuckled. "At any rate, those costs would be lower than providing sufficient containment for acid treatment, d'you see?"

S.S. Hobson thanked the mining engineer, asked for a written report, provided a handsome check for his consultative services, then dismissed him. After Lloyd had departed, the banker swiveled his chair to stare out the window at Lewistown's muddy main thoroughfare, then swiveled back to say to Jake Hoover, "We're talking a bunch of money here, and you haven't even

51

started your ditch yet."

The black moustached man simply sat in his ladderback chair, legs crossed, arms folded, hat in lap, waiting for the banker to continue.

Hobson didn't disappoint him. "Bouvet will be here next week. He'll want to see the mine, as well as our plans for development. Is there any way we can get a carriage up to that plateau?"

Hoover nodded. "Give me Russell and Munger for a week, along with a draft horse or two, and we'll pioneer enough of a road to get Jim to the claims."

"I can do that. What about the ditch survey. When is your man coming for that?"

"He'll be here next week, too," Hoover replied. "But it'll only take me a couple of days to line him out on where we want the water delivered, then he'll have to figure how high up on Yogo Creek we'll need to go for the diversion. After that, I can take Jim on a tour."

The banker shook his head. "Jake, we're talking about a lot of money up front. Forty thousand might not be enough to get us going, especially now with a tunnel, and probably accumulating ore into dumps for a year in advance. We may be faced with an assessment of the principals."

Hoover's laugh boomed around the room. "Well, don't look at me, Hob. Pretty quick, I'll have to go out and find me an honest job in order to eat; say, go on a couple of roundups, do some market hunting. Or you'll have to give me an advance for being your manager at the mine."

"It may come to the point where we'll have to take in other investors, Hobson muttered.

Chapter Eight

As luck had it Hickson, the surveyor, and his helper, arrived at the Glendennan Ranch on the same day S.S. Hobson arrived with the sapphire mine's third partner, James Bouvet. It was mid-May, during spring run-off, and the streams were high and muddy.

"The river crossing was a little dicey," the banker said to Jake Hoover as he climbed from the buggy. "Will there be any problems getting Mr. Bouvet up to the mine?"

"None I can see. Two crossings, but they're good ones. Besides, I think the run-off peaked yesterday and will be getting easier every day now." Jake turned with a wide grin to the bespectacled portly little man who was rounding the buggy. "Well Jim, I see they let you out of jail. Ain't that a wonder?"

"How are you Jake?" Bouvet said, grabbing the outdoorsman's hand and vigorously pumping it. "I'll tell you it feels good to be back in Montana again, breathing clean, crisp mountain air, seeing horses and cows that run free every night and most days."

Jake turned back to Hobson. "The problem is the surveyors came in earlier this morning and I've got to spend a day or two getting Hickson and his helper started on the ditch. After that, I'll be free to show Jim around." He turned again to the third partner. "How long do you have, Jim?"

The portly man shrugged, holding out his hands palms up. "I'm on no schedule."

Jake nodded. He said to Hobson. "I'll put a packstring together and pull out with Hickson first thing in the morning, then come back for Jim in two days. Will that be okay? Charlie and Ben helped me put a wagon route of sorts up to the claims. That

53

way Jim, you can get up there without having to straddle a bronc."

Bouvet blurted, "Might it be possible for me to go along with you and the packstring? I'll try not to get in the way of the surveyors." When Jake raised an eyebrow, Bouvet added, "I want to see as much of this country as possible. I can ride a horse and I'll carry wood, wash dishes, whatever you'll let me do to share your burden."

Jake glanced questioningly at Hobson. The banker shrugged, so the outdoorsman said to the city refugee, "You got anything besides them town clothes? Something you won't mind getting greasy and smokey and full of horse sweat, and maybe a little of your own sweat?"

"I do."

"Well, I have a tent already set up on the Judith. It's big enough to hold another body, at least for a night or two. And I'd reckon we can round up some blankets here at the Glendennan. If you don't mind sleeping on the ground, then you're on. Just be ready an hour after the sun climbs over yonder horizon."

Bouvet nodded, eyeing the Big Snowy Range to the east.

* * *

Jake kept a close eye on his portly partner all the way up the Judith, watching for some sign that the soft Chicagoan was beginning to flag. He'd been amused when Bouvet loomed at the corrals while Jake was still sorting horses. Bouvet wore leather jodhpurs held up by bright red suspenders. The man's feet were encased in sleek, black, knee-high boots. And his shirt was rich wool plaid; it was overlain with a rough-out leather coat with big lapels and a double row of buttons down its open front. There was a silk bandanna big enough to cover a dining room table, carefully folded and knotted at the neck. All was topped by a white cavalry hat Hoover would've bet was freshly liberated from its delivery box that very morning. Jake had to admit, however, that the

54

ensemble, complete with steel-rimmed eyeglasses didn't seem out of place on the eager, bouncing Bouvet.

At any rate, Jake watched Bouvet carefully at the first water crossing and was pleased at the way the man followed his instructions to keep his eyes fixed on the far shore and rein his horse angling against the current to guide him to the exit point.

Hell no, Jake snorted. It wasn't Bouvet where the problem was, but with that idiot young helper Hickson brought along. He was the one letting his horse drift until Jake had to fire a rifleshot in front of the horse in order to get the pimply-faced young bastard's attention!

And now, nearing the end of their day, it's the kid who's the one whining, not the dude from Chicago. And on top of all that, storm clouds were building in the west, and sure as hell to bring rain.

At their Middle Fork camp, Bouvet practically fell from his saddle and stood motionless for a moment, holding to saddlestrings. When he turned though, there was a broad smile on the greenhorn's face, and he quipped, "I'll say this much, Jake: that was a fine brisk ride on a lovely day." Then the man slipped off his horse's bridle and began undoing the saddle girth. "As soon as I'm through here, you tell me what to do, so I may help."

Again, the kid was worthless. At least Hickson stayed out of the way, but the damned kid kept feeding branches to the fire on which Jake was trying to cook, standing in the way every time the outdoorsman reached for a pot or pan. Finally Jake lost his temper and told the kid if he caught him within twenty feet of the fire until supper was over, "I'll personally turn you bottomside up and beat your pointed little butt until it's raw."

After that, Hickson kept the kid busy polishing survey instruments.

* * *

55

The next morning, they all climbed to the headquarter's site in the rain, and Jake pointed out the delivery point for their water flume. Then, after after their noon meal the party rode up what Jake had begun calling Sapphire Mountain to the trail into the Yogo drainage. "We'll drop down here," he told Bouvet, "in order to give Hickson a feel for where he might pick up a head of water for the coming ditch." At that point, the party split up, with the surveyors returning to the Judith River base camp, and Jake and Jim riding on up Yogo Creek.

Hoover breathed a sigh of relief with Hickson's and his helper's departure. Bouvet, though, was something else, proving a fine companion, eager, though dumb as hell about how one gets along in the western mountains. At least he could saddle his own horse and was good to carry in wood—though most of what he fetched wouldn't burn if you threw it into a Shay engine's flaming firebox. Neither did the man know anything at all about cooking. But he did do a mean dishwashing turn. And he was surprisingly good at helping to tend their horses.

Nope, Jake thought, the only real problem with the guy is his insatiable curiousity about everything. Every tree type, brush type, wildflower; Bouvet wanted to know everything about them. And he displayed excellent retention. The man had an eye for beauty, too, seldom passing an opportunity to pause, drink in, and exclaim over a distant vista or an especially intriguing land formation. But the thing Jake admired most about him was his partner's unflagging cheerfulness. Apparently the man was never dispirited.

Since Jim asked nothing of him except the chance to tag along on Jake's next adventure, Hoover figured the man was his to mould as he wished. That squared well with what the outdoorsman had in mind, for he'd not taken time for himself since that November day almost seven months ago that he learned Tiffany's

56

had paid $3,500 dollars for a cigar box filled with a bunch of blue pebbles. And it'd been three months longer than that since he'd been to Yogo Gulch, seen to his claim there, seen to Millie, guzzled whiskey with Bill Logan and Pete Weatherwax and Bedrock Birchbaum.

Jake was surprised to see Etienne back at his claim; further surprised to see the little Metis building another cabin in the exact same place, with a corner hanging out over Yogo Creek. After introductions had been made, Jake said, "Ain't you afraid you'll lose this one to a flood, too?"

"No, no," Etienne waved dismissively. "The water, she's go down now. No more flood. No more ever." The dark little man waggled a forefinger near his temple. "Etienne, he knows. She bites once, that is all."

Jake grinned. "Whatever you say, old friend." He swung back on the gray, waited for Bouvet to remount, then said, "We'll be heading on up creek, Etienne. It don't get dark so early this time of year, but a man still wears down all the same."

The Logan family was gone, Jake shook his head as he rode past their empty, doorless, sightless cabin. So was Bedrock. The wall on Dutch George's cabin had finally lost its long struggle with gravity and he assumed Settler and Silas Crabtree were no longer there. But Pete Weatherwax strode from his rocker to hold out a welcoming hand; so did Lawless Laulis and Dud Dichard.

"I'll say you're a popular man," Bouvet said as Jake reined his gray toward a woman industriously shoveling gravel into another rocker. "Mayor, eh? That, of itself, is an accord of honor."

The woman had her dress hiked up and pinned between her legs at knee level. She leaned on her shovel and watched the riders approach, no expression at all on her face. Bouvet was surprised to see that she was dark; he saw, too, that her hair was straight and black and hung to the waist. The woman's lips were

57

thick. Black blood there somewhere, thought the portly man.

"Howdy Millie," Jake said, leaning on his saddlehorn. "Been awhile."

"Ain't no fault of mine, Jake. I've not hardly moved from my claims. It's you that's been a little flighty. But then we heard about your sapphire discovery."

"Got a man I'd like you to meet, Millie." The two men swung down. "This is Jim Bouvet. He may look a little funny dressed the way he is, but he's not bad company for a cowboy whose been working his butt off for way too long."

Bouvet strode forward smiling, hand outstretched. Millie's smile appeared faint, with a touch of reserve. Still it was a transformation from the stern Masai matron of a moment before. Her hand was firm and the grip she returned pained the newcomer. "Good day, Mr. Bouvet," she said in a soft melodious voice the man thought must be accompanied by harps strumming in the background. "You, sir, are traveling in what most people who really know him would agree is most esteemable company."

"Indeed," Bouvet said, while retrieving his hand with only the tiniest grimace, "I myself believe so, too."

Jake, gazing up the Gulch, said, "Population's falling off some. The Logans are gone. And Bedrock. They'll be missed."

Millie said, "Bill and Nettie Mae left with Willy before winter set in. Bedrock was gone almost as soon as you left last time. The others sort of trickled away. You're losing your constituency, Mayor. Soon it'll be only me and Pete left."

"Lawless is still here. And Dud."

"So is Henry and Eli. But they'll be leaving before another winter sets in. What brings you back, Jake?"

He laughed. "What else? Gold. You. Not necessarily in that order."

Millie glanced at Jim Bouvet, then returned eyes to await

58

more from the stocky, black mustached frontiersman. "Jim and I'll be camping at my cabin for a few days, Millie. Wonder could you provide meals for us during that time. Jim told me coming in that he'd be willing to pay double the going rate just to get away from any more of my cooking."

Millie noted the look of surprise on Bouvet's face, but very seriously said, "Yes, I will do that. Suppers will be at seven, and so will breakfasts, unless you men desire an earlier start." She glanced at the sun and smiled. "Now I must ask leave if I'm to meet my own supper schedule."

As Jake and Jim walked their horses to Hoover's cabin, Bouvet said, "I'm surprised. That's a cultured lady, Jake. What's she doing in a remote place like this?"

Hoover grinned at his partner. "Nobody knows. Some folks without class has asked and got nowhere." Then he stared soberly down at the trail they trod. "And as you can see, ain't no body big enough, nor tough enough in this gulch to force her to talk."

* * *

"Ma'am," Jim Bouvet said, pushing his plate aside and patting his belly. "That chicken was absolutely delightful. As was the creamed potatoes and dumplings and apple pie. I heard what Jake said about paying double, and I can assure you that no matter what the charges, triple would not be enough."

"I'll swanny, Mr. Bouvet, that's enough to turn any girl's head."

Just then, there came a sharp cry from an adjoining room, and Millie dashed away, returning a few moments later with a baby in her arms. She passed the infant to the dumbfounded Jake without a word. He glanced once at the bundle of swaddling clothes, then his black eyes rose to stare at Millie as she deftly swept up the dirty dishes and carried them to a sideboard where

59

the washbucket sat. "I ... I didn't know, Millie," Jake stammered. "How ... when ... why didn't you send somebody after me?"

She wore the fetching red dress with the white stripes that he so admired. Beneath the hem, Millie wore shoes that she seldom brought out except for the most distinguished company. Her shining black hair was gathered and bound with a red ribbon, and she wore imitation pearls around her throat. Jake could see she'd scrubbed her cracked hands until they nearly bled, and the fingernails had been pared and cleaned since she'd leaned on her shovel earlier that afternoon. The woman planted herself to tower in front of the seated Jake Hoover. "His name is Naseby Ringgold, Jake. He was born on April Fool's Day, and he's been some colicky ever since. But he's mine. All mine. And I'm as proud of him as I can be."

Jake chucked at a tiny chin, then when the child screwed up its face to squall, handed the baby back to its mother.

"May I hold him, please," Jim Bouvet said. Millie eyed the portly newcomer for a moment too long, then delivered her baby to Jim's lap. Bouvet pulled the blanket from around the youngster, looked inside the diaper, turned him over and gently patted him on the tiny back while expertly bouncing him on one knee. When the child burped, then began to cry, Bouvet swept him up and peered into its open mouth. Finally he laid the underside of one wrist on the crease between neck and shoulder and said, "I believe he's a sound infant, Miss Millie, though a little undersize. He'll grow out of the colicky stage, but it'll be some time before he does. I may have some medicine with me that will help."

Millie took the baby back, new-found respect shining in her eyes. Jake said, "Are you a doctor? Hobson didn't tell me ..."

Bouvet shook his head. "A veterinarian, Jake; but a good one nevertheless. Simeon never told you, probably, because he didn't think it was necessary for our partnership.

60

"At any rate, Millie, the baby is a fine one, and growing up here, in this environment, I can imagine he will, in time, sprout hair on his chest."

Back at Jake's cabin, the two men poured a nightcap. Bouvet said, "A remarkable woman, Jake. Remarkable woman. So refined, yet so formidable. One can almost overlook her color because of so many fine attributes." When Jake said nothing, Bouvet mused, "I wonder who the little bastard child's father is?"

Jake threw his glass against the stove and stalked out, slamming the door behind. A moment later, the door popped open and Jake thrust his head in. "I'm sorry, Jim, but the baby is mine. You take the bed. I'll be sleeping at Millie's."

Chapter Nine

Jim Bouvet had the run of Jake Hoover's cabin in Yogo Gulch for two additional nights. Hoover's and Bouvet's first full day in the Gulch was spent visiting with each of the remaining miners, watching them pan and sluice and rocker for gold. Jake also took Jim around his own discovery claim at the mouth of Skunk Creek, actually letting the Chicago veterinarian dig and pan for his own splash of color.

Bouvet, of course, tried as soon as the two men were alone to apologize for his blunder of the evening before. Jake dismissed the attempt by simply saying, "I never heard a thing."

If Millie Ringgold knew Bouvet had belittled the birth of her child, she gave no evidence, remaining her cheerful, efficient self. That she and Jake Hoover were very much in love was, after the film had fallen from his eyes, without question to the bespectacled doctor. That he was basically a kind man without manifest prejudices also permitted him to appreciate the woman's capacity for fine cooking, her surprising serving talents, and her intelligent discourse. And he told her so often.

Millie, of course, swelled at the doctor's compliments. Jake, meanwhile, listened good-naturedly; it was Bouvet's kindness to Millie that seemed to remove the last shred of rancor the outdoorsman might have harbored against the doctor.

To the woman, Bouvet's offer of medicines—a paregoric and a magnesia for her infant's colic—made the doctor ten feet tall to the isolated woman. "All I had to treat little Naseby with was alumroot," she told the men, "and it's hard to gather while snow still covered the hillsides."

Bouvet patted her hand and said, "Children usually get over colic after about three months, so he'll probably be getting better on his own. On the other hand, he's undersized, so it may drag on for four or five months, but he'll be over it in any event pretty quick." Then, while his head was down as he rummaged in a black bag, Dr. Bouvet added, "The best thing for that boy right now is a ready source of nourishing milk, and it looks to me as though he has an abundant supply close to hand."

Millie regarded him steadily with no apparent embarrassment; Jake, oblivious, picked up his hat mumbling that he'd wrangle their saddlehorses.

* * *

Jim Bouvet was made of stern stuff. Though he was by nature diplomatic, it wasn't within the man to shrink from a topic he felt strongly about. So, when he and Jake were halted by snowdrifts far up Yogo Creek the veterinarian said, "Why have you not married the woman, Jake?"

"Not because she's black," the outdoorsman said, twisting in the saddle to catch the doctor's eye. "I asked her to leave the Gulch with me. She won't."

"I see. That would be a problem."

"It's an even bigger problem now," Jake said, obviously referring to the child.

The owl-like eyes of Bouvet flashed from behind his glasses. "She's obviously a lady of some refinement. Cultured isn't she?"

Hoover twisted to face forward, but he said over his shoulder, "Near as I can tell. But I'm not what anybody could call a refinement expert."

The two men spent the day drifting back down the miners' trail, Jake prospecting along the way, Jim simply relishing an adventure amid western mountains with a companion who could handle himself so competently in the wilds.

* * *

63

On the following day, Jake loaded their packhorse, kissed Millie goodby, and chucked his son under the chin. Then the mayor of Yogo Gulch and the veterinarian from Chicago headed downstream to check on the surveyor, Hickson. They were pleased to find a ditch level already roughed in, and Hickson and his helper busy surveying the placement for a diversion abutment and its associated flow spur.

Jordan Hickson slapped at a particularly pesky mosquito and asked Jake, "Will you be for bringing in the Chinks?" When Hoover nodded and told him Han and his boys should begin in a couple of weeks, the surveyor said, "Good! Just the roughed-in route will be good enough for those bastards, as much experience as they've had with the ditches."

Hoover asked, "Any idea how long the ditch will be?"

"Looks like about five miles, give or take. If you'll take our horses back, me'n Luke will mark the route more clearly on our way back to camp tonight."

Jake rubbed his chin as he stared at Hickson's diversion stakes. "Will a dam hold here, Jordan? In a flood, I mean."

The surveyor nodded. "Should. That's why I picked here to put it." He pointed to the limestone sidewalls of the little canyon. "Won't be no new channels cut here." He nodded, as if pleased with himself. "This is where the water runs, and this is where it'll stay—if you properly set the anchor pins. It'll be up to you to put in a solid abutment during low water, one that'll hold when she runs high."

Jake nodded. "We'll be back to camp tonight. Right now Jim and me'll mosey on up to the claims so's he can look 'em over. First one in can make up enough biscuits for company."

Hickson chuckled. "That'll be you, Jake. Me and the boy will be tied up here till late afternoon. Then doin' a better marking job for the Chinks will take most of the rest of the daylight."

Jake Hoover and Jim Bouvet spent the remainder of the day roaming along the fissure providing the basis for their mining operation, identifying claim locations, sifting through marmot mounds for blue stones, digging for chunks of the soft gemstone-bearing ore. At one point, Jake crouched at a marmot mound and cursed.

"Something wrong?" Bouvet asked.

"Yeah, somebody's been pokin' around here ahead of us. See the bootprint?" Then he shrugged and grinned. "That's one of the problems of ownership, Jim: keeping out them as wants to steal from you."

"Tell me about it," the doctor said. "Thieves broke into my Chicago home a couple of years ago and stole ten thousand dollars worth of artwork."

Later, the two men led their saddlehorses down the steep grassy slope to where Jake had his rock samples weathering on a limestone slab. He was pleased to see the soft igneous samples crumbling even more under the onslaught of rain and snow. He tossed Jim an egg-shaped sample with the edges of two sapphires extruding from its sides. "Take this one home with you, Jim," he said. "Put it outside where it's exposed to the weather, then watch it crumble until you can pick out the sapphires." Jake waved a hand across the hundred-foot circumference of weathering samples and said, "If my idea works, we're going to be able to recover the sapphires without a big crushing operation, without acid vats and expensive rendering." Bouvet's spectacles flashed in the sun. "Of course," Jake continued, "the idea means we'll have to mine a year ahead of the washing and screening, stockpiling a hell of a bunch of ore, then spreading it to help it weather. But the cost won't amount to much compared to doing it the hard way, with crushers and stamps and vats and stuff."

Bouvet nodded. "Hobson told me the engineer thought we should give it a try." Then he chuckled. "Old 'S.S.' would always jump at the chance to save a nickel—he's frugal."

Jake grinned. "I'd call him so tight you couldn't shove a needle up his bunghole."

* * *

The following day was spent at the headquarter's site, with Jake pointing out the placement of their proposed buildings, ore storage points, the washers, and catchment riffles. Then, leaving the surveyors, Jake and Jim headed up the South Fork to Hoover's cabin. The following day found them on their way to a picturesque series of meadows called Russian Flats, near the pass into the Musselshell drainage.

"I'll swear, Jake, I've never been in a more beautiful place. These wildflowers! Have you ever seen so many different kinds in your life?"

Jake laid a last piece of slivered kindling wood on the tiny tipi of slivers he'd already propped there. Then the man flicked a match aflame with his thumbnail. He chuckled, held the match to the firewood, then said, "Every time I come up here, Jim."

Bouvet hugged his knees. The leather jodhpurs were showing the wear of hours spent in the saddle and soilings from many campfires, as well as much mucking and panning for splashes of color at myriad tiny creeks. "Do you know them all?"

Jake laughed. "Not on your life, especially if you want their scientific names. I don't do Latin. But that one over there is a 'sugarbowl,' and that one is a 'shooting star,' and that one a wild crocus . . ."

"We have crocus at home," Bouvet interrupted.

Jake waved a hand. "Look out over the meadow. See the taller sea of blue down by the creek? That's iris—you got them at home, too. Higher up the slope is a wave of deeper blue—that's camas. Indians counted on 'em for their diets. We'll dig some of the roots for supper."

"What about the orange ones over by that pile of rocks?"

"Paintbrush. You should have them in Illinois, too."

Bouvet laughed. "We do. I was testing you."

"Ask, then, about the whites. They're strawberry, or mariposa lily, or death camas. Remind me not to dig any death camas roots."

Bouvet watched the fire lick its way up the kindling wood, watched Jake carefully feed larger pieces to the blaze, watched the outdoorsman push the blackened coffeepot close to the fire with his boot. "Jake," the older man said at last, "I envy you your outdoor knowledge, your outdoor competence. But most of all, I envy you your robust good health. I hope you appreciate how important that is to life, liberty, and the pursuit of happiness."

Hoover stared at the fire, then out at their grazing horses. "I hope so, too, Jim. But I'm not sure if I do, having never had any other kind." He rummaged in their gear for a shovel, then added, "Still, I get an occasional hitch in my get-along. And my head hurts if I swig too much rotgut whiskey."

Bouvet laughed. "You're going after the camas roots?"

"Yep."

"Then let's."

* * *

Later, Hoover said of the boiling roots, "They taste a lot like potatoes, but not quite so mealy. They're best roasted in an oven, but to do it right takes a night and a day. And we'll have to get back to see how Hickson is doing before they'd be ready. Besides, first I want to ride to the pass and see if we can spot any elk."

"We're not hunting them are we?" Bouvet asked.

"Nope. If we were, we would've shot the cow at the ranch

67

this morning. But I like to look at 'em."

"Yes. I'm fond of viewing them, too."

Hoover tasted the camas broth, then added a pinch of salt. Then he impaled a couple of raw steaks on sharpened sticks and propped them before the fire. "The cooking won't be as good as Millie's," he said. "But it'll be filling."

Bouvet's eyeglasses glinted as he stretched his jodhpur-clad legs. "Don't try too hard, Jake. I'm not the marrying kind."

* * *

Jordan Hickson was wrapping up his survey report when the two mine owners returned. "Finished the surveys yesterday, Jake," the man said. "You look over the drawings and the report to see that everything is okay. With your approval, me'n Luke will head on back in the morning."

Jake took the diagrams and report and ambled toward a quiet spot along the Middle Fork. "Want to check these over with me, Jim?" he asked over his shoulder.

The doctor shook his head. "I wouldn't have any idea what I was looking for. I trust you."

Hoover returned an hour later. "What about the flume trestles?" he asked. "I don't see anything in here about those."

Hickson shook his head. "You won't either, unless we run a minute survey, with each inch laid out on grade and identifying the exact dimension of each trestle. But you don't want that, Jake. It'd cost way more than you and Hobson laid out to me. Besides, the Chinks will be able to build to their exact needs as they move the ditch along."

"How do I know how much lumber to buy?"

Hickson laughed. "You won't until it's done. Just get 'em enough to begin, then keep 'em supplied. That's what I'd do. If you wind up with any left over, you can use it at the mine mouth."

* * *

68

Hoover and Bouvet rode to the Glendennan with the surveyor and his helper. There, Jake signed off on the bill Hickson presented and the two surveyors climbed into their buggy to head for Lewistown and payment from the Fergus County Bank President. It was the following day when Hoover and Bouvet mounted up for the ride to the same town; S.S. Hobson had sent a letter out to the Glendennan that he was calling for a syndicate meeting as soon as they returned from Bouvet's tour.

The two friends stopped off, however, for a drink at the Utica Bar. And it was the following afternoon before the two bedraggled comrades again pointed their horses east. They met Hobson ten miles out of Lewistown; one look at his hung-over partners and Hobson wheeled his buggy around without a word, leading the cavalcade to town at a punishing trot. At Lewistown, though the hour was late and his partners debilitated, the bank president insisted on convening a mining company board meeting in his Fergus County Bank office. "I want to go over a few things, Jake. One, this bill from Hickson. It seems excessive."

Jake shrugged. "Didn't seem that way to me. That's why I signed it."

"I paid him half. Told him I'd see about the other half after talking to you. Are you telling me the job took eight days!"

"Nope. Two of those days were for travel. We agreed to pay him for his travel to and from the job."

"What about this line item for his helper? One-fifty a day, for Christ's sake! We could hire somebody right out of Dartmouth for that!"

Jake yawned. "He had that in his estimate, Hob. What the hell's got you on the peck anyway."

Hobson threw Hickson's bill on his desk. "The Chinese and the ditch will take the bulk of our capital reserve. Then headquarters construction and the tunnel will take the rest. There's no way we can afford to hire miners and work them for a season on the reserve we presently have. We're either going to have to take in more partners, or subscribe more capital from ourselves."

Jake grunted, "I already told you, Hob, I'm struggling to eat as is. You can't get blood out of a ..."

"Then Jim and I will have to subscribe for your portion by buying some of your one-third ownership."

Jake stiffened and his black eyes narrowed.

Bouvet spoke for the first time. "Let's see our financial report, Hob."

"I don't have one prepared. I just know ..."

"You don't have one? You don't have one! Then why did you call this board meeting if you're not ready to supply a financial statement?"

Tap-tap-tap, went Hobson's pencil. He said, "Perhaps we should adjourn until morning."

Bouvet said, "Personally I think that would be a splendid idea." Then he slapped his knees with both hands and pushed to his feet. "Meanwhile Jake, what do you say to Hob popping for a drink for we thirsty travelers?"

Hoover rolled to his feet; both men faced the seated bank president. Slowly, as if fighting himself for the idea, the banker threw down his pencil and reached into his pocket for a silver dollar. He slid it across the desk. "I'm afraid I won't be able to join you boys. It seems I'm going to have to stay up late in order to put together a financial report."

70

Chapter Ten

It turned out that it was mid-afternoon of the following day before a quorum could be assembled for the first board meeting of what came to be called, before the three-day meeting ended, the Yogo Sapphire Syndicate. The reason for the tardy call to order was soon apparent to the angry Syndicate Chairman, S.S. Hobson as he spied his other two partners' bloodshot, half-lidded eyes, their flushed faces, their unwillingness to face bright sunlight or absorb loud noises.

"I can't believe you both reached your present conditions on the fruits of my single silver dollar," the banker growled as he slammed his office door behind the veterinarian. It was apparent that neither visitor had washed or bathed. Both were unshaven and both had obviously slept in the clothes in which they'd arrived in Lewistown the evening before.

The visitors crept to chairs facing the imposing desk of their host. Hobson handed each a financial report. Both began reading. Hoover was soon snoring. The owlish eyes of Bouvet's swept to Hobson, however, and he said, "This item for eastern travel for Hobson and Hoover: how do you propose to justify this when I was not yet a partner?"

The banker picked up a copy of the statement for himself. "I paid for the entire trip, obviously. Jake doesn't have a pot to piss in. Surely, Jim, you realize there were expenses involved during the run up to establishing the venture."

"Of course I realize that. I also realize Mr. Hoover had many expenses during his search for the gemstones, as well as during the exploration of the lode's dimensions and its proper staking."

71

Hobson nodded. "That's right. However, as his grubstake partner ..."

"As his grubstake partner," the other man quickly broke in, voice rising, "you are entitled to a share. You, nor I are entitled to a lion's share!"

Tap-tap-tap went the pencil. "All right, Jim," Hobson said, "let's be reasonable about this. It's clear we won't have sufficient capital for development, isn't it?"

The flushed veterinarian looked back down at his financial statement. "No, it's not. Not when I see we still have well over thirty-five thousand in reserve."

"I'm trying to look ahead ..."

"I see." Bouvet pulled off his spectacles and squinted at the banker. "But wouldn't it be more prudent to wait at least until we're able to phase in the final cost of the ditch before running like the sky is falling? I, for one, am unwilling to consider an additional subscription until we're able to better project our expenses, probably some months from now. Especially one that would so obviously inconvenience one partner in particular."

Tap-tap-tap.

Bouvet continued, "It seems clear that Jake—as the man indicated last evening—isn't in favor of a subscription at this time either. So it would appear to me that there are two votes against. That leaves only you, Hob. How do you vote on that one?"

Tap-tap-tap. At last, Hobson said, "Then there is little purpose for this meeting, is there?"

Bouvet laughed, then winced at his hammering temples. When the pain subsided, he said, "I think there are important matters to come before this board. But I'll make a motion we adjourn until tomorrow."

Both men glanced at the snoring Jake Hoover. Bouvet said softly, "I do believe Mr. Hoover is in support of the motion."

"I don't have another appropriate time on my calendar."

Bouvet placed his glasses back upon his nose and stood. "Then Jake and I will continue the meeting without you. It only takes two for a quorum when there are only three principals to engage."

Hobson took a deep breath and nodded. "What time would you gentlemen find most appropriate?"

"I'm suggesting tomorrow morning at ten o'clock."

"Very well."

Bouvet started for the door, then turned. "Oh, and one other thing Hob: I don't particularly like this arrangement with you behind a desk and us as supplicants out front. Either bring in a table with three of the same kind of chairs, or find another room where we can meet—perhaps the Odd Fellows Hall down the street."

Tap-tap-tap. Finally Hobson said, "I'll get word to you about the meeting place."

As Bouvet quietly closed the office door, S.S. Hobson was trying to shake Jake Hoover awake.

* * *

The very first order of business as the board meeting of the unnamed sapphire syndicate reconvened, this time in a corner suite in the American House Hotel, was to find a proper name for their mine.

"I propose the Yogo Sapphire Syndicate," S.S. Hobson said.

"I'll second the motion," James Bouvet said.

"All in favor ..."

The second order of business was a proposal by James Bouvet that the Syndicate compensate Jake Hoover for his time as manager of mine construction and operation. Hobson asked if the Syndicate would also care to compensate him for his

73

effort as financial comptroller?

"Of course," Bouvet said. "Especially if the job requires your full attention, as Jake's does."

Hobson looked around for a place to tap his pencil, but since he sat on the suite's single bed he slipped the pencil into the inside pocket of his suit coat.

"I'm curious, Hob," Bouvet said. "How much time have you actually spent as the financial officer of this enterprise?" When the banker merely stared at him, Bouvet said, "An hour? Two hours? Five? Ten? Has it interfered with your present job? With any of your ranch operations?"

Bouvet looked at Jake who appeared bewildered. "I know Hoover has put in several months working on the field end of things. That's several months just since I bought into the partnership. For which he's received nothing."

"Hey men!" Jake cried. "I'm asking nothing." He thought a moment, then added, "Well, maybe enough to let me buy a slab of bacon and a sack of beans."

"How much do you propose Jake should be paid?" Hobson asked.

Bouvet shrugged. "I'm told a miner in Butte gets two dollars a day. I should think our mine manager should get at least as much."

"Would you go for twelve dollars a week until we get the mine producing?" Hobson asked.

"Is that a motion?" Bouvet said.

"I'll make it one."

"Then I'll second it."

"All in favor ..."

"Next order of business," Hobson said. Turning to Jake, he asked, "How will you employ the Chinese? Where will they start? How will they proceed?"

Jake shrugged. "I figure to leave it to Han Lee to decide how to handle the work. I imagine, though, he'll want to do the diversion dam first, but I don't know. Right now I'm more concerned with getting material out there for where the flumes crosses gullies. Hickson said there'll be three—maybe four if Han Lee don't want to dip his ditch back into Jenkin's draw."

"What about the storage heaps?"

Jake stroked his chin. "Well, Hob, I'd like to strip the topsoil off the limestone and see if we can store there. Han's crew can do that after they finish the ditch. But I imagine we'll have to pour some concrete in a few places in order to make a smooth surface as the lode rock deteriorates. Then we'll have to build wings in order to channel the material when we turn the water on it; guide it into the sluice, and finally the sieve." The outdoorsman shrugged. "If we can't use the basement rock, then we'll have to build storage platforms." He shrugged again, adding, "We'll just have to wait and see."

"The thing is," Bouvet said, "you're trying to hold expenditures as low as you can, right Jake?"

Hoover nodded. "If we can use the limestone as base, it'll save us some. By letting Han's crew water-grade the ditch, we saved a bunch over getting a detailed survey and ..."

"What about the mine tunnel and the buildings we'll need for headquarters?"

"I've already talked to Han about putting up a few buildings, one for equipment, one for a barn, then a bunkhouse, a kitchen and dining room, an office."

"Can we hold down initial cost by housing the crew in tents? Perhaps put the office in a tent temporarily?" It was Hobson again.

"Yeah, sure. Until mid-October, maybe. But you can't wait that long to start building winter quarters, Hob."

75

"Are you planning to use the Chinese in the mine?"

Hoover ran a hand over his face. "I don't know. They're the best there is on ditches; I don't know how they are on tunnels. You got any thoughts on it?"

Hobson had his pencil in his hand again. Again, he found no place to tap it. He said, "I question how trustworthy they'll be when it comes to something as easy to conceal as a sapphire."

Bouvet said, "One could say the same thing about gold, too. Or diamonds. Or emeralds. And one could say it if the workmen were white. Or black, brown, red or green. It's a management problem that's still in the future."

"There's some of this stuff I don't know about, boys," Hoover said. "I've never been a hardrock man, so maybe we'll have to learn some things as we go along."

Hobson, still uncomfortable without a surface upon which to wield his pencil, said, "Jake, is there any chance at all of producing sapphires this summer? Anything at all?"

The outdoorsman spread his hands. "Well, sure. I'll try. It may be that when we get water set up at the rendering site that we can bring some ore down from the top, then flood it. Maybe it'll break down faster than we think. Then there's always the chance we can work the gopher mounds for some loose stones. But I sure wouldn't count on us producing a whole lot."

"Even another cigar box. Or two."

Bouvet cleared his throat. "Are we talking about anything that is actionable as far as this body is concerned? Or are we merely visiting?"

Hobson raised an eyebrow to Hoover. "How about it, Jake? Do you have anything you want to bring up?"

Hoover shook his head. "Not if I got approval to go like we planned when we got together in Chicago."

Bouvet said, "You two have management authority to

make any necessary immediate decisions. Right?"

"What about the next meeting?" Hobson said. "Probably we should convene again before winter sets in."

* * *

Han Lee Song led a crew of thirteen industrious Chinese laborers who specialized in water transportation: ditches for sluices, irrigation, municipal supply. They were also experts at constructing flumes, diversion dams, and control headgates. Han Lee's crew was considered such experts, and their work proved so much in demand throughout Central Montana's mining districts that potential employers often had to wait weeks for their services.

Han Lee himself spoke fluent English. He was a jolly little fat man, given to big cigars, and probably the occasional opium pipe. He habitually wore the green corduroy and black leather, low-heeled boots affected by engineers. His crewmen were all clad in their traditional straw hats and gowns, or in loincloths when hard at work.

The Chinese labored as a unit, at a daily unit price that was an unnegotiable thirty-two dollars per day, plus food and shelter.

When Han Lee arrived at the Glendennan to be met by Jake Hoover he was accompanied by a slender assistant with bushy black hair who, Hoover soon understood, spoke no English but was the actual construction boss.

The men went by wagon to the claims, then hiked down to the headquarters site and followed the survey route around to Yogo Creek where the diversion dam was to be placed. Jake stood to one side while Han Lee followed his stern-faced assistant around, taking notes as the other rattled to him in Mandarin.

The assistant gazed around the narrow canyon, then rattled again to Han Lee. "My assistant wishes to know where you will put tents while the diversion dam and headgate is being constructed?"

77

Jake led the two men to a bench a hundred yards above the stream, showing them how he'd cleared space for four tents. "Tell him the tents will be set up by the time his men arrive."

Then the party again followed the survey line back, Han Lee sweating from every pore. The assistant studied each ravine that must be crossed by flume. "My assistant wishes to know," Han Lee said, "if you will be able to reach this spot with the necessary construction lumber?"

Jake nodded. "I have the flume designs back at the Glendennan. All the lumber can be brought in by packhorse."

* * *

The Chinese arrived at the Glendennan on the following Tuesday, and were transported to the top of the plateau by wagon, then the men hiked, carrying their personal belongings, down to their initial camp near the Yogo Creek diversion point.

Meanwhile, Jake worked like two men, moving via packstring their tools and equipment, form lumber for the dam, sack after sack of cement and lime, even some sand. As much as he wanted to do so, Jake found no time to visit Yogo Gulch. There were long packstring loads of lumber to be dropped at each flume crossing; there were massive amounts of rice and vegetables to be packed to the ditch builders' mess tent; there was the ever-incessant need for something unforeseen or something forgotten to be rushed in. Trowels, wheelbarrows, mud buckets, tea cans, mud hoes for stirring concrete, scoop shovels for scooping sand or cement.

As anticipated, Yogo Creek was dropping, allowing a diversion to one side of the canyon while a three-foot dam was constructed halfway across the streambed. Then the stream was routed over the half-dam that was in place and the dam's remainder was finished. Meanwhile, other Chinese labored on the headgate, then began digging the ditch with picks and shovels;

always Han Lee's assistant was there, directing, ordering, checking.

Jake was standing nearby when the first trickle of water was turned into the short ditch; saw the excitement among the laborers as the trickle of water reached the ditch end; then stood in open-mouthed amazement as the gang of singing, happy pickmen and shovelmen continued digging the ditch as the trickle flowed along its bottom, leading the water ever onward, using the tiny stream itself as a water-grade level to keep the ditch on its proper slope.

If in their happy labor, the water proved the ditch to be dipping too fast or rising too much, then progress forward ceased while corrections were made. Occasionally word had to be passed back to Han Lee, the headgate tender, to stop the flow while corrections to the ditch's depth or direction was achieved. Once, flow was stopped while a rock outcrop was tunneled through with rock drills and dynamite. Work never halted on the ditch, however, as the level was continued on by Han Lee's assistant eyeballing the grade and giving instructions.

Jake soon sensed that the real leader of the team was the assistant, and Han Lee merely the language vehicle for communicating to their surrounding world. "Your assistant?" Jake asked Han Lee one day. "What's his name?"

"Ahh, yes. I'm afraid you could not twist your tongue enough to say Chinese name. But he answers to 'San'."

"San? Just San?"

An explosion sounded around the curve of a hill and Jake set out at a jog-trot along the ditch bank. He was soon met by a runner rushing to tell Han Lee to send more water through the headgate. The outcrop had been magnificently breached with a short tunnel. "Excellent!" Jake breathed to no one in particular. It was then that San moved to his side nodding, and they waited together for the water's return along the ditch, watched it flow through the tunnel, then tramped happily together down to the ditch end.

In another hour the laborers trooped back along the ditch to their camp. In a single day, they had brought water along the mountainside for almost a mile, to the first ravine. Tomorrow they would begin the first span.

Not all the Chinese worked on the flume, however. Instead, a small crew went ahead to blow another hole through a second outcrop. "How does your people know they'll do it at the right level?" Jake asked Han Lee.

"Ahh, San say the survey is very accurate." He shrugged and added, "If San is wrong, then there will be two holes in the mountain."

"And if he's right," Jake murmured, "you won't have to stop the water while his men does the drilling."

San placed a headgate at each flume, enabling the gate tender to stay sufficiently close to the leading end of the ditch extension so that he had a fine-tuned control over the need for water, simply spilling what wasn't needed into the ravine below.

Another day and the ditch again flowed along the hillside; miraculously it swept through the second tunnel without any need for reshaping, and on to the second ravine. That second ravine was a longer span, requiring a day and a half to complete. This time, when the crew was split up for flume construction, the second group hiked on to the third flume and started its construction as San trotted between the two construction sites, overseeing both jobs.

On day six of the ditch construction, with the ditch nearing its halfway point, Jake took leave in order to move the Chinese camp down to the Middle Fork, where they would remain until their work was completed. After that, he spent three days packing supplies from the Glendennan to the new camp. At the end of that period, near the end of July, if he listened carefully Jake Hoover could hear shouts and singing as the ditch neared the yet-to-be-constructed mine site.

* * *

There was a celebration to be remembered when water trickled from the ditch's end, above the headquarters site. S.S. Hobson was there, along with a couple of his Glendennan cowboys, including Jake's friend, Charlie Russell. Pete Weatherwax was down from Yogo Gulch, too, as was Raphael Etienne from below the diversion dam. Where the Chinese came up with the fireworks, Jake never learned. Nor where they came up with the rice wine.

Hobson brought a congratulatory telegram from Chicago. He also brought more questions, more complaints on Jake's expenditures, though the ditch was completed well under Hobson's time estimate, at a total cost of less than half both men's projections.

"Let me get this straight, Hob," an angry Jake Hoover said to his partner as both men stood to one side watching the ditch crew's celebration, "you want me to lay the Chinese off without them putting up even one building, without working on the road, or without clearing the dump pad?"

"It seems like a splendid opportunity to cut expenses and spend that money on a mine crew."

Hoover spat between his feet. "And where did you figure we could house the miners?"

"You could temporarily put them in tents. That's what we discussed at the last board meeting."

"The hell it is! You discussed tents! Well, mister, talking about it isn't the same as deciding to do it. Not with winter coming, probably before we can get a bunkhouse up."

Hobson folded his arms and turned to watch a particularly explosive rocket.

"And how about a road? We can't even get any mining equipment up here without a road."

Hobson sighed and turned to his angry partner. "Jake, anybody can build a road. We can get people to work on a road without paying top dollar to the Chinese."

"But can you get men to do the job as fast and as well as those slant-eyed little bastards! I tell you, Hob, the reason the ditch is done now is because we paid good money to men who did one hell of a fine job—a job done better and cheaper than if I'd used the ones you wanted me to use in the first place."

When Hobson ambled toward his saddlehorse, Jake gripped him by the shoulder and spun him around. Though fire flashed from the darker man's black eyes, his voice was soft ... and even. "I'll tell you what I'm going to do, Hob. I'm going to put the Chinese on the road and you're going to say no more. If you got any more complaints, you bring 'em up in the next board meeting."

Hobson twisted away to mount his horse. After he seated himself, he said, "I still pay the bills, Jake. I wouldn't recommend your taking on more than you're authorized to do."

* * *

As things turned out, Jake Hoover didn't put the Chinese to work on the road. Neither did they strip the overburden from the limestone on Jake's proposed ore dump, nor start construction on a single building.

"So sorry, Jake," Han Lee said, "but Mr. Hobson, he say we work no more. So we go to next job."

"That sonofabitch! Forget him, Han Lee. What I'm telling you is we need you here."

82

"No, no. We do not wish to anger Mr. Hobson. He's a big man. He controls all the money. Tomorrow we leave."

Chapter Eleven

Jake Hoover brooded as the Chinese packed their belongings preparatory to hiking out to Hobson's Glendennan Ranch where they would find transport to their next employment. He packed their duffel, tools, and bedding onto packhorses. Later, after dropping the Chinese's gear at the Glendennan, he returned to the camp on the Middle Fork of the Judith, struck the tents, saving only one to use for storage. Finally, Jake packed his horses with all the food remaining after Hobson laid off the Chinese and took it to Millie Ringgold's place in Yogo Gulch.

After spending a few days with Millie and bouncing his son Naseby on his knee, Jake Hoover took up the chase as a market hunter. One month went by. Two. Three. Charlie Russell found him in the Utica Bar.

Jake turned when he heard his name. He didn't smile. He didn't shout. Instead, he slid his whiskey bottle in front of the younger man and said, "When is it?"

"When is what?"

"The thing you're here to summon me for."

Russell poured a generous dash, then leaned over to splash Jake's glass half full. "Next Saturday. Old 'Ess-ess' said to tell you it'll be in his office after the bank closes."

"Will Bouvet be there?"

Russell shrugged, then asked, "Will you be there?"

Hoover threw off most of his whiskey. "Wouldn't miss it for anything, Charlie."

"Hobson said he'd like to talk to you before the meeting."

Jake's smile was grim. "You can just trot right on back and tell him I said that me and him have already talked way too goddamned much."

Russell grinned. "You know, Jake, I might do just that—tell him on my way out of the country." When Hoover failed to ask what he meant, Charlie added, "I'm pulling stakes. Heading for Great Falls. Thought I'd ought to do it before winter."

Hoover nodded, sipped on his remaining whiskey, nodded again, then muttered, "I might come with you."

* * *

Jake Hoover tied his dapple gray to the bank's hitchrack at twenty minutes 'til six on Saturday evening, October 20, 1894. The blinds were drawn inside, but lights were burning. S.S. Hobson let him in at his first knock. "Good you could make it, Jake," he said, as affable as the man ever allowed himself to be. Jake ignored him, striding rapidly across the bank's lobby as Jim Bouvet struggled from his chair, face wreathed in smiles.

Later, after good-natured laughs and backslapping and handshakes, the three men sat around a table, each in equal chairs, while the fall meeting of the Yogo Sapphire Syndicate's Board of Directors began. Hobson called attention to a financial statement he'd prepared and laid before each member. Bouvet expressed surprise that no expenditures were listed after mid-August.

Hobson said the reason no expenditures were listed is because none had been reported.

"Why?" Bouvet asked, though Hobson had already filled him in on Hoover's absence from the mine site.

Obviously annoyed, obviously dreading the impending confrontation, the banker spread his hands and said, "Mr. Hoover has apparently resigned from our employ."

Bouvet pushed forward in his chair. "Is that right, Jake?"

Hoover laughed. "Tell him why, Hob."

"I have no idea."

"You're a lying sack of shit!"

Bouvet held his hands out to separate both men. "All right,

85

it's obvious to me that something is going on that I don't know about. Why don't each of you tell me what it is. Start with you, Hob."

Bouvet's directive caught the banker by surprise. "I already told you my side ..."

"Yes, I know. But Jake hasn't heard your side. In order to clear the air, wouldn't it be better if both parties aired their griefs in the open?"

Hobson shrugged. "In order to hold down costs, after the ditch was done, I suggested to Jake that he terminate the Chinese and employ workmen at a lesser rate."

Hoover laughed again. "I don't suppose you'll admit that you fired them without my knowledge."

"How could I do that, Jake? They were working for you."

Hoover nodded. "So that's your story."

Bouvet said, "All right, Jake. What's yours?"

"Han Lee told me this lying sonofabitch told them their work was finished. When I tried to argue with Han, he said they weren't about to mix it up with the banker—that he was the money man."

Bouvet turned to the banker. "Mr. Hobson, did you in fact tell the Chinese they were being terminated?"

"I talked to Jake about it ..."

"The hell you did! You fired them when I was dead set against it!"

"... I thought he would understand the need for employing people for less money."

Bouvet picked up the financial statement, ran quickly through it, and said, "Well, it seems to me that the ditch ... it is completed, right?"

Both Hobson and Hoover nodded.

"And didn't it come in much lower than our estimate?"

Again both men nodded. Hobson said, "But ..."

"No trouble with them, Jake?"

"You mean the Chinese? Hell, they're less trouble than a corral full of sheep. Worked like the devil was after 'em all day, every day. Got by on a bowl of rice and all the tea they could drink. I wanted them to grade out a wagon road up to the headquarters site, then put up a bunkhouse and a cookhouse, maybe a barn and an office building."

Bouvet looked again at the banker. "Have you really looked at these figures, Hob? Went over their work on the ground?"

"The figures, yes. Of course. On the ground, no. That's Jake's job."

"Well, then, why didn't you let him do it?"

Hobson leaned back in his chair, stared at first one, then the other of his partners. At last he said, "Perhaps I shouldn't have interfered."

Bouvet pounded the table with the flat of his hand. "Now that that's settled, what's the next order of business?"

Hobson looked at Jake. "What are your plans for the mine now?"

Hoover's grin was lopsided, his statement flat. "None now. It's too late this season to do anything more."

Bouvet smiled at Hobson. "Your move," he said.

Hobson said, "Tents? It's surely not too late to grade a road."

"Nope," Hoover snapped. "By the time we round up the men, set up a camp, get their equipment up there—teams, fresnos, scrapers—it'll come freeze up, or a 'norther' will blow in and we'd have to shut it down on account of snow. We lost the only chance we had before winter sets in. And we did that last August. Now the soonest anything can be done is next April maybe, or May. That's the way it is. And that's it!"

Hobson shrugged. "If that's it, then that's it."

"Not for me, it's not," Jake snapped. "I won't be back next April either if I'm going to be second-guessed while I'm out there."

Bouvet cleared his throat. "Calm down, Jake. Your role can be clarified in this board meeting. I'm making a motion that S.S. Hobson be relieved as President of the Yogo Sapphire Syndicate and I be appointed instead."

Hobson turned red, but he recorded the motion. "Do I hear a second?" he murmured.

Jake Hoover said, "I'll second that."

"The vote will not be necessary," Hobson said, sliding his notepad over to Bouvet. He added, "The President is also the Recording Secretary."

"Now," Bouvet said, "I have another motion to make—I'd like to make a motion that S.S. Hobson be relieved as Treasurer of the Yogo Sapphire Syndicate and that duty also be transferred to me."

The rout of Hobson was so complete, the banker himself seconded the motion.

Jim Bouvet smiled at the blocky man with the black moustache. "Your instructions, Jake, is to be in the field as quickly as you can in the spring. That means getting a road in as quickly as possible. Put up buildings as quickly as possible. Do whatever else is necessary to get actual mining operations up and running as quickly as possible. Then get those sapphires out of the ground, dammit."

"Which reminds me," Jake said, pulling two full leather pouches from his coat pockets and throwing them to the table. "You might be interested in these."

Hobson opened one pouch and spilled its cornflower-blue contents across the table. He looked up at the outdoorsman with a raised eyebrow.

"Those came from the cleanup of the samples I spread across a piece of flat limestone last spring."

Bouvet spilled the other pouch.

"They're only maybe a third of a cigar box," Jake added, "but they seem proof to me that my weathering idea will work. Our big problem is to get a bunch of crumbled lode rock out where it's exposed to the weather."

* * *

Jake Hoover spent much of the winter of 1894-95 stockpiling equipment for the Syndicate's summer assault on the sapphire lode. Most of what was needed, he purchased second-hand in Butte: the pneumatic drill and compressed air pump, a fresno and handlebar scraper, two ore cars and six thousand feet of rail. He arranged for April and May use of teams from local farms and ranches in the nearby Judith River Valley; those teams were to be driven by their owners during road construction to the headquarter site. He arranged, also, to have lumber for the planned buildings wagon-freighted to Bill Givens' place above Utica. And when he found that the Chinese had not forgotten S.S. Hobson's instructions to terminate employment at the Yogo Mine, Jake caused handbills to be printed and circulated along the Judith that temporary work was available. "Inquire Jake Hoover, Utica Store, Weekdays, 4 – 6pm."

As soon as ice went out of the ground in late March, Jake Hoover started things moving. Farmers hitched up their teams, and they and their teen-age sons converged on Jake's road, gouging and scraping and picking and shoveling through cuts and dumping fill at the side. "We'll eventually rock it with tailings from our tunnel," Hoover told Givens.

Other laborers from as far away as Lewistown hiked ahead of the road to the mine site and were put to work scraping overburden from the base limestone. After the soil was removed, a

89

mason began work on a retaining wall at the lower end of the scoured limestone, leaving only a headgate through the barricade.

With two dozen men hired, Jake had a tent "city" erected along the Middle Fork. And as soon as the road reached the headquarter's site he had space enough gouged out of the hillside to move the camp nearer the work.

By then, he had a skeleton crew begin work on the tunnel, experienced miners with hardrock experience. Soon they were spilling blasted rock into farm wagons parked below the tunnel mouth; when full, the wagons carted the rock down the road, where men and boys shoveled the slag onto the road surface.

* * *

Then a carpenter picked the best workmen from the lot, and began erecting buildings. With so many men working for wages, armed guards were employed to bring payrolls to the Yogo Mine. When Jim Bouvet visited the operation on the first day of July, the road was in, storage pad and retaining wall cleared and in place, and the buildings half up. The crew was then down to five miners and six carpenters.

"Impressive, Jake," Bouvet murmured.

Hoover shook his head. "The Chinese could've done everything we have here for less money—except for the tunnel—and we'd be a year ahead."

"Will you stockpile before winter?"

"Some. But we'll try to run through the winter as much as we can."

"How long before you reach the lode?"

"Lloyd, the engineer, projected twenty feet per day at three thousand feet. We're doing a little better than that, but we'll still be at it until the first of October."

"Can you go two shifts?"

Jake seemed startled. "I don't know, Jim. I'd have to think

on that; maybe talk to Perkins." He added, "He's the boss on the tunnel."

"Think about it," Bouvet said.

When the veterinarian climbed into his carriage for his return down valley, he said, "The board meeting will be at the Glendennan Sunday afternoon. You'll be able to get away, right?"

Jake nodded. Then he said, "Hobson didn't come with you. Is there a reason?"

"I certainly hope so," Bouvet said. "I instructed him to stay away."

Chapter Twelve

The 1895 summer meeting of the Yogo Sapphire Syndicate didn't amount to much. President James Bouvet's inspection of the mine site had found a beehive of activity, with much of the needed construction actually ahead of expectations. As consequence, the Chicago veterinarian made a motion that Jake Hoover's efforts as mine manager be commended and that his salary be advanced to fifteen dollars per week.

S.S. Hobson seconded the motion, but made an observation that he was still concerned that expenses were so rapidly outstripping income that they would soon be financially in arrears. That caused the three owners to pay close attention to the financial report provided by Bouvet.

Even Jake could see the red line creeping toward their reserve limit. Hobson moved to explore outside investment capital. The motion fell for want of a second, but during the discussion following the motion, Bouvet agreed that an assessment of the principals might be required before another year was out. To Hoover's agitation, Bouvet said, "Don't worry, Jake. If it becomes necessary, I'll advance you your share at no interest."

Hobson stared out the Glendennan's cookhouse window.

* * *

Jake Hoover, after talking to the tunnel foreman Perkins, decided against going two shifts in the tunnel. Instead, he pulled the experienced miners from the shaft to the plateau atop the seam, wagon-freighted the pneumatic drill up to them, then had the crew drill several shallow powder holes. After preparing charges and tamping them into the holes, two hundred yards of the sapphire-bearing dike was dynamited into crumbling rubble. Jake then sent the experienced miners back to the tunnel and employed some of his farmer friends to bring their teams and wagons and strong backs to shovel and wagon-freight the rubble down from the high plateau to the weathering pads.

As the rubble piles grew, Jake turned water from the Yogo ditch on the rock, accelerating the soft rock's weathering.

Though the weathering pads accommodated the gem-bearing rubble from above, it soon became apparent that when the tunnel penetrated the gem-bearing dike there would not be adequate storage room for the mine's routine production. On his own initiative, Jake had his farm crews begin clearing soil from nearby limestone to create additional storage pads.

By then, July had faded into August, and soon August faded into September. It was on the 29th day of September when the tunnel crew holed out of limestone into the soft gem-bearing dike rock. The 29th of September was two weeks to the day until the Columbus Day board meeting of the Yogo Sapphire Syndicate.

* * *

The October board meeting of the Yogo Sapphire Syndicate centered around their mining venture's critical financial position.

"Less than a thousand dollars in reserve!" S.S. Hobson cried. "Jim are you mad? We won't even be able to meet the miner's wages in another month!"

The President, James Bouvet, took the wire-framed glasses from his bulbous nose and said, "Jake, there's more costs in mining than we anticipated here; more people employed. The wagons. Teams."

Jake Hoover nodded. "We talked about it being important to get ore onto the weathering pads; you know, more of it so we could produce more jewels come spring. If I'd waited until we holed the tunnel into the gemstone dike, we'd only just now be able to begin stockpiling." In the ensuing silence, he added, "Well,

93

I talked to Perkins about two shifts, as you suggested, but he didn't think the idea would work until we actually hit the sapphire drift. That meant we wouldn't have much on the weathering pads if I'd waited to do something. So I decided to go after some of the surface ore from the top ..."

"There's nearly two thousand dollars in wagons and teams!" Hobson cut in.

"Ye-e-a-h," Jake said. "But how else you going to get the surface ore down to the pads without we take it the long way around by wagons from the top to the pads? Hell, men, it'll pay off come spring, when we wash it out. We'll have so goddamned many sapphires we'll flood New York with 'em." Jake knew he was rambling, but the cold, hard financial facts rattled him, too.

Additional discussion followed. Bouvet finally said, "It looks like we're either going to have to submit to an assessment, or secure a line of credit for operating expenses from some lender. Hob, give us your advice."

"Well, I wouldn't commit my bank to such a line of credit until we see how the washing process is going to produce in the spring. I don't believe any other Montana bank will be any more likely to do so. Perhaps you know someone in Chicago who'll provide loan guarantees."

Bouvet smiled. "Then that leaves an assessment."

"Or selling some of our shares to outside investment capital," Hobson said.

"Will you go along with an assessment, Hob?"

Hobson sighed. "I'd rather sell shares. But lacking that, I'd rather just close down the operation until next spring. Then see how the cleanup goes."

"Jake?"

The outdoorsman spread his hands. "You boys know I ain't got a pot to pee in. So unless somebody advances me money

94

on my ranch or gold claim or share of the sapphire mine, I'm out of an assessment." He took a deep breath. "But, God! Shut the mine down?" He shook his head, clearly unable to grasp the thought.

"Can you run through winter?" Bouvet asked.

Hoover nodded. "We're underground now, where it's warmer. Moving the ore carts outside will be tough when a 'norther' blows in. But the tunnel mouth and weathering pads— hell, the whole operation—is on the south side of the mountain, so we'll pick up any sun and whatever 'chinooks' blow in from the southwest." He sighed, "Oh, there'll be days when it won't pay to get out of bed. And keeping a wagon road open up there might be a little tough, depending on how bad is the winter, but ..."

Bouvet said, "How about a thousand dollar assessment, Hob? I'll put up Jake's thousand and mine. A thousand from you might give us enough to run through most of the winter. What do you think?"

"I'll do it, but grudgingly. I'd prefer to shut down now, lay the crews off until after we see how the spring cleanup goes."

"Jake?"

The outdoorsman shrugged. "I'd rather not get into debt to you or anybody else. But I don't really want to shut down, either." He turned to stare out a Glendennan ranchhouse window. When he turned back, he said, "I'll leave it to you boys. Whatever you decide is what I'll do."

"Hob?"

Hobson said, "I'll make a motion we terminate further mining operation at the Yogo Sapphire Mine until after spring cleanup."

Bouvet looked steadily at Jake for several long seconds, then said, "Okay, I'll second the motion. Further discussion?"

"Where does that leave me?" Jake said, eyeing Hobson.

The banker said, "Will you consider, say, reduced pay? For reduced work, I mean."

Hoover laughed. "Not on your life. I'm taking me off the payroll and going back to market hunting. Or maybe to my claim over on Yogo Creek. I ain't been over there for four months."

Hobson nodded, satisfied. "That means we won't have any further expenses until cleanup. Is that right?"

Jake laughed again. "It may not be as clean as you think. We've got a lot of money already invested up there in equipment and buildings, let alone all the ore on the weathering pads. We can't just walk away and leave it to the mercies of whoever wants to pick it over. That means a watchman. Maybe two."

The banker said, "You could watch over it from time to time."

Hoover muttered, "So could you. Or Jim could run out from Chicago to keep an eye on things."

Bouvet cleared his throat. "A watchman is necessary, Hob. What about one of your cowboys?"

Hobson nodded. "But we'll have to pay him. I'll send Terwilliger up. He'll work for thirty-and-found."

"Done!" Bouvet said. Then he asked, "How long before you can button things up, Jake?"

"A week. Then I'm going elk hunting."

"Can I come with you?"

Hoover grinned. "Don't know why not." He glanced at the banker. "You can come along, too, Hob. How about it?"

S.S. Hobson actually considered it, then shook his head. "We're starting roundup. I can't get away."

* * *

It took a little more than a week for Jake Hoover to lay off his miners, get them to Lewistown where they could find transport to the outside, then close up the company buildings at the mine.

96

Before leaving, Jake introduced the mine and its equipment to the crippled old cowhand Hobson sent. "There may be somebody up here from time to time, wanting to pick over the ore we got in those heaps yonder," Jake told the new watchman/caretaker. "You'll have to discourage 'em, that's all."

"I reckon I can do that, Mr. Hoover. Mr. Hobson said he'll send out a bunch of 'No Trespassing' signs for me to put up. Soon's they're up, won't be no reason for nobody to come a-calling."

* * *

Before Jake Hoover and Jim Bouvet disappeared into the mountains elk hunting, Jake took a couple of days to visit Millie Ringgold. It was the first time in almost five months since he'd seen the woman and her child. "He's growing, Millie. And he's over his colic, you say?"

The eighteen-month-old Naseby gurgled with delight as his father bounced him up and down on a knee.

"Just like the doctor said he would, he outgrew it."

Jake studied the woman as she bustled about her kitchen. She sure as hell don't put on either weight or airs, he thought. "You getting along okay?"

She paused long enough to trail fingers along his broad shoulders. "I'm all right, Jake. That twenty-five dollars you send up every month puts me and Naseby in the land of milk and honey, honey."

His mouth corners turned down. "Yeah, that's one thing I got to tell you, I got laid off at the mine. I'll send what I can from here on out. But there won't be any twenty-five a month until spring and the mine starts up again."

"You need money?" she murmured. "I don't spend near all you send. You can have what I got left—almost fifty dollars."

Jake lifted the baby, inspected his diaper, then grinned

97

down at the wet spot on the knee of his woolen trousers. He handed the baby up to Millie. "You keep it. That's your nest money in case anything happens to me. I'll send more anytime I can. After spring when we come into fat times with the mine, things'll get better."

Millie thrust diaper pins into her teeth while lifting the infant by the heels with one hand and spreading another diaper beneath with the other. "How goes the mine, Jake? Is everything all right? Or is Hobson still trying to pull the strings?"

Hoover shook his head. "Jim's got him on a tight leash. But we ran out of money. It takes a pile to make a pile, I guess." He stood up to pour himself some coffee, eyeing her with a raised eyebrow. When she told him no, he continued on: "We got enough ore stockpiled to send New York a bunch of cigar boxes full of sapphires. Soon as we get our money back on them, we'll be all right, I guess."

Millie pulled the shoulder of her dress down to shake a breast free, then turned Naseby's eager lips loose on the nipple. "You'll probably turn too much of a hob-knob to come see me," she murmured.

He dug for his pipe, filled it, lit it, then said, "Likely. When I get my own phaeton, with four white horses to pull it and a postilion to hold my cane and a footman to spread the red carpet, then I might find you a little too dusky to fit my taste."

She chuckled. The chuckle was rich and deep, from far off bayous and saltwater marshes. Then she laid Naseby face down in his homemade crib, patted him for a few minutes, then straightened to turn out the kerosene lamp and come to Jake's arms....

* * *

It was the following morning when Jake Hoover told Millie Ringgold what she didn't want to hear. "I don't know,

98

Millie," he said, "I'm not sure I'm meant to be rich. Seems to me like there's too much garbage goes with it."

She turned from the wash bucket to dry her hands. "What in the world do you mean?"

"Like you. I been way too busy all spring and summer and fall even to take a day or two off to visit you. Only time I ever see my friends is on business. Then when you got riches somebody else might want, you got to guard it. Where's the fun in all that?"

She refilled their coffee cups, then took a chair across from him. "It won't always be that way, you silly man. When you do your cleanup in the spring, you'll be able to buy some help. Besides, when they see how much money you made for them, Mr. Hobson and Mr. Bouvet will give you a raise big enough to buy two phaetons and enough darkies to do you well."

"Maybe," he grunted. "But maybe there's some folks whose head ain't shaped for money. Maybe money ain't all that important to them folks. Maybe just watching the sun come up over the Snowies, or a flight of wild geese heading south is more important than enough silver to buy all the whiskey in town. Maybe just holding your hands out to a blazing fire beneath a spruce tree, or listening to horse bells tinkling in a meadow is worth more than a gouty foot propped on a pillow in the finest drawing room of the best club on Fifth Avenue."

Millie drained her coffe cup, then stared down at the dregs in its bottom. The things she saw made her sigh. But she understood; Jake valued his freedom. Just as she valued hers.

* * *

They found the herd of elk over the top, drifting down into the Musselshell drainage. Snow had been deep while following their tracks up and over the pass from Russian Flats. But they'd taken their time and had been amply rewarded by the huge six-point Jim killed with one shot from his brand-new Krag rifle.

"One's enough, Jim," Jake Hoover said, slipping his Winchester back into its saddleboot. "He'll be a load just getting him up and over the top, down to my cabin. I'll do my market hunting a little closer to civilization."

They spent the night in a copse of trees near the butchered elk, letting the quarters freeze for easier packing. The night was bitterly cold, but both men carried wood for the fire and stayed awake most of the night while feeding it.

"Horses are a little gaunted up," Hoover said as he loaded elk quarters the following morning. "So we'll spend another night when we hit the first grass good enough for 'em to paw through."

"You're going to a lot of bother for me," Bouvet said at the next evening's camp. Their tent was pitched alongside an icy stream, just down the hill from a mostly snow-free meadow.

Jake chuckled. "Hear 'em, Jim? It's about the prettiest sound a man can hear out in the mountains."

"Horse bells?" the veterinarian asked.

"Be damned! You're trainable after all."

Both men were silent as they watched tongues of flame eat dead spruce limbs. Slicked-clean tin plates containing only pocket knives and spoons lay at their sides. On the other side of the fire lay a greasy frying pan and a Dutch oven. Steam drifted up from a metal bucket squatting near the coals.

"Jake," Bouvet said in a low serious tone, "I'm a little concerned about you and Hobson, your relationship. There seems to be some subdued animosity that I think should not be there."

The outdoorsman pursed his lips and was still thinking when Jim gently nudged him with a boot toe, "Right or wrong?"

Nodding at last, Jake murmured, "I suppose you're right. Me? I don't want it that way, but I can't help it. He's too niggardly for my taste." He broke another branch for the fire. "I try to get above it, Jim. But if it stands out that plain to you, then I'm not

100

doing a good enough job of hiding it. Maybe I got this thing about folks with money, but I don't think I feel that way about you. And you got more money than God and almost as much as the Pope."

Bouvet laughed. Still chuckling, he said, "I think you're taking Hob too seriously. It's true he's a frugal man, but that's a handy trait to have in a banker. It's also a handy trait to have as a watchdog on a board of directors for the Yogo Sapphire Syndicate." Jim waved a dismissive hand at Jake's attempt to interrupt. "I know, and you know, and Hob knows that you are doing a splendid job as a mine manager. But the man is worried about our finances. It's his place to worry about our finances. We all should. What you must understand is that there's nothing personal about you when old 'S.S.' questions your expenditures."

Jake remained silent too long Bouvet added, "The man was wrong—dead wrong—to interfere with your management, as he did with the Chinese. But I have him broke of that." When the other nodded, Bouvet added, "He's basically a good person, Jake. You must believe that about Hobson."

Hoover growled, "You going to wash dishes? Or do you figure to preach all night?"

* * *

A small herd of elk had apparently grazed around Jake's cabin in the early hours before dawn of the same day Bouvet and Hoover brought their packstring to the door. "Well, would you look at that," Jake drawled. "Why in hell did you have to go clear over to the Musselshell to kill an elk when you could have shot one from the cabin door?"

"I was just following my guide."

"Well, help me get these packs off the ponies and I'll go see if I can rustle up enough more meat to make our time worthwhile."

Jim grained and curried their horses, then turned them

out to graze. He was packing in an armload of firewood for the kitchen stove when, in the distance, he heard Jake's Winchester bark once, then again.

With Jim Bouvet's six point and Jake Hoover's spike bull, and a young cow Jake brought down at the same time he downed the spike, the hunters put together an impressive packstring as they wound down valley with their load of meat. First, though, they thought they would swing by the Yogo Sapphire Syndicate's mine to see how their watchman/caretaker was doing....

Hyrum Terwilliger wasn't doing anything. In fact, Hyrum Terwilliger would never do anything again. Hyrum Terwilliger was dead.

Chapter Thirteen

Jake Hoover found Hyrum Terwilliger lying face down on an ore heap. He'd been shot twice; once in the lower right side at some distance, then in the back of the head at close range.

The two mine owners suspected that something was amiss by a lack of smoke arising from the stovepipe of the tiny office cabin the caretaker had chosen as his winter quarters. Inside, Hoover and Bouvet discovered a three gallon bucket of water on the sideboard and a half-filled pot of coffee, both frozen solid.

"Scrambled eggs—looks like he just finished breakfast."

Hyrum's horse was in a stall in the mining operation's barn. By the great gaps and splintered boards of his stall, the gaunt gelding had apparently not been fed in several days. Bouvet brought a pail of water, then fed the ravenous horse carefully regulated amounts of hay from the loft.

Meanwhile Jake began a search for Terwilliger. Fearing foul play and reasoning the only thing really worthwhile for thieves to steal would be found at the ore dumps, Jake began his search there. Though the body was half-covered with a dusting of fresh snow, it was easy enough to spot.

Returning to Bouvet, Jake instructed the veterinarian to stay away from the body. "We'll want to leave the place as clean of our tracks as possible, so the sheriff can investigate. Poor Hy is dead, so bringing him in won't help."

Then Jake hung a nosebag filled with oats on his dapple saddlehorse and started dropping frozen elk quarters from packhorses. "You'll have to take care of the ponies until I get back, Jim. Probably in a couple of days. I'll pick up a fresh horse at the Glendennan, then trade him off for another at Hanford's Ranch."

When he swung into his saddle, he peered down at his friend. "You're not scared are you?"

"No, of course not," Bouvet snorted. "Besides, I'm armed."

"So was Hyrum, I think. Leastways there's no long gun at the cabin and I know he had one. If it's like I suspect, he got into a shooting match with somebody and lost it. That somebody took Hy's gun when he run off." The outdoorsman studied the veterinarian for a moment more, then said, "There's a bushwhacker out there somewhere, Jim. That means you only tend the animals after daylight and stay holed up in the cabin for the rest of the time. Got it?"

Bouvet nodded. "I got it." Then he slapped the rump of Jake's dapple with his hat.

* * *

Jake Hoover returned from Lewistown in late afternoon of the day after he'd left the Yogo Mine. Sheriff Walker Thompson of Fergus County rolled in driving a buggy twenty hours later. Thompson was accompanied by two deputies and S.S. Hobson, President of the Fergus County Bank.

The Sheriff's investigation disclosed only that Hyrum Terwilliger was killed "... by a party or parties unknown." The subsequent Coroner's Report placed time of death as "... one week—more or less—prior to the victim's discovery."

When the Sheriff and his deputies left, shaking their heads over their inability to uncover any evidence, S.S. Hobson remained to participate in an emergency board meeting with his two partners.

"Well, that cuts it," Hobson said, stuffing another piece of stovewood in the cabin's tiny stove. "What's our plan after this?" Both Hobson and Bouvet waited to hear what Jake had to say.

"There was only one," Hoover said. "I didn't tell the Sheriff because it would've only confused things in his mind, but I

104

found where the killer tied his horse."

"Where?" Hobson and Bouvet asked together.

"To the hitchrack at the blacksmith shop. Reason I found it at all is because it's under roof where no snow covered it."

"Anybody could've tied up there," Hobson said.

"Yeah, that's right. But I shoveled that floor clean myself and even pointed it out to Hy when I was making my rounds; told him this is the way we wanted things to look come spring."

Bouvet peered up at the pacing Hoover through his steel-framed glasses. "What is your interpretation of this, Jake?"

"Well, I thought it over on my way to Lewistown and back. Way I figure it, somebody wants to cut themselves into our sapphires real bad, but they don't got even as good an idea how to recover them as we do. Way I figure it, they just thought they'd go out to the ore heaps and help themselves to a pocketful. So that had to be before the first snow fell—about two weeks ago...."

Bouvet poured three cups of coffee and sweetened each with a generous dash of whiskey. "Go on," he said after he'd handed the cups around.

"Whoever it was knew Hy, or was known by him. That's why he killed him, because if Hy lived, he'd spill his guts about who was trying to steal our gems." Jake took a big sip of his whiskey-laced coffee, then added, "Everything fell together when I found the pile of horse biscuits under roof at the smithy. Two of 'em really. Big piles. The bottom one was frozen when the top one splattered down on top of it. That means a horse stood there twice. Since he shit in more or less the exact same place, it could mean more than just that he was tied in the same place; odds are good it means he was a stud."

"Why a stud?" Hobson asked.

"Studs most always shit in the same place." Jake looked to the veterinarian for confirmation.

105

Bouvet nodded. "That's right. Especially if they're in a corral, or small paddock. I'm not sure if it'd be true in a stud tied to a hitchrack, though."

Jake paused to let the other two wallow his words around in their own minds while he studied the mine layout through the office window. Then, still staring, he said, "Whoever it was knew Hyrum well, probably called him a friend. Knew him well enough to tie his saddlehorse in the stable and come inside for a cup of coffee. If what I think is true, he might even have offered Hyrum a partnership deal for the two of 'em to help themselves.

"I'm guessing they argued. Then the other man went away for a day or two while Hyrum stewed over the fact that his friend wasn't his friend any more. The killer was less sensitive than Hyrum, however, and didn't really know he was no longer welcome at the Yogo. So he rode back and tied his horse under the smithy overhang and, since Hyrum probably wasn't up yet, ambled out to the ore heaps to pick himself a handful of sapphires. Hyrum discovered him out there, fired a warning shot over the killer's head and got wounded in return. Then the killer executed him."

"Hyrum Terwilliger was the most inoffensive man I ever knew," Hobson murmured. "This is awful!"

"How widespread were the dead man's acquaintances, Hob? He worked for you. Did he have many friends?"

The banker shrugged. "He'd only been at the Glendennan for a couple of years. Came here with Shorty Rathdrum from over on the Yellowstone. Rathdrum might be able to help with Terwilliger's acquaintances, but he's in the 'Old Folks' home in Great Falls now. Went there last summer. Couldn't hold up doing his share."

"Well, I'm pretty sure there ain't no stud horses over in Yogo Gulch. And nobody I know with farms along the Judith has time nor patience enough to have a stud horse around. How about the Glendenan, Hob? Any stud horses there?"

"Only out on the range. None of my cowhands rides one—except sometimes Ben Munger when he's breaking a horse that hasn't been cut yet. But Ben? No. Him and Hyrum were friends."

"What about securing our mine?" Bouvet asked. "We can't just leave it unguarded."

"It seems obvious," Hobson said, "that Jake will have to remain on duty. He's known to be both capable and dangerous."

"At the same rate as we were paying Hyrum Terwilliger?" Bouvet said. "Thirty-and-found?"

"Get yourself somebody else," Jake growled. "I've still got a bunch of frozen elk meat hanging in the barn that's got to find their way down to people who'll pay for 'em."

"All right!" Bouvet said, voice rising. "I want you both to stop feuding—we have serious business to conclude. Jake, how much would you have to have to watch this place the rest of the winter?"

Jake shrugged. "Under the circumstances, half pay might bring me back. But more to the point, I think we need two guards here. What happened to Hyrum wouldn't have happened if somebody else had've backed him up."

"That's out of the question," S.S. Hobson said. "We haven't sufficient funds to buy that kind of protection."

Bouvet said, "All right, here's a motion: I'll make a motion that the Syndicate retain Jake Hoover at half-pay; seven-fifty per week to oversee the maintenance and safety of our Yogo Sapphire Mine facilities and assets, AND that the Syndicate authorizes Mr. Hoover to retain a second watchman at nominal wages until normal operations begins in the spring."

Hobson stared at his fingernails until Jake murmured, "I'll second the motion."

"Money?" Hobson asked.

"We'll go back to our assessment of one thousand each," Bouvet said. "I'll put up Jake's share. Surely, Hob, these circumstances warrant the assessment, if for no other reason than to protect our investment."

Jake's mind was elsewhere. After Hobson finally capitulated by agreeing to the assessment, Jake turned from the window and said, "Whoever's out there found out he just can't walk out and pick up the gem stones. He'll soon figure out that the real pay-off will come with the cleanup in the spring, when we 'riffle' the crumbled ore through the sluices and bag the gems. If he's going to try again, that's when he'll come back. By then, he'll figure we've forgot all about Hyrum and be so intent on our own eyes sparkling over the sapphires that we'll get careless. That's why I'm going to see if Pete Weatherwax will spend the winter down here with me. That way, when we start sluicing come April or May, we'll have a good sluice man already on the job. And with Pete sluicing and me watching, we'll get the son-of-a-bitch who killed Hyrum Terwilliger."

"What if Weatherwax won't work for what you'll offer?" Bouvet asked. "For thirty a month and his board and bed?"

Jake chuckled. "Then I'll offer him enough of my wages to get him to say yes. Pete's tough enough to be the man I want."

S.S. Hobson tap-tap-tapped his pencil on the office table. "Revenge isn't nearly as important as bringing in the gems, Jake. Remember that."

Hoover again chuckled. "You got your priorities, Hob. I got mine."

* * *

Jim Bouvet volunteered to remain at the Yogo Mine while Jake visited Yogo Gulch to recruit Weatherwax for guard duty. Jake's visit to the Gulch meant spending an evening bouncing his son on his knee and sleeping in the arms of Millie Ringgold.

At breakfast the following morning, Jake casually asked, "Nobody here owns a stud horse. Right Millie?"

"Not that I know of. Why you ask?"

"Anybody been gone recently? Say in the last three weeks?"

"Nobody except you. I'd know if they had—there's not that many left here now that I wouldn't know. Again, why?"

He told her about the murder of Hyrum Terwilliger, and his suspicion that the killer must have been the man's friend.

She shook her head. "Far as I know, everybody here has stayed put. Anyhow, I wouldn't know it if anybody was friends to—Hyrum Terwilliger, you say? I can't recall ever meeting him."

She continued stirring the pot before her as whatever delicacy was inside simmered. Then she blurted, "You're not safe, Jake. You better take a friend or two from the Gulch back with you. Take Pete or Dud. You and Pete get along well and he's tough enough to stand off a cavalry regiment if need be."

He pinched her butt through the gingham dress. "That's why I'm here, Millie. To offer him the job."

Chapter Fourteen

It proved an uneventful winter for Jake Hoover and Pete Weatherwax; a pleasant, enjoyable time for both. Their companionship was amiable. Their accommodations as good as either had experienced during most of their rugged outdoor lives. Each took occasional leave from their job—Pete to wear elbow grooves on the rough plank surface of the Utica bar, Jake to spring occasional surprise visits to his family in Yogo Gulch.

When one man took leave from the mine, the other went into double-watchful defense mode, veturing outside only after carefully studying the surrounding buildings and terrain; then only to carry water from the ditch or pack wood from the rick behind the cabin.

On one visit to Utica, Pete brought back a small "fice" dog, a yapping mixed breed: rat terrier, perhaps a little dachshund, maybe a touch of beagle, and a whole lot of vinegar and alum. The dog didn't so much take up at the mine, as he did take *over* the mine. He slept in the barn with Pete's and Jake's horses, but when the first smoke belched from the office's stovepipe at dawn, the mongrel could be found sitting on the front stoop, yawning as if he didn't care whether anyone fed him or not, but pissed as hell if they didn't. However, there wasn't so much as a jackrabbit could hop in the valley below, or the ridge above without setting off the mutt's annoying yap.

It was Jake Hoover who did most of the perimeter patrols, while Pete Weatherwax, accompanied by the tail-curved-over-his-back fice, kept an eye close in, checking the buildings and the ore dumps daily.

Once, Jake found a fresh set of horse tracks on the ridge

110

above their buildings. And again, somebody had ridden up the wagon road to within sight of the mine, but never came on in. After spending a great deal of time studying each sets of tracks, the outdoorsman finally grinned and nodded—the tracks came from ice shoes on the same horse. In each case, however, he was unable to follow the tracks back to their source, losing them in the maze of prints left by numerous saddle and work animals traveling the main road. They did however, he was able to ascertain, come from down-canyon. From civilization. That fact, in Jake Hover's mind, freed anyone from Yogo Gulch from any taint of suspicion.

* * *

The fice put up a barrage of yapping, ushering S.S. Hobson's buggy into the yard. "Call this damned mutt off or I'll take a bullwhip to him!" Hobson shouted after pulling up in front of the office.

Jake was on patrol, but Weatherwax called the thousand-pound grizzly bear of a five-pound dog off, allowing Hobson to dismount from his carriage. Inside the cabin, the banker was brusque as he slipped from his mittens and out of a heavy buffalo coat: "Where's Jake?"

"Out." Weatherwax made no move to help Hobson from his coat; instead the man stood just inside the door, with his arms folded and a half-sneer on his cadaverous face. The banker guessed that Hoover had filled the miner with a bunch of lies about him. Still, the gaunt, almost skeletal miner with the shaggy black hair and the long waxed moustache twisted into sinister points made him shiver.

"Any idea when he'll be back?"

"Prob'ly any minute. If I know Jake, he saw you coming in."

Weatherwax was right. Hoover blew through the door ten minutes later, slapping snow from his trousers and coat. "What

111

brings you here, Hob?" he asked.

"Can we talk privately?"

Jake glanced at Weatherwax, but Pete was already shrugging into his sheepskin coat. "Want me to put your horse away, Jake?"

Hoover nodded. When the gaunt miner closed the door, the outdoorsman raised a questioning eyebrow.

"I'll make this quick. I'm having Munger watched. He's disappeared from the ranch twice, once around Christmas for an overnight, then again last week for a long day. No one saw where he went, but his horse was well-lathered when he returned both times. The man had to be out for more than just a training ride."

"Stud?"

"No. But that means nothing. He might have had a stud available in November, but none now."

"Can you find out if the horse he rode last week had ice cleats on?"

"I'm sure he did. Most of the stock we keep corralled for winter use at the ranch are shod with ice cleats."

"Anyone else gone from the Glendennan this winter?"

"Not that I've heard about."

Hoover nodded, as if satisfied. He poured coffee for two without asking if the banker wanted any, then added a double ration of whiskey and handed one to the visitor. "Somebody has watched the ranch twice this winter, once around Christmas from up on the plateau, once last week from down on the wagon road. Same horse. Same shoes. Same ice cleats."

"Other people shoe with ice cleats." When Jake said nothing, the banker asked, "Does Weatherwax know there's a killer on the loose?"

Jake nodded. "He knows about Terwilliger. I haven't told him we're being watched, but the man's not plumb dumb. He

112

knows I'm spending so much time out for a reason."

"He'll try again?" Hobson asked.

"Of course. But he's smart enough now to know what he wants he can't get by picking over the ore heaps. By now he's figured out that he should wait until after cleanup, until we've got a bushel of the raw gems. I'll get him then."

Hobson took his coat from its peg.

"Sure you won't stay the night?" Jake asked.

The banker shook his head. "I told them I'd be back to the Glendennan tonight. Lewistown tomorrow. Thought I'd better warn you, though."

Hoover walked the other man to his buggy. After Hobson took his seat and picked up the reins, Jake reached out and squeezed the visitor's knee. "Thanks, Hob."

The older man studied his younger partner with unblinking eyes, then murmured, "We're all in this together, Jake."

* * *

One minute, it seemed, there was a blinding spring blizzard, piling snowdrifts into roadcuts, and on the lee side of buildings. Then there was an eye squinting sunball bursting upon leaden and soggy slopes, spreading torpor amongst the inhabitants of the Yogo Mine operations.

Pete Weatherwax eyed a meadowlark perilously perched on a dead mullein stalk waving in the breeze. "You want to start the cleanup pretty soon, don't you Jake? Sure hope so, 'cause I'll want to get back to the Gulch as soon as the run-off is over."

Jake Hoover nodded. "Yeah, I think. You go ahead and get the sluices ready while I put in a day or two on the circuit. Then we'll turn the water on and open the pad gate."

Weatherwax studied his troubled friend. "You think he's still out there, don't you?"

Hoover snorted. "I know he is, Pete. I can feel it in my bones." He thought a moment, then said, "Here's what I want to do: I want you to do the cleanup on your own; at least what you can. You can turn the ditch onto the ore heaps as it's needed. You can open the holding pen gates and handle the sluices. You can clean the traps and box whatever you find ..."

"You trust me to do that alone?" the scarecrow broke in.

Jake's smile was thin. "Why you think I rode over to the gulch to bring you back by the scruff of your neck? No stouter than you are, you couldn't pack off as many sapphires as your pockets would hold. Anyway, where you'll have trouble will be moving the sluices to slice off a different pile. Otherwise, maybe you can handle the rest pretty much alone."

Weatherwax nodded. "I know where you'll be. And I take some comfort in knowing it."

* * *

The wind came up fresh from the valley, with a modest bite to it. There was a flash of blue, a scuff of wings, and the harsh calling of a magpie. Jake Hoover fiddled with the offside billet strap on his saddle, the big dapple gray's body between him and the horses he could hear clip-clopping toward him from around the bend of the wagon road. The rider paused at sight of the dapple, then came on with a face wreathed in smiles. "Pon my word. Jake Hoover! Boy, are you a sight for sore eyes!"

The stocky outdoorsman finished fiddling with his billet strap, then stepped from behind his horse. "Well, pon my word, too. What the hell are you doing riding this way? And with a packhorse, yet?"

"I'm pulling stakes, Jake. Leavin' Hobson. I'm tired of bronc-stomping and want to see different parts. How about you?"

"Ridin' to the Gulch. It's been all winter since I seen to Millie and my baby son."

114

That Millie Ringgold had a baby, most of Fergus County knew. Many also thought Jake had a part in making it, but Jake actually admitting to paternity was news to Ben Munger. It was also news—good news—to Munger that Jake planned to be gone from the sapphire mine for a day or two. But how to explain his own presence up on the plateau so as not to make the tough outdoorsman suspicious? "Truth tell, Jake, I ain't never seen it down to Yogo Gulch. Been here goin' on three years and never seen how it was down there. Maybe we can ride along together."

Jake swung atop the gray, taking a place alongside Munger's sorrel. "New shoes," he said, eyeing the sorrel's hoofs.

"Put 'em on yesterday. Figured, since I was leaving the Glendennan, that I'd use Hobson's iron."

The horses paced on. Munger asked, "What brings you up here on top the bench? And at the same time I come along? I'd call that just plain lucky."

Jake laughed. "How else am I gonna get from the mine to the Gulch? It's the only trail into it. I see Millie, I got to go this way." Though true about the horse trail from mine to Gulch, Jake saw no reason to mention that he'd spent the night in the hills above the Glendennan Ranch, had watched Ben Munger saddle up and head for the Yogo country, then rode like hell to circle ahead and intercept him.

The two men jogged stirrup to stirrup for awhile, Munger's packhorse trotting along behind. Then the Glendennan broncbuster asked, "You boys started washing your ore dumps yet?"

"My God, yes. And was we surprised! Filled three cigar boxes and we're only a quarter done. Didn't really want to leave, but Millie and the boy is worth something, too. And one man can handle the sluices." He fell silent, then added, "I told Pete to keep the office locked, though, and the key in his pocket."

The wagon road along the top of the mining operation

ended, narrowing into a horse trail. Jake deftly maneuvered Munger into the lead, with the packhorse between. "Ain't nothing dicey ahead Ben."

"Etienne has a place down here, don't he?" Munger called over his shoulder as their horses plunged down the hill to Yogo Creek.

"Yeah," Jake sang out. "It'll be the first one we come to. But he likely won't be home. That's one man who spends more time prospecting than anybody else I know."

They crossed the ditch taking water from Yogo Creek to the Yogo Sapphire Syndicate Mine site. Actually they crossed under the ditch at the first flume, near the canyon bottom. Though Munger's packhorse stopped abruptly and wall-eyed the flume, Munger's sorrel paid the intricate cross supports and the sound of rushing water no more attention than did Jake's dapple gray—good reason, Jake figured, to think the sorrel had been down the trail before.

Etienne was, as expected, gone. But Munger, as Jake thought he would, elected to stay at the little Metis's cabin. "This is far enough from Hobson to hold me for a night or two—before I amble on up to wherever it is the gold claims are. Besides, that way I won't mess up your homecoming with the woman and your kid."

Jake waved him goodby, then, out of sight, trotted swiftly up to the diversion dam, then up the hill to the flat where he'd placed the now abandoned Chinese camp. There, he tied up his horse, jerked off the bedroll behind the saddle, and unwrapped the sawed-off, double-barrel shotgun. He quickly snapped barrel to stock, then slipped the Winchester from its saddle scabbard and, carrying both guns, ran down to the dam, then began trotting along the ditch bank, along the shorter foot route to the Yogo Mine; the one he'd neglected to mention to Ben Munger.

116

* * *

The killer crept into place by mid-afternoon, only a few minutes after Jake expected him. The outdoorsman had already decided there was only one really good place from which a careful bushwhacker would make his ambush. Ben Munger crawled from the tiny draw to the rock outcrop and the clump of concealing junipers, less than one hundred yards from where Pete Weatherwax busied himself cleaning out sluicebox riffles.

Munger studied the layout for a few minutes, then inched his Remington lever action rifle over the rock, eared back the hammer, started to take a bead, then stiffened when twin clicks of hammers eared back on a 12-gauge double-barrel brought him up short. "Naughty, naughty," Jake Hoover drawled.

Ben Munger held his Remington out without turning, then let it clatter to the rocks. "You tricked me," the ambusher said.

"I did that. I surely did. And ain't it a pitiful thing to take advantage of the trust of a friend so's a body could cut him down, like I aim to do to you."

Munger slowly swung his head to peer back over his shoulder. What he saw brought an involuntary shiver. "Jake, we been friends for a long time."

"Yep. And I hope you'll think on it the same way poor Hyrum Terwilliger got to think on it just before you blowed off the back of his head. Now pick up that rifle, because whether you hold it or whether you don't makes no difference to what I aim to do."

"God, no! At least take me back for a trial!"

Jake's laugh was hollow and forbidding. "Pick up the rifle, Munger. At least die trying. At least have the guts to give it a try."

"No, I won't." Munger started to roll over to confront his enemy. The move was an ill-disguised attempt to cover drawing a handgun from his belt. Just as the snub-nose .38 revolver cleared leather, the roar of the sawed-off 12-gauge's twin barrels seemed

117

to suspend time. It was the last thing the ambusher heard as two loads of double-ought buckshot nearly cut him in half.

Chapter Fifteen

Ben Munger's 'hideout' snubnose .38 was still clattering its way down the rocks as reverberations from the shotgun's blast reached Pete Weatherwax at the sluice boxes. The gaunt miner ducked and jerked a rifle from behind a brace post. Then Jake stood away from the junipers and waved to his friend.

This time it was Pete Weatherwax who rode for the Sheriff. Meanwhile Jake covered the body of Ben Munger with a canvas tarp, then hiked back along the dike to his horse. It was dead dark by the time Jake reached the dapple gray and started back up the long trail from Yogo Creek to the plateau above. By the time Jake reached Munger's two horses, the Big Dipper had made a quarter-turn; he loosed the horses with saddles on so they could find their own way back to the Glendennan.

* * *

Sheriff Walker Thompson arrived to investigate the second death at the Yogo Mine two days after Munger died. Thompson was accompanied by Deputy Silas Avens, and Fergus County Bank President, S.S. Hobson. Thompson's investigation disclosed the salient facts as laid out to him by Jake Hoover: the deceased had been apprehended by Hoover in an attempt to kill mine employee Pete Weatherwax and died in an attempt to shoot his way to freedom. The Remington rifle, lying where it fell among the rocks was one piece of evidence, the .38 revolver another.

Sheriff Thompson climbed the hill to view the copse of trees where Munger had tied his two horses prior to descending to the ambush spot. Try as hard as they might, neither Thompson nor Avens could see any other reason for Munger tying his horses where he did, except to approach the mine unseen.

119

Rafael Etienne gave supporting testimony when he told the Sheriff he'd returned to his cabin by mid-afternoon on the same day Hoover and Munger had visited there. "Fresh horse tracks— these were there. Three horses only little before Etienne, he come home. Etienne, he always welcomes the—how you say it— visitings." The little Metis poured thick, black coffee for Sheriff Thompson and S.S. Hobson. "Just like for you, Etienne make welcome, pours coffee. What else have I forgot, eh?"

"Back to the visitors."

"I disappoint. Nobody here. I look at tracks. One go up these creek, toward the camp on the Gulch. The other two horses, she turn around and go back up the trail where they come down."

"Did all the horses leave at the same time?" Thompson asked.

"Thees Etienne does not know because all were gone when he comes home. But Etienne, he's lonesome for talk, so I'm go up creek to visit other peoples. Then I see where horse that goes up creek turns off trail at rock dam. But the trail she takes I know don' go nowhere, so Etienne follows it up to old camp for Chinese. There, Etienne finds horse b'longs to his friend, Jake Hoover. Etienne knows thees horse. He knows his friend, too. So he follows Jake's boot tracks back to dam, where they go out on bank of ditch. I follow them more on that ditch bank until I come back to the trail down where is my cabin. Etienne is tired. He don' go no more looking for Jake Hoover. Instead, he goes to his cabin and goes to sleep."

"Did you hear Jake Hoover come back and get his horse?"

The little Metis shrugged. "No, no. Etienne, does no bad things, so bad things don' keep him awake. When he go to sleep, Etienne sleeps until he wake up." The Sheriff started to ask another question, but Etienne held up a hand. "But the horse, she is gone the next morning when I walk up to where he tied to see if it's hungry or thirsty."

On their way back to the Yogo Mine, Sheriff Thompson said, "Well, Hob, I can't see any reason for Ben Munger to turn around and go back except to do what he tried to do."

Hobson nodded. Then he reined his horse in front of the Sheriff's and halted. "And didn't Pete give testimony that from the time he heard the shot and looked up, Jake was in sight all the time until he climbed up there? So there couldn't be any made-up evidence: the rifle, the six-gun, the ambush spot. It seems clear to me that Jake Hoover performed a public service."

"That's the way it looks to me, too, Hob. But I'll want to talk to some of your boys at the Glendennan. See if Munger told anybody anything about where he was going. We'll want to tie this investigation down as tight as we can. Jake deserves that."

* * *

Jake Hoover had not been entirely forthcoming about other things with Ben Munger, on their ride down into Yogo Creek. For instance, Pete's cleanup of the sluice boxes had not yielded five cigar boxes full of sapphires, but two. Though it was true that they'd already ran a third of their ore heaps through the sluices, it was also true that much of the ore had not sufficiently broken down to yield the gems they contained and would have to be hauled back up to the weathering pads and left for another year.

"Still," Jake told S.S. Hobson, "we should clean up at least four boxes. Maybe a little more."

"That's not enough," Hobson said. "Maybe ten, maybe fifteen thousand. That won't run your mine crew for a year."

Hoover nodded. "But there's probably another ten to fifteen that didn't weather out of the ore we had. It'll just take a little longer time to weather it is all."

"Two years to weather means more front loading, Jake. We can't afford that right now." Hobson bit his lip. "Well, let me take the two boxes we have and I'll make a run back east with them. "If we can show another check from Tiffany's, maybe we can find some short-term financing on the strength of it."

"Meanwhile, what about us?" Jake asked. "Do I hire another mine crew, or not? What about the remaining cleanup?"

Hobson's lips pinched, but he flashed a grim smile. "According to Bouvet, I'm not even supposed to be out to the mine site talking to you. So you can't consider anything I say as anything but suggestions. But I wouldn't think about hiring another mine crew until after we talk to Tiffany's, and after I visit with Jim in Chicago."

Jake nodded. "What are we looking at—three, four weeks? Or can you get a telegram out to me?"

"Wait for word." Hobson swung his head to peer down at the sluice boxes. "As far as Weatherwax goes, he told me he wants to get back to the Gulch anyway."

"That's what he tells me, too."

Hobson said, "Can you continue the cleanup alone—now that the threat Munger posed has been eliminated?"

"I don't see why not. Send me another dog out, though, will you? Pete'll take his fice with him."

After the banker swung atop the big Tennessee walking horse, Jake gripped the headstall's cheekpiece and said, "By the way, I'm back to the full fifteen a week now."

Hobson smiled, then reined the Walker away. "We'll take it up at the next board meeting; President Bouvet will come back with me, do doubt. I'll put in a recommendation that we make it retroactive to today."

"Does Jim know about Munger?" Jake called to the retreating banker's back.

"How could he?" Hobson said, reining his long-legged horse around in a circle. "We left town too quickly to get off a wire. Besides, no one, inside or out, knows anything until the Sheriff's investigation is filed."

* * *

With freedom to move about without fear of a bushwhacker, the cleanup of the remaining ore dumps proceeded rapidly. Each morning, Jake would crank open a gate valve feeding into the huge fire hose. Directing the stream onto a portion of the remaining ore heap, he'd slice off a section to wash down the weathering pad to the retaining wall at the bottom. Then he would open the gate to the sluices and turn water from the ditch to flood onto the pad, thence down the sluices boxes, carrying the crumbling ore with it. Much of the residue went out in mud and sand and small gravel, passing through a screen at the bottom to wind up in the Middle Fork of the Judith, far below. But much of the ore was too large to fall through the screen, and had to be scraped off into a pile for further weathering in order to yield its treasure of the tiny blue stones. The loose gems, themselves, being exposed by the weathering process and composed of much more dense, heavier material than the surrounding decomposed rock in which they'd been imbedded, would fall into the riffle traps at the bottom of the sluice boxes.

That pretty much explained Jake's days. In the morning to move a mass of ore down to the head of the sluice boxes, then passing ore down the sluices until he would have to stop sluicing and shovel the screen free of large ore clumps. Then repeat the sluicing cycle. Occasionally, he would clean the traps of gemstones.

Jake completed sluicing the ore heaps to a total cleanup of four and one-half cigar boxes filled with sapphire gemstones. After finishing his cleanup, the man began the onerous chore of shoveling the larger poorly-weathered ore that had not passed through the washing screen onto a wagon, then transporting it

123

back up to the weathering pad. He was still engaged in that task when S.S. Hobson drove into the mining complex in his buggy. Jake watched the oncoming buggy while stuffing his pipe and leaning on a shovel.

"I'm afraid I bring ill tidings," the grim-faced banker said without preamble, as he pulled his buggy horse to a halt. "Jim Bouvet is dead."

"Dead!" Jake blurted.

"Not only that," Hobson growled. "Our sapphires aren't worth as much as we thought."

"Dead. Jim is dead?"

"I said our sapphire mine isn't as valuable as we thought."

Hoover waved a dismissive hand at the banker's second revelation. "What happened to Jim, for Christ's sake?"

Hobson set the buggy's brake, wrapped the reins around the brake handle and clambered down. "Massive heart attack is what came in on the wire. When I saw him last week, he looked a little peaked. And he turned even more peaked when I told him what Tiffany's said. But he acted anxious to get out here and look the mine over."

Then the banker murmured, "How much more did you get with the cleanup?"

Jake pitched his shovel on the ore wagon, unhitched its draft horse and started him for the barn. "Sorry, Hob. But with the news of poor Jim, I ain't got the heart to talk about sapphires just yet."

In the office a few minutes later, S.S. Hobson said, "You may not wish to discuss business right now, Jake, but I'm afraid there are certain realities that must be faced."

Hoover kindled a fire in the cookstove, then poured two glasses to the half with cheap whiskey. S.S. Hobson threw off half of his, while Jake gulped all. The outdoorsman stared moodily out the little office window. "For this," the morose man muttered, "I've taken three years out of my life to do things I didn't really want to do, killed a friend, ignored the woman I love and my own child, and got into arguments with the man who was kind enough to grubstake me when I needed it. What in the hell am I doing with my life!"

Hobson downed the rest of his whiskey, coughed into his fist, and said, "So you think it's all over, do you? You're ready to run scared because a friend died and we have a little run of bad news?"

Jake poured them both another half-glass. Then he shoved a ladderback chair toward Hobson with a foot and pulled out another for himself. "All right, dammit. I can see you ain't a-leaving until you tell me what's wrong with the sapphires. So what is it?"

Hobson sat down, lifted the glass to study its amber contents and said, "The sapphires are too small, Jake. Tiffany's only wants the larger ones—ones big enough to facet for jewelry. They say most of our production is too small for anything except industrial uses, like cutting tools or abrasive equipment. They say there's a market out there for industrial gems, but those uses are outside their market."

Jake took a big slug. "What about the boxes full of rocks?"

"They wanted to pick through them. Came up with a handful that was large enough to be faceted. They called them first- and second-grade stones, say from one-tenth of a carat up."

Jake sighed. "Carrots don't mean nothing to me, Hob. How much of our two boxes met that measure?"

"Perhaps a fourth. They offered twenty-five hundred for the lot, provided they could pick them over."

Hoover strode again to the window and stared out. "Did you...?"

"I did not. Instead I thanked them for their time, suitcased the boxes, and left for Chicago to talk to Jim. But I must tell you, Jake, Jim was as perplexed as I am. We know there's a market, but it's probably international instead of American in scope."

Jake turned from the window, hands in pockets. "What now?"

S.S. Hobson stared at his remaining partner for several seconds, then said, "Bouvet is gone, Jake. He won't be coming back. It's up to us to pick up the pieces. But we won't be able to start production of the mine anytime soon, for obvious reasons. We have no money."

Jake shrugged. "I was market hunting before, I can market hunt again."

"Don't be ridiculous!" Hobson spat. "Mine production is our first priority. But we've got to obtain additional financing. I think I know where we can find an investor for Jim's one-third, but that won't add any addional operating capital unless we make another assessment of the principals."

Jake kicked his chair out of the way and began pacing.

Hobson said, The possible investor is Matthew Dunn from Great Falls. I think Dunn will put up additional investment capital, but the catch is we'll have to sell him some of our shares. He says he wants fifty percent to become involved...."

Jake shrugged, as if he didn't care.

"... but he says he'll accept forty-nine percent voting interest."

The outdoorsman paused at the window, stared out for what seemed hours, then began pacing again.

"Jake, will you listen! He doesn't want operational control. That means you and I will still have operating control of the mine. But what we don't know a thing about is gemstone markets. Dunn says he has overseas gem contacts. He might be able to us find the kinds of sales outlets we need for our sapphire production."

Still staring at the mine yard, Jake said, "And you want some kind of decision from me. Right? Well, what is it you want, Hob? Tell me and I'll do it, agree to it, fight for it. Lie, cheat, steal." He turned. "What the hell is it you want, Hob?"

Hobson said, "Will you sell eight and one-third percent of your shares to Matthew Dunn if I sell an equal amount of my shares?"

Again Jake shrugged as if he didn't care.

"If it works the way I think it will," Hobson continued, "Dunn will pay us each ten thousand for our shares and throw in another ten thousand to the kitty for his share of operating capital. With ten thousand each, that'll give us ..."

"Twenty thousand," Jake said, pausing before the seated banker and staring down at him with piercing black eyes.

"What?"

"I said twenty thousand. If each of us puts up ten thousand for operating capital from our one-quarter share, then Dunn damn well better put twenty thousand up for his one-half share." He began stalking the room again.

S.S. Hobson was obviously flustered. "Well, yes, but I ..."

Again Hoover paused before him. "You and Dunn worked all this out before you came out here to see me, didn't you? What did you do, Hob, ride the stage into Great Falls as soon as you heard about Jim? Or did you meet him half way?"

"Look, Jake, you're right about the share assessment. I just never ... Dunn was the one who made the proposal. I suspect he knows we're in straightened financial circumstances. I'm not sure he will ..."

Jake smiled—grimly, but a smile nevertheless. "Well, Hob," he said, "Dunn will have to agree to twenty thousand or he'll have to get along without my shares. Instead, I think I'll just head on out into mountains and see if I can make contact with Jim out there somewhere.

Chapter Sixteen

One of the ironies of civilization is how we attach artificial values to objects of little real worth. Money, for instance; it makes little sense to value money, whether paper or gold, except that the system governing us—whether national, international, tribal, family, or communal group—places artificial value on what we hold in wallet, purse, safe, or under a mattress. If that system breaks down, the only real value to you of a fifty-dollar bill might be in its use as fire tinder (think Confederate paper money.) Gold? Yes, should a perception of its value vanish, one could hammer it into a digging tool or a spoon, perhaps. But even then gold would be a poor substitute for baser, stronger metals.

In short, the real worth of most precious metals lies in the artificial value we place on them. Often, that value is predicated on rarity. Silver was once held to have a value only slightly below that of gold, until silver was produced in such quantities that the bottom dropped from our perception of its high value.

Much the same could be said of precious gems; their value lies in our perception of their rarity. All else, the appeal of their translucence, opalescence, iridescence, are products of Madison Avenue creativity, even though the initial Madison Avenue was probably a camel path through a Babylonian bazaar.

Perceptions of value for rare gems and precious metals are usually heightened during cataclysmic upheaval: wars, famine, natural disasters. Often during those periods, people of means convert substantial property into more transportable and easily hidden precious gems or gold coins providing some economic assurance for their future. That their perception of value is actually based on a chimerical fancy means nothing; to them, at that point in time, investing in precious stones and metals provide the best game in town.

Similarly, during periods of social and economic instability such as rampant inflation, deep economic depression, government turmoil, widespread crime, one can see investors turning to precious stones and gold as a hedge enabling them to protect their riches. But to reiterate, the values of those investments are based on perception alone—a perception that the gems are rare and desirable and can, when needed, be converted into such fluid capital as necessary to buy beans and porridge.

In short, wealthy individuals buy precious gems because they can, sometimes as symbols of status or station, but more often because they're frightened by internal circumstances or outside affairs and see the gems as good investments. They are selective, however. The larger the diamond or emerald or ruby or sapphire, the more value is placed upon it. One cut and polished sapphire of five carats size is worth many times more than five hundred sapphires of one-tenth of a carat size.

What exactly is a carat?

A carat is the unit of measure used in rating the weight of gems. A carat is equal to one-fifth of a gram. Carats actually go back to those first Madison Avenue hucksters from Babylonian bazaars who needed some standard of measure to sell by. Their choice for a unit of measure was the carob seed.

Carob trees, a member of the legume family sometimes growing to fifty feet in height, are scattered throughout much of the Middle East; indeed, throughout much of the warm, dry regions of the world. Carob seeds and pods are edible. The ground seeds are used as a substitute for cocoa and ground pods can be baked into a kind of cake known as St. John's bread. The pods are commonly used as cattle feed. Carob fruit appear in foot-long reddish pods that usually shell out five to seven seeds.

130

One notable fact about carob seeds is, though they may differ in shape and size, they are all within a fraction of an equal weight. Before the invention of standardized units of measure, Abdullah measured gem weights in relation to carob seeds. This weight proved to be approximately one-fifth of a gram. When metric weights were developed, the unit of measure was standardized and this division of a gram was dubbed, out of deference to the useful carob seed, a carat.

* * *

Here are some end-of-the-nineteenth century faceted sapphire values relative to Yogo sapphires: According to a U.S. Geological Survey Report of the period: "... larger Yogo gems, those weighing several carats when cut, were valued at $75 a carat and that the smaller stones retailed at $30 to $40 a carat." That compares to the actual average value of Yogo gemstones in the rough of less than one dollar per carat, indicating that the per-carat value of the gems mushroomed upon cutting.

Becoming more analytically trenchant: because of size, only about fifteen percent by weight of the total production coming from the Yogo mine was of gem quality. One must also consider that each gem usually lost around seventy percent of its size during faceting. That means a Yogo gemstone weighing three carats in the rough would actually cut out at about one carat. In short, a sapphire which brought three dollars in the rough would bring thirty or more when cut and polished.

What then are we talking about in sapphire quantities of as much as a filled cigar box?

In the troy weight world, a carat equals one-fifth of a gram. That's not an overly pretentious weight when one considers that a gram is but a little over three one-hundreth of an ounce. There are twelve ounces to the troy pound measurements used for gems and precious metals. And say a sapphire-filled cigar box might weigh

131

somewhere around twenty pounds avoirdupois weight. Though one might grow confused with the math, one can soon imagine a lot of carats in a cigar box filled with sapphires.

When Tiffany's returned their first check for thirty-five hundred dollars, it is said they quoted the current (1893) London market values as follows: six dollars per carat of first quality, a dollar and a quarter per carat of second quality, and twenty-five cents per carat for gleanings.

There must have been somewhere in the neighborhood of eleven thousand carats of sapphires in that cigar box. Even if all of them rated as "gleanings," there would've been a check for nearly three thousand at the going rate. Actually, the tiny sapphires—the gleanings—totaled ninety percent of the box's contents. The remainder were taken up by both "first" and "second" quality sapphires, which should've produced at least another thousand dollars of value to the box and its contents.

At the least, one can see that Tiffany's obtained a bargain!

Why didn't Tiffany's leap at their second chance to obtain cigar boxes filled with Montana sapphires? Simply because, as they said, they're a jewelry firm, not gem wholesalers. One would think, too, that jewelry firms had only limited outlets for industrial grade stones, even though it was clear that a market did exist.

Besides, when Fergus County Bank President S.S. Hobson showed up on their doorstep with two additional boxes filled with sapphires and hinting at many more to come, the man posed the threat of flooding their markets.

Chapter Seventeen

Matthew Dunn appeared to be everything Jim Bouvet had not. It was obvious from the beginning that the discoverer of the Yogo sapphire lode was of little interest to the Great Falls investor. It was also soon obvious to Jake Hoover that Matthew Dunn had significant money in more of S.S. Hobson's business affairs than merely the Yogo sapphires. So Jake turned up his collar, pulled his hatbrim down, and retreated into his own thoughts as the first board meeting of the reconstituted Yogo Sapphire Syndicate convened in Hobson's Fergus County Bank office (with Matthew Dunn ensconced behind Hobson's desk and Hoover and the banker ranged before him). The date was July 27, 1896.

To Jake, Dunn was medium-sized, fox-faced, and as nervous as if he was an ice cube on a red-hot stove. The man's suit was tailor-cut and freshly pressed. He wore a vest with the mandatory watch chain across his spare middle. There were spats on his sharp-toed shoes and a four-in-hand tie that Jake would bet money the man didn't know how to knot on his own. Jake sneered inwardly at how comfortable Dunn appeared in command. He soon discovered, however, that the fox-faced man was discomfited by anyone not showing sufficient deference to his august presence.

"Matthew asked how soon the mine could be up and running, Jake?" It was Hobson.

Hoover tipped his hat to the back of his head and said, "A month, more or less."

"Not soon enough!" Dunn snapped.

Jake yawned and pulled the hat back over his eyes. "Then do it yourself."

"Why so long?" Hobson asked.

Jake tilted the hat back and said, "Good miners don't grow

133

on trees, boys. I'll have to go where miners can be found: Butte, maybe. Black Hills. Maybe even to the Mesabi Range. Then it'll take a little time for them to get here, get set up, start production. A month, more or less." He tilted back down his hat and appeared to go to sleep.

"If it wouldn't be too much trouble, Mr. Hoover, Matthew Dunn snarled, "we'd like to have your attention."

"You have it, Mr. Dunn," Jake drawled from beneath his hat.

Matthew Dunn glared at S.S. Hobson, who spread his hands and shrugged. Dunn said, "Am I to understand that we can't get started producing ore before the end of August?"

"That's right."

"And then you plan to dump it in heaps and let the weather break down the ore, then clean up the ore next spring?"

Jake sat up and tilted back his hat. "Maybe not even then for the ore we produce this year. One thing I found during last year's cleanup is that it may take more than a year for the ore to weather before we can really get at the sapphires."

"Then, using your method, we won't see any sapphires produced until the spring of '98?"

"No, that's not entirely true. We've still got the unrendered ore leavings that we ran through once this year; the ones I hauled back up for another round of weathering. That should be a prime producer next year."

"And how much would you estimate that residue will produce?"

Jake shrugged. "Probably half what we got this year." He looked at his hands, then said, "Besides, you still got over four cigar boxes that you haven't yet peddled."

"That's another agenda item for this board meeting," Dunn said. "Right now we're talking about getting the mine up and

134

running, and how you can do it sooner."

Jake leaned back and pulled his hat down again.

"I'm concerned about our mine manager's lack of responsiveness," Matthew Dunn said.

Hobson tried. "Is there a way to extract the sapphires more rapidly, Jake?"

Hoover said from beneath his hat, "We've been over that at least a dozen times before—yes. But it'll cost one hell of a lot more to set up crushers and stamps. It'll cost one hell of a lot more to operate. And we'll lose a hell of a lot more gemstones to damage and wastage."

Jake tilted back his hat, pushed to his feet, and leaned over the desk to go face to face with Matthew Dunn. "*Mister* Dunn. I told you what I know, gave you an answer to the best of my knowledge. If you can't accept that, then you better get another boy to run your mine. I'm about fed up with it anyway, AND a whole lot fed up with you—and I don't even know you yet."

There was a flash of fear in Dunn's eyes. After all, this is a man who kills when angered! "Please sit down, Mr. Hoover," the Great Falls man said. "We'll move on to another agenda item."

Jake strode to the door and jerked it open. "First a breath of fresh air." To Hobson's anguished cry of "Jake!" he said, "Don't worry, Hob, I'll be back. It's my bladder. Go on with your board meeting, it don't make no difference to me. Or you can adjourn for the ten minutes it'll take me to piss and toss down a double dose of whiskey."

The office door slammed solidly enough to rattle its glass. "He's his own man," Hobson mused, gazing through the window at his partner's retreating back. "He can and will do wonders, but he'll never be driven anywhere."

Dunn stared through the same glass. "I think we need a different manager," he said. The banker made no reply.

135

* * *

When Jake Hoover returned to the board meeting of the reconstituted Yogo Sapphire Syndicate, he found another individual in the room.

"Your ten minutes took an hour," Matthew Dunn said without looking at the latest arrival. "So we reconvened without you."

Jake grinned. He strode to the newcomer and, holding out a hand, said, "I'm Jake Hoover."

The man leaped to his feet and took the hand. "George Wells. Quite pleased to meet you, Mr. Hoover. You're the talk of the bloody street in Great Falls, you know."

"George is originally from England," Dunn said. "Though he won't admit it, he's a 'remittance man' who's been cast out of some titled family. He plans to buy a ranch and settle down here. But the real meat is that the man has some knowledge of gems and the gem market." When both Hoover and Wells continued standing, Dunn said, "Hobson, bring in another chair."

After each was seated, Dunn said, "All right, George, you were saying ..."

"Right. As you've discovered, the bulk of the world gem market is on the other side of the Atlantic, with the most of it controlled by my countrymen. Unfortunately, I know twiddle about sapphires, except that most of the production comes from South Asia: India, Burma, Siam, and Ceylon. It's the Siamese who are the middle men. They sell sapphires in the rough to Oriental and Arab potentates, but mostly they sell to the English who employ Dutch gem cutters. It's the English who actually furnish most of the finished gems to world markets."

George Wells finished his brief dissertation by saying, "I'm sure that's where your American firm—Tiffany's is it?—obtained their supplies until you came along. I would presume they employed their own cutters to facet your raw stones. It's quite possible they had a bad experience with their own faceters, or it may have been more expensive than they presumed."

When Wells stopped, Hobson asked, "What are the chances of us making contact with the London buyers, Mr. Wells?"

"Oh, easy enough I should think. But it would require a personal presentation. And it should be delicately handled, since what you've done, as was indicated by your New York firm, is threaten to turn the market topsy-turvy."

Dunn growled, "George, do you know anything at all about the market for industrial uses, for what is called 'gleanings'?"

Wells shook his head. "No I don't, old chap. But I'm sure my contacts would. Even if the major purchasers do not ordinarily accept what you call gleanings, they are certain to have some as residue from the cutting process. The result of that would be that they would needs find an industrial market for them."

Matthew Dunn swiveled his chair to stare out an office window. Tap-tap-tap, went Hobson's pencil. At last, Dunn swiveled back and asked, "George, would you consider returning to England to act as our representative to your contacts?"

"Pshaw!" the Englishman replied. "I'm over here in America to become a gentleman rancher, not to seek employment with a gem company. Someday, perhaps, gentlemen. But my immediate concern is finding suitable ranching property."

Tap-tap-tap went the pencil. "Perhaps we could help you there," said S.S. Hobson. "What do you think, Matthew?"

"Absolutely! We can look for suitable property, put a little money down to hold it, then wait for your inspection and selection. That is, provided you're in England in our behalf."

"Now wouldn't that be white of you!" Wells exclaimed. "I would be proud, indeed, to work for you on those kinds of terms."

Chapter Eighteen

Jake Hoover's heart was no longer in his sapphire discovery. He tried to install new spirit into his flagging will, but he could no longer find the energy or enthusiasm of former days. "It's no good, Millie. This new guy and me ain't about to see eye to eye. Jim Bouvet I counted as a friend. Matthew Dunn is the kind of asshole I can't see ever bending elbows with."

The man and woman sat on blocks of wood before her Yogo Gulch home. "There's still Mr. Hobson," she said.

"Yeah, there's still Hob."

"And didn't you tell me this Dunn don't want management control?"

"Yeah, that's what he *said*. But what he *does* is different from what he *says*."

"And didn't you tell me that you and Mr. Hobson are getting along better now?"

"Yeah, we're getting along okay. But what I didn't know going in is that this Dunn probably has a big bite of the Fergus County Bank, as well as a bunch of other investments old S.S. is probably into, too. That means Hobson won't vote his sapphire shares against Dunn in anything important."

The woman picked up the naked boy running around her Yogo yard and plopped little Naseby onto Jake's lap. "What are you going to do, Jake?"

The man wiped a calloused palm across his face, then began bouncing the boy. At last, he said, "I don't know, Millie. Quit managing the mine for one thing. Maybe sell my interest for another. I hear there's new gold fields showing up in a place called the Klondike, up in the Canadian Yukon. Maybe that's where I should be: after a man's placer gold, instead of dancing around a bunch of shyster investors chasing women's jewels."

Millie came to stand in front of her man. "You're not talking sense, Jake Hoover. And you know it."

He set the boy to the ground, then ran a hand over his face again. "Aww, I know it, Millie. I sold out every other time too soon. And I'll probably do it again now. But there's nobody can say Jake Hoover don't live free, beholdin' to no man." He searched her face, then added, "Who knows, if there's anything you like most about me, maybe that's it."

She studied him for several seconds, then murmured, "Maybe it is, Jake Hoover. Maybe it is."

* * *

Though his spirit wasn't really in it, Jake Hoover had so maintained the buildings and organized the Yogo mining operation when it sputtered that he was able to organize operations to begin anew within the specified month. With a crew of ten miners, a foreman, powder monkey, cook, and blacksmith, along with a team of draft horses to haul the freight wagon to and from town, and a mule to move ore trucks within the mine, the Yogo Sapphire Mine was a beehive of activity on the mid-August day when Jake's partners, Matthew Dunn and S.S. Hobson, arrived for an inspection.

Ore had been piling in impressive heaps for two weeks, but Dunn dismissed the heaps, saying, "We need equipment to process this ore, Mr. Hoover. What do you have in mind for accomplishing this need?"

"And what kind of equipment did you have in mind, Mr. Dunn?" Jake asked.

"Stamps, shakers, rendering machines. Perhaps acid tanks. This is not really my field of expertise, Mr. Hoover. But one assumes it is—or should be—the province of the mine's manager."

139

The broad-shouldered outdoorsman nodded. "I believe it is, Mr. Dunn. My recommendation is to build additional weathering pads. Stairstepped and probably out of lumber. Car-decking would be ideal. Then we'll need more catch-dams, with headgates into additional sluice boxes, and a trestle system of overhead tramways to dump the ore trucks. Any quick estimate will disclose that such construction would be but a fraction of the initial cost of setting up any kind of stamp mill and acid treatment vats. Not to mention the cost of operation after the initial investment."

"I disagree."

Jake smiled as he eyed the distant Big Snowy Mountains. "Then why don't you voice your disagreement and exercise your vote at the next board meeting?"

"I intend to do so."

Jake tried to catch S.S. Hobson's eyes, but the banker studiously avoided looking at him.

* * *

The 1896 fall meeting of the Yogo Sapphire Syndicate was called to order in S.S. Hobson's Fergus County Bank office on Thursday, October 22. Matthew Dunn was once more ensconced behind the desk, while S.S. Hobson, Jake Hoover, and George Wells was arrayed before him. The meeting began with a report from George Wells on his exploratory sales trip to England. Wells told of his first stopping in New York for a final offer from Tiffany's.

"I began by holding out the carrot of their being the Syndicate's exclusive marketer. They perked up like a stud in heat, but the blighters wouldn't move on having anything to do with industrial grade stones. They did say they'd go a little more than what they quoted to Hob here, when he was first to see them. But their offer was only for first and second grades."

The others sat patiently as Wells shuffled through several

sheets of notes. "I called first to visit my father at our ancestral home at Norwich. While there, I came in contact with a Miss Bessie Reed, who is a favored customer of a famous London Gem firm, Messrs. Johnson, Walker, and Tolhurst, LTD."

Wells looked at the others and smiled, exposing prominent yellowing teeth below a shaggy straw-colored moustache. "Miss Reed is a somewhat unusual lady, given to some degree of ardor for my aging father, you see."

Dunn drily said, "That's fascinating, I'm sure."

"Well, Miss Reed gave me a letter of recommendation to Messrs. Johnson, Walker, and Tolhurst, which I exercised most diligently. Miss Reed was quite emphatic that I take a cross-reference quantity of gems with me for the firm's inspection. I think it quite fair to say Johnson, Walker, and Tolhurst was disposed to a bit of interest, though they wanted to see more. With that, I returned to Norwich for the rest of my trunks and the case filled with rough sapphires."

"And what was their final disposition?" S.S. Hobson asked.

"As I cabled to Mr. Dunn, they are interested in an exclusive agreement with the Syndicate, provided they obtain at least a one-fourth share in your Yogo Sapphire operation." A feather falling would have thundered through the still office, until Wells added, "Pending, of course, their inspection of the property."

Hobson said, "You no doubt told them we agree."

"Mr. Dunn advised me to that estate, yes."

"I've already agreed to transfer half of my stock to their account," Dunn said. "Their money is in escrow."

Hobson wanted to ask what price Dunn had placed on twenty-five percent shares in the Yogo sapphires, but instead asked, "When are their inspectors to arrive?"

"No date has been set," Wells replied. "I trust Johnson, Walker, and Tolhurst are in abeyance until they hear the outcome of this meeting."

"I move we welcome Johnson, Walker, and Tolhurst, Ltd as member stockholders in the Yogo Sapphire Syndicate." It was Hobson.

"I'll second the motion," said Matthew Dunn, looking pointedly at Jake Hoover.

Jake thought about raising the point that Dunn was only voting a one-fourth interest with his other one-fourth held in escrow to the English gem merchants. But instead he said, "Count my vote in favor."

Wells then continued by saying the English firm agreed to the market prices originally quoted by Tiffany's, including the gleanings. "But," Wells added, "they'll want to limit production for three years while they further develop their markets to absorb the possible influx of unanticipated quantities of sapphires from America."

"What do they want to limit it to?" Jake asked.

"They'll have that answer when they arrive to inspect the mining operation."

"And they'll arrive," Hobson said, "soon after this board cables them that we approved both Mr. Dunn's transfer of stock and the agreement in principle for them to be our sole marketing agents."

"That's jolly well it," Wells said, gathering up his notes.

"Then I suggest this board thank Mr. Wells," Dunn said, "and excuse him while he leaves to cable London, and hopefully to get a timing for their inspectors. Then I wish him well as he retires to savor his new Utica ranch property."

* * *

Mr. Brownstone Tolhurst exercised the Johnson, Walker, and Tolhurst option on Matthew Dunn's relinquished twenty-five percent. Tolhurst did so on behalf of himself and Messrs. Walter C.

and Ernest A. Walker as tenants in common. But it was mid-January before Tolhurst, accompanied by a man he introduced as a Johnson, Walker, and Tolhurst sales specialist, Edward A. Keller, along with two mining engineers, were able to visit Montana and the mining property. By then, Jake Hoover was gone.

Hoover kicked over his traces when a decision was made to once more lay off the Syndicate's mining crews due to production uncertainties brought about by the pending exclusive sales agreement between the Yogo Sapphire Syndicate and the London gem firm, Johnson, Walker, and Tolhurst Ltd. When Jake was again ordered to close the mine, he did so, then joined the exodus himself by selling his twenty-five percent interest to George A. Wells for five thousand dollars.

* * *

When Jake Hoover stopped by Millie Ringgold's home in Yogo Gulch on Christmas Eve, 1896, she met him at the door, a tall, handsome, grave woman who said, "You went ahead and did it, didn't you?"

"I did," he replied, entering and dusting powder snow from his coat and britches, then pulling off mittens, hat, scarf, and buckle overshoes. Seriously, he took her hands in his and said, "I'm off to the Yukon, Millie, soon as I put things to rights on my ranch." Then he took her in his arms. "What I'm here for is to take you with me—you and Naseby."

She returned his hug while Humphing! and telling him she was going no farther than maybe to Utica for a New Years Eve blowout.

"I'm serious, Millie," he said, holding her out at arms' length.

"So am I, Jake."

"You'll be by yourself, woman. You and Naseby. Even if you tried to get word out, I won't be anywhere around."

143

"I'll make do. Won't be long before Naseby'll be my little man. Besides, it's not as if you've been just around the bend of the Creek when I needed help before. Pete's still in the Gulch. So is Lawless."

"What if they leave?"

"Then it'll be me and Naseby."

He dropped his hands and moved to the stove, it belching a steady roar. Later, while playing with his son, he gave the toddler an envelope and told him to take it to his mother. When she took it, he said, "There's twenty-five hundred dollars in there, Millie. It's half of what I got for my share of the mine. The rest I'm taking to Alaska. That should run you for a few years, 'til I get back from the frozen north with enough gold and furs to last us all until we pass over the rainbow."

She took the envelope, folded it, and thrust it beneath a stack of pewter plates in her cupboard. Then she busied herself at the stove, saying, "I can't believe you sold your mine for five thousand dollars, Jake."

"You think I'm lying!"

She wheeled and slapped her forehead, "No! God No! I just can't believe you'd have sold out for so little!"

"I wanted out. Now I'm out. Now I want to go as far away as I can get from the stink of sapphires and the people corrupted by sapphires." He shook his head. "I want you to go with me, too, Millie. But I knew you wouldn't, so lacking that, I want you to be as safe as I can make you while I'm gone."

She knelt before him. "Jake, Jake. My poor Jake." Then she took him in her arms and rocked back and forth, while their son tried to scramble between.

144

Chapter Nineteen

While Millie Ringgold and Jake Hoover were ushering in the New Year in a momentous farewell blowout at the Utica Bar, a quieter, more sedate meeting was underway in the library of Matthew Dunn's Great Falls mansion.

"We're better off without Hoover!" Dunn said in a voice brooking little argument. "Without his carping, we can implement new ideas for increasing production."

S.S. Hobson murmured, "I hope you're right, Matt. But I was with Jake longer than either of you two and I found him hard-working and earnest." With Dunn's frown, Hobson said, "But there's no doubt you two struck raw nerves."

Dunn waved dismissively. "What we've got to do now is ready ourselves for the Englishmen's visit. "George, have you been to the mine?"

George Wells nodded. "Everything is buttoned up. Hoover did a good job there. Let's just hope the weather holds for Mr. Tolhurst and company."

"And they're bringing engineers?" Hobson asked.

"Two."

Dunn said, "That's when we'll find out what kind of equipment and facilities we'll need for proper expansion."

An elderly matron among them refilling claret glasses.

Matthew Dunn sipped daintily, then patted his lips with a linen napkin. "We've maneuvered well, gentlemen. We've tied one of the most prestigious jewelry firms in the world to our operation, yet we have voting control. They have the money, we have the source of supply." The man stared at crackling flames in the room's fireplace, then smiled at his guests. "I believe we are ready to receive them."

* * *

Brownstone Tolhurst proved gargantuan, both in height and girth. Six inches over six feet tall, with a girth to shame a shorthorn bull, Tolhurst, what one could see of his florid face, had a bulbous nose and puffed cheeks that were cross-hatched with blood vessels and pockmarks. As both engineers helped the Englishman from the coach, Simeon Hobson whispered to George Wells, "He'd dress out at least three-forty."

Dust-devils whipped in the street, joined by tiny crystals of a just-beginning-to-blow snow. One engineer handed Tolhurst a top hat, then pulled out a small brush and whisked off the gem dealer's topcoat. Another man emerged from the coach, a tall, slender, hatchet-faced man with muttonchop sideburns who looked down his nose at the wind-whipped cowtown.

George Wells stepped forward, thrusting out a hand. "Good to see you in Montana, Mr. Tolhurst." As soon as the first Englishman acknowledged his presence, Wells tipped his hat to the muttonchop man to whom he was introduced as Edward Keller. Wells then presented S.S. Hobson, followed by introduction of the two mining engineers. With that, the English party was led to the nearby American House Hotel, and after each had freshened and rested from their tiring two day stagecoach journey from the Northern Pacific Railroad terminal at Big Timber, they gathered for a reception at the home of Simeon S. Hobson.

By then, the weather had further soured with heavier snow and wind whipping tiny flakes level with fence wires until the flakes lodged into drifts. In addition, the temperature plummeted. When told they would travel to Hobson's Glendennan Ranch on the morrow, then to the actual mine the following day, Brownstone Tolhurst guffawed and boomed that he had gone as

146

far into the New World's Indian frontier as he had any intention of traveling. Edward Keller echoed the big man's sentiments, adding that Johnson, Walker, and Tolhurst engineers would accompany the Yogo people to the mine for an assessment of the operation. "Meanwhile, we'll make the best of this cowtown gomorrah," Tolhurst boomed.

* * *

The following week proved a trial for most of those concerned. Though Brownstone Tolhurst seemed more or less content to read quietly in the lobby of the American House Hotel, or perch his enormous bulk at the bar while talking to cowboys trying to recover spirits lost to the winter's first raging blizzard, Edward Keller paced endlessly up and down the board sidewalks of the snowy little hamlet.

It was originally intended that Hobson and Wells would accompany the English party to the Glendennan, and that was where the cook brought in from Great Falls was ensconced, along with copious quantities of imported foodstocks and a wide range of liquors. But one result of the group being split in the face of the winter's first major blizzard was that only George Wells and the two engineers traveled out to make a mine appraisal. A second result was that Simeon Hobson was required to play Lewistown host to the two London merchants.

Fortunately, Matthew Dunn arrived from Great Falls on Thursday and George Wells and the English mining engineers returned the following Saturday. The first stockholders meeting of the reorganized and newly named New Mine Sapphire Syndicate took place at the Odd Fellows Hall, beginning at ten in the morning, Monday, January 25, 1897, Matthew Dunn, President, presiding.

Brownstone Tolhurst suggested that Johnson, Walker, and Tolhurst mining engineers, Lansing McWilliams and Reginald P.

147

Kensington, make a report of their findings.

McWilliams began by complimenting the mine's management. "Everything was properly buttoned up. The bunkhouse and cookhouse, barn, and blacksmith shop was clean and orderly. Both wood and coal was stockpiled for immediate use. The machinery, when last retired, seemed to be freshly oiled and in proper working order."

The engineer turned to the mining operations. "Mr. Kensington and I examined the mine tunnel and found it well sited, with no obstructions. Rail track for ore removal was properly laid and on grade. Ore trucks seemed in good repair and adequate for the operation that had been conducted." The man briefly referred to his notes, then said, "The tunnel itself runs for twenty-nine hundred and eighty-three feet through what, in America, is called Madison limestone, a quite vigorous rock capable of bearing its own weight with only limited shoring.

"When the actual gem-bearing dike of igneous rock itself is reached, the tunnel forks, both right and left to follow the dike. The dike, of course, is the feature that gives the property remarkable value. It is intrusive, of igneous origin, carrying sapphires, and cutting the bedded limestone, which is the prevailing country rock of the region."

Here, Lansing McWilliams paused for a drink of water before continuing. "The dike has been traced on the surface for a distance of about five miles, striking approximately north eighty degrees east, south eighty degrees west, with a dip to the north of about five feet to a hundred feet of depth. The average width is eight feet or more, in places widening to double that width or more, while seldom narrowing to less than five feet."

McWilliams paused for questions, received none, then continued. "The limestone dips slightly to the east, with some local rolls, but the fissure may be said to cut the bedding planes at right angles, making an ideal condition for mining operations. The dike is believed to be the only known one in existence carrying gem sapphires, and wherever it has been opened, sapphires have been found."

Brownstone Tolhurst interrupted to ask, "What about other dikes in the area?"

Reginald Kensington replied, "Records kept by the previous manager disclosed the existence of another similar dike approximately six hundred feet to the north that contains no sapphires."

Matthew Dunn blurted, "Why wasn't I aware of that?"

Hobson shook his head. "I didn't know it either. Jake was like that, though. That's why he's a born prospector. But if he reported every lead he looked into that failed, we would've been buried under the information."

McWilliams looked from one man to the other. "Is it proper for me to proceed?"

"Proceed," Dunn snapped.

"The dike rock, or trap, is easily distinguished by its bluish or gray-green color and porous texture, and carries limited amounts of iron in its composition. In places, it includes fragments of wall rock and clay with red or yellow tints from oxidation of the iron. It appears there is often a distinct gouge with slickensides produced from movement. It also appears the dike filling can be drilled by hand with a coal auger, yet it stands well."

"How deep does the dike go?" Matthew Dunn asked.

"I can see no reason to suppose that the present condition of the dike will alter in depth for many hundreds of feet."

At this point, Tolhurst proposed a brief recess. When the New Mine Sapphire Syndicate's board meeting resumed, he asked the engineers for their assessment of sapphire volume contained in the dike rock.

Lansing McWilliams responded, "It seems impossible to arrive at a per-carat estimate of a ton of pay dirt, though we tried. The reason why it's difficult is because the sapphires are unevenly scattered throughout the mass. Using the log reported by the mine's previous manager, it seems that approximately one hundred and twenty pounds troy weight of gemstones has thus far been removed from the property, for an estimated total of around two hundred and forty thousand carats, perhaps fifteen percent of which were of cuttable gem size.

"Since there was nothing in the log providing any coherent figures on the amount of ore actually removed and processed, Mr. Kensington and I did a very rough calculation—hampered of course by the fact that a sizeable quantity of ore had been removed from the dike surface that is now covered by snow—and concluded that somewhere in the realm of one hundred carats of sapphires exist for each mine car of eighteen cubic feet of broken ore."

Hobson and Dunn scribbled furiously and the mining engineer courteously waited until both men looked expectantly up for more.

"One might inquire about the mine's reserves, and it can be confidently said that even if just the known area of the dike is cleaned out before venturing down with a shaft, that there is sufficient gem-bearing ore to last for a century. And that statement is not to be construed to mean that gems do not exist below the present level. They do. In short, gentlemen, the Yogo deposit is virtually endless, and probably equals the total of all known sapphire deposits throughout the history of the world."

Silence fell across the room as Lansing McWilliams shuffled his loose papers and prepared to take his seat. Matthew Dunn cleared his throat and said, "A few more questions, Mr. McWilliams."

"Yes sir."

"You never said anything about ore processing and gemstone recovery. Can you share with us your expert knowledge of the requirements to turn the mine into a highly efficient operation?"

"Good question, sir, of course. Reginald, do you want to take it?"

Reginald Kensington leaped to his feet. "Naturally we made an assessment of the present mining operation—you know, its facilities and equipment. What's there seemed more than adequate for the use that it's been put to in the past. But ..."

Dunn interrupted, "I'm not talking about what has been our practices in the past. I'm talking about the equipment needed to turn the operation into a major sapphire producer—stamps, whatever processing machines are needed. That sort of thing. Have you made any sort of appraisal there? Can you report out an estimate of the kind of capital expense necessary to bring the mine up to where we want it?"

The younger mining engineer seemed confused. "Perhaps a little better tramway system. Perhaps more storage pads. Is that what you mean sir?"

"I do not," Dunn snapped. "Obviously what we have is something designed by children playing games. I want to know what two European mining engineers would suggest if they were retained to design the most productive mine at the Yogo site that they can imagine."

McWilliams pushed back his chair to stand beside his younger counterpart. "Are you under the impression," he asked, "that a different process should be utilized in recovering the gems?"

"Of course. Everyone knows that."

The two engineers looked at each other. Kensington grinned and waved to the older man while dropping into his chair.

151

"Mr. Dunn, the process currently in use is an extremely effective way of extracting the sapphires. It's economical and results in little damage to emerging gems. I cannot in good conscience—nor can Mr. Kensington here—imagine any other process being employed. Stamps or crushers would obviously result in damaged gems. Any other rendering method than the simple weathering that is presently being employed—acid, for instance—would result in much greater expense, as well as much greater risk to both workmen and the surrounding lands."

Matthew Dunn shifted uncomfortably. "I don't believe it!"

McWilliams stared at Brownstone Tolhurst, then turned back to Dunn. "Sir, you asked for our opinion. We offered it. You are certainly welcome to seek out other opinions, but you have no right to say you don't believe that our opinion is our opinion!"

"Is your report completed, Mr. McWilliams?" Matthew Dunn asked evenly.

Simeon Hobson cleared his throat and said, "I'd like to ask the engineers a question or two, if I might."

"Proceed."

"Mr. Kensington, you mentioned a better tramway system and more storage pads. Can you explain?"

The younger man pushed to his feet. "Yes sir. The problem with the present rendering system—the weathering—is that in its present form it's labor intensive. To break down properly, much of the ore will have to be exposed for two years. Perhaps some will even take three. But there is only two weathering pads, one catchment dam, and one sluice system. Presently the ore that fails to break down properly must be wagon freighted back up to the weathering pad. That is a horribly inefficient method. If and when the operation gets properly under way, both Lansing and I recommend that additional weathering pads be stairstepped down the hill, complete with their own ore transport trams and sluice systems. That way, there would be no heavy labor involved in ..."

Dunn again interrupted. "What would such a complicated arrangement cost, Mr. Kensington."

McWilliams growled, "Half as much as your proposed stamps, Mr. Dunn. And the system would produce far more undamaged gems at less than a quarter of the cost to operate."

Brownstone Tolhurst said, "Might I suggest a recess for tea? Or do you provincials still call it dinner?"

* * *

The Board of Directors of the New Mine Sapphire Syndicate reconvened at 2:00 p.m. without the two mining engineers.

"I wasn't through questioning them," Matthew Dunn said, with some annoyance.

Brownstone Tolhurst smiled. "Dear me. And I dismissed them."

"Can you get them back?"

Tolhurst smiled again, this time showing teeth. "Mr. Dunn, forgive me for pointing out the obvious. But the engineers are working for Johnson, Walker, and Tolhurst, not the New Mine Sapphire Syndicate. I asked them to make their report here out of courtesy, not to become embroiled in a debate over proper mining methods for extracting sapphires. Should you wish the New Mine Sapphire Syndicate to further pursue exploring various mining methods, then perhaps it'd be proper to pursue that idea with a motion to this board to hire additional engineers to make additional appraisals."

No emotion flickered across Dunn's face as he said, "Further discussion?" When there was no response, Mathew Dunn said, "Then let's take up the matter of the exclusive marketing agreement between Johnson, Walker, and Tolhurst and our new New Mine Sapphire Syndicate."

"Quite right," Tolhurst agreed.

"As I understand it, Mr. Tolhurst," Dunn said, "as an addendum to the agreement, your firm wants to limit production from the Yogo for a period of three years?"

"Indeed, yes. The time is needed for Johnson, Walker, and Tolhurst to expand their own markets for the added sapphire flow."

"And what is the limit you would require?"

"One hundred thousand carats per year."

"One hundred...!" Dunn spluttered. "You can't be serious! That's one-half of our previous production and one-tenth of what we're capable of without expanding present production capacity. That's strangulation, sir. And to that we'll never agree."

Brownstone Tolhurst slid an empty chair nearby, then lifted a gouty foot onto it. "Gentlemen, let me explain how the entire gem industry functions so you will understand the impact that your discovery has made—or could make—on the world sapphire market."

The big Englishman paused to unlace and slip off his patent leather shoe while Edward Keller folded an overcoat and placed it beneath the big man's foot. Tolhurst sighed and continued: "The market for gems is strictly limited, controlled entirely by demand. While Johnson, Walker, and Tolhurst is the leading jewelry manufacturer and gem wholesaler in the world, we are still controlled entirely by that single factor: demand.

"One must understand that there are only so many lovely necks and fingers to display precious gems; only so many diadems and crowns and scepters. One must understand that throughout the world there are many firms who would like to place their gems into those diadems and crowns and scepters, and onto those lovely necks and sturdy fingers. Your Tiffany's is one. From Africa comes De Beers with their diamonds. Emeralds from Ecuador. Topaz from Persia.

"To this time, it's recognized that the world's highest quality sapphires come from Ceylon and Kashmir. Others of high quality also stem from Siam and Burma. If you haven't already picked up on those facts, gentlemen, all known sources for high quality sapphires are Oriental. That means that of the existing limited demand out there, Oriental sapphires are the ones sought.

"Then suddenly there's this eruption of sapphires from America! If what our engineers tell us is true, America can drown the world in sapphires but for two factors: One, America doesn't have *Oriental* sapphires; and Two, there is little demand across the world to be submerged in sapphires."

"Does this mean ..?" S.S. Hobson began.

Tolhurst held up his hand. "Not at all, Mr. Hobson. Our firm sees opportunity with your Yogo sapphires. But with that opportunity also comes parallel peril. To avoid the peril of a market flooded with unlimited American production, we need to manage the Yogo gems entry into that market carefully and judiciously. Johnson, Walker, and Tolhurst is the foremost gem dealer in the world. We're the ones who can indeed implement a favorable market strategy, based on careful and controlled flows of American sapphires, coupled with judicious market expansion efforts."

When it became obvious to the others that the gem dealer was finished, Matthew Dunn filled his flushed cheeks and expelled. "I'm afraid, gentlemen, that your strategy, while perhaps beneficial for you, would be disastrous for us."

Tolhurst chuckled. "We're only talking about three years, Mr. Dunn."

"And you're talking about three years of outgo and little income for us."

"Be advised that Johnson, Walker, and Tolhurst is now part of your 'us'. We exercised our option, you know."

"Well, Mr. Tolhurst, we have yet to sign your exclusive marketing agreement. I, for one, am opposed to doing so if our production is to be limited to one hundred thousand carats per year."

This time the huge Englishman laughed aloud. "Mr. Dunn, the production stipulation might be even more restrictive than you think. What it really says is Johnson, Walker, and Tolhurst will accept only one hundred thousand carats of uncut gems per year. You already have two years' supply of that total in the rough stones you have on hand. And our engineers are persuaded there's at least another year's supply in the ore you already have weathering. That means we're insisting that no further production occur for three years—until we have the opportunity to put into place an effective plan for marketing the stones."

"Impossible!"

"Dear me," Tolhurst sighed. "We hoped you would see our position."

"Hob," Dunn said, "I would entertain a motion that we thank Johnson, Walker, and Tolhurst for their time and effort in proposing their exclusive marketing agreement, but that we find its terms too restrictive for the New Mine Sapphire Syndicate, and therefore decline to further consider it."

After some hesitation, S.S. Hobson murmured, "So moved."

When Matthew Dunn seemed as if he would move on, Edward Keller, the other Englishman, said, "I presume you'll call for a vote on the motion?"

Dunn said, "All in favor signify by raising your right hand." He and S.S. Hobson did so.

Both men stared pointedly at George Wells who spoke for

the first time, "Point of order, please. I believe it fair to have a brief discussion of the motion before the vote."

"All right. What do you wish to discuss, George?"

"For one thing, it's the fact that the motion makes if final; that we'll never consider the offer of exclusive representation by these people again. Is that wise, Matthew?"

"Not at all. Let them come back with an agreement we can live with and I, for one, will consider it." When the supposed reasonableness of his response appeared to have no effect, Dunn muttered, "What do you propose to do, George, nothing?"

"What Mr. Tolhurst said sounds reasonable to me. An exclusive marketing agreement with the most prestigious gem firm in the world seems worth the wait. I think you and Hob aren't properly appreciating the problems associated with even approaching a reputable firm such as Johnson, Walker, and Tolhurst."

Hobson said, "Is there an amendment that would be acceptable to all parties?"

After a pause, "Keller said, "Call for the question."

Dunn murmured, "All in favor?" Hobson and Dunn raised their hands.

"Opposed?" Tolhurst, followed reluctantly by George Wells, raised their hands.

In shock, Dunn muttered, "Where do we go from here?"

Edwards said, "The motion failed to carry."

Brownstone Tolhurst said, "I'll move that the Syndicate sign the proposed marketing agreement with Johnson, Walker, and Tolhurst."

George Wells said, "I'll second the motion."

Dunn waited. Edward Keller said, "Call for the question."

"All in favor?" Wells and Tolhurst raised their hands.

"Opposed?" Dunn and Hobson raised theirs.

"Motion failed!" Dunn said. "So it seems obvious that we do not have an exclusive marketing agreement with Johnson, Walker, and Tolhurst. That means we can begin production while searching for another marketing source."

Brownstone Tolhurst sighed and shifted his great bulk. Edward Keller folded his arms and waited.

"The thing now," Dunn continued, is to decide whom to employ to manage the mine, and when we should direct the new manager to begin operations."

Tolhurst drawled, "I move we do not authorize mine operations throughout 1897."

George Wells raised his hand and said, "I'll second the motion."

"George! Have you gone mad?"

"There's a motion and a second," Edward Keller brusquely said. "Will there be discussion?"

Matthew Dunn stared at the slender Englishman, eyes narrowing. "Mr. Keller, you have no standing in this meeting. You cannot inject your thoughts into the discussion. Nor claim any rights. Therefore, I'll have to ask you to leave."

Brownstone Tolhurst cleared his throat and said, "One moment, old chap. Mr. Keller happens to be the legal counsel for Johnson, Walker, and Tolhurst. He's here to provide legal advice to the voting delegate of the firm's block of stock. As such, you may find it difficult to eject him from this meeting. And make it stick."

"There's always the town constable, Mr. Tolhurst."

"And a judge," Keller said. "Because if I'm ejected, Mr. Tolhurst will find recourse in a court of law."

Dunn leaned back in his chair. "I did not think I needed legal advice for this meeting, Mr. Tolhurst. I'm surprised you feel you do."

Tolhurst smiled. Keller said, "Call for the question."

Dunn grimly said, "All in favor of the motion that we suspend mining operations at the Yogo Mine throughout 1897 raise your right hand." Tolhurst and Wells voted for the motion.

Dunn stared through George Wells as he said, "Well, it's obvious that you've effectively blocked production for this year, Mr. Tolhurst. Which, it appears, is your intent in order to restrict the flow of our sapphires into your competing markets. But you do know we still have nearly two hundred thousand carats of rough stones already mined. I can—and will—assure you that I'll try to get them to outlets that will hurt your firm the most."

The English barrister said, "Recriminations can be bitter provenance, Mr. Dunn. Besides, it is sometimes better to recognize that half a loaf is better than no loaf at all."

S.S. Hobson said, "Please! Let's hold on a minute. Matthew, I'm not willing to shoot myself in the foot in order to take revenge on someone else." The other four men eyed him, waiting for him to continue. "The way we're going now will see no return from the mine this year, and probably next. At least they're offering something. Therefore, I'd like to reconsider the motion that we sign the exclusive marketing agreement with Johnson, Walker and Tolhurst."

"Et tu, Brutu," murmured Dunn.

When the motion was brought forth again, there were three votes in favor, one opposed. Dunn stood from his place at the head of the table and said, "I won't sign that agreement as President of this Syndicate. Therefore, I'm resigning my position.

Hobson, as Vice President, took up the gavel. Tolhurst droned, "I move that Simeon Hobson be moved to the position of President of the New Mine Sapphire Syndicate." As authorized, S.S. Hobson signed the Exclusive Marketing Agreement with Johnson, Walker, and Tolhurst, Ltd, of London, England to

159

represent Yogo sapphires worldwide.

Little business remained: only a decision to continue to employ the watchman presently at the mine, and to authorize plans for spring cleanup of ore presently on the weathering pads. Johnson, Walker, and Tolhurst Ltd had no objections. In return, Brownstone Tolhurst and Edward Keller received the four and one-half cigar boxes filled with Yogo sapphires, signed for them, and promised to grade them upon arrival in England.

"We'll apply the first one hundred thousand carats to this year's quota," Tolhurst said, "then place the rest against that of 1898."

When the meeting broke up, the gloom of evening was already clamping down. Simeon Hobson and George Wells departed at the same time. As Hobson held the door for his new ranching friend, he said, "Just one question, George."

Wells, pushing through the door, said, "Of course, Hob. Anything."

"Were you voting your shares in there today? Or someone else's?"

Wells peered up at a clearing night sky. "I dare say it'll grow colder tonight, what?"

Chapter Twenty

At the close of the New Mine Sapphire Syndicate board meeting, where the victory of Johnson, Walker, and Tolhurst, Ltd's London jewelry firm seemed complete, the rest of the evening was spent by the Englishmen's preparation for the following morning's departure on the hundred-mile stagecoach journey to the Northern Pacific Railway Station at Big Timber, and to giving instructions to the two mining engineers who were to return to the Yogo Mine for further appraisals. With the stage due to depart at six a.m., there was little opportunity for Brownstone Tolhurst and Edward Keller to recap their meeting.

As chance had it, there was limited opportunity to discuss the meeting on the first leg of their stagecoach journey either, for the coach was crowded until it reached the Moore Relay Station, where the other passengers disembarked to change coach for Great Falls. In fact, it appeared the two Englishmen would have the stage to themselves until a late arriving passenger checked in just as their driver prepared to pull out for Judith Gap.

The blocky newcomer wore a floppy wide-brimmed black hat, heavy wool-lined mittens, and a huge buffalo coat with the hair side out. Shiny-worn wool trousers were tucked into knee-high black leather boots that had mud and snow clinging to them. The man also carried a Winchester rifle whose snout preceded him as he shouldered into the coach. The man both Brownstone Tolhurst and Edward Keller took for an Army Indian scout, or possibly a buffalo hunter, or a wagon train guide eyed the two English gentlemen sitting across from each other, noting the way the two held themselves to the far side of the coach. Then the newcomer took a place beside the door through which he'd just clambered, stretched his legs so that his muddy boots rested on the

161

seat across from him, shrugged more deeply into his buffalo hide coat, and promptly fell asleep.

As the coach rolled up the long grade to Judith Gap, Keller asked, "Were you pleased with the way things went yesterday?"

"Quite."

"Our man Wells acquitted himself splendidly. Demonstrated your perspicacity in choosing him as your agent, Brownstone."

The passenger on the far side of the coach shifted, then began softly snoring.

Tolhurst chuckled. "I thought Dunn would have apoplexy. Made the whole trip worthwhile, eh?"

"What is our plan, now that we've halted gemstone production."

"Just for a year."

Keller cried, "Only one? We have the power to block their production longer. Isn't it possible we may need to do so if they clean up the ore they have on those weathering pads this season. We are committed to buy sapphires produced there, right?"

Tolhurst chuckled again. "Only in good time, my dear Edward. Only in good time." Before Keller could comment, the big man added, "Surely it hasn't escaped you that we already have this year's allotment, and most of next."

"True."

"And that their cleanup will probably fulfill our three-year limited production requirement."

Keller nodded. "But after the end of that grace period. What then?"

Tolhurst took his time answering, glancing at their sleeping companion, then leaning conspiratorily to Keller. "By then, we'll have complete control of the New Mine Sapphire Syndicate and all its operations. By then, also, we'll have

162

expanded markets established. By then we'll be in position to see what the Yogo Mine will produce."

"Who will be next to go, Hobson or Dunn?"

"Oh, Dunn. The banker demonstrated a little flexibility. He came into the meeting Dunn's man, but he went out with a somewhat broadened perspective."

Keller, idly staring at the slumbering figure, asked, "What will it take to acquire Dunn's stock, do you think?"

Tolhurst guffawed. "My dear Edward, it all depends on how little Dunn thinks will be returned from the mine. As far as either of the other two principals are concerned, they should never learn that we intend eventually to turn the Yogo into a multi-million carat production."

The two Englishmen continued discussing their American mining venture until the coach pulled into the stage stop at Judith Gap for a change of horses and, though the sun was well past its zenith, a noon meal of baked beans, roast mutton, and boiled cabbage was ready for the passengers. Though the hungry Englishmen ate with gusto, their fellow coach companion took his nourishment in the room next door, bootheel draped over a brass rail.

"It's all downhill," the driver shouted down to his passengers as he climbed to his perch. "Clear from here to Harlowtown; we'll make good time."

"How far is Harlowtown?" Keller wondered, taking a watch from his waistcoat pocket. Glancing at their drowsing companion, he asked, "I wonder if our friend here can talk?"

Tolhurst murmured, "It may be that he can't speak English."

The two men launched into a discussion about how Johnson, Walker, and Tolhurst would actually operate the mine when time came to do so. Brownstone Tolhurst said, "McWilliams

163

and Kensington seemed to believe former management had a good system—one that will cost little to develop and less to operate."

"Don't you find it amusing that Dunn wants to change rendering methods?"

Again Tolhurst guffawed, this time holding his oversized belly. "A good thing he won't be there when we begin actual operation."

The coach rolled on at a steady six miles per hour on a gradual descent for the nineteen miles into Harlowtown. It arrived at that Musselshell River town at dusk, pulling up before the newly constructed stone hotel. The frontiersman climbed from the coach first, wandering down the board sidewalk toward a lighted building from which raucous music thundered. The two weary Englishmen went directly to the hotel dining room and wolfed down another meal of mutton, cabbage, and beans. Then the two men retired to their rooms where they slumbered through the night.

The following morning, Brownstone Tolhurst punched his companion on the shoulder as Keller climbed into the coach. "I dare say our friend did not fare as restfully as did we."

The bleary-eyed, greatly hung-over frontiersman clambered up to ride with the driver as a Norwegian farm family of six crowded into the coach after the Englishmen. "I wonder if these yeomen speak English," Tolhurst muttered.

The father leaned across the mother and said, "Yah. I speak English good. So does Olga here, and three of the boys."

Edward Keller asked, "Where are you people going?"

The pink-cheeked man, still leaning across the wife, said, "To the railroad. Olga's family, dey live in Bismarck, Nor' Dakota."

Keller asked, "How can an entire family leave a farm this time of year?"

"When else? It is wheat we raise, not milk cows. Is good to

164

get away just now."

Tolhurst said, "Must be difficult raising sufficient funds from a small farm for a family to travel."

"Not so hard when you marry an Olga." The father's blue eyes danced. She squeezed his hand. "Her father and mother, they send tickets. Dey own the biggest dry goods store in Bismarck."

* * *

It was a twelve hour stagecoach journey from Harlowtown to Big Timber, with several icy stream crossings and low divides to pull over. Horses were changed at the Melville Station, and the passengers had a quick meal of boiled mutton, cabbage, and baked beans. For most of this day's journey, high peaks from the formidable Crazy Mountains towered to the west in snowy grandeur.

There was trouble coming down the grade into Big Timber Creek, and one wheel of the stagecoach slipped off the frozen road. All passengers debarked from the coach's left side, onto the frozen roadway, and the baggage unloaded from both top and rear compartments. Then stout poles were cut for levers and boulders rolled into place for fulcrums. With all of the men and three of the boys straining on the lever poles, the coach was at last ratcheted back onto the roadway. Then one of the lever poles was shortened and lashed between the spokes of the rear wheels to keep them from rolling on the coach's way down the remainder of the icy grade. At last the baggage was reloaded and the driver gingerly took his seat. With brakes set, and a firm grip on the reins, the man encouraged his team to shuffle on down the hill to the bottom. Meanwhile, the passengers walked the remaining half-mile down to the coach.

At the Yellowstone River, ice had jammed the ferry crossing and the only alternative was to transport the passengers and their baggage across the open leads via rowboat where they were met on the other side by a stage company carriage that shuttled them on into Big Timber.

"What comes of bein' late gettin' here," the carriage driver said. "Y'all missed the eastbound train. But the westbound is due in about ten minutes. If we hurry, we can still make it."

As chance had it, the frontiersman was the only passenger riding west. He made his boarding, waving at his fellow travelers as he mounted the railcoach steps.

The carriage driver took the farm family and the two Englishmen on to the hotel, where they took rooms. While the carriage driver helped Brownstone Tolhurst and Edward Keller with their trunks he said, "I reckon you must be the English fellers what's takin' over the sapphire mine up Yogo way."

The Englishmen looked startled. Keller said, "I dare say we're hardly taking over the mine, my good man. Where did you hear such a thing?"

"Hoover told me on the way up from the river."

"Who?"

"Jake Hoover. He's the one what rode in with you on the stage. He's the discoverer of the sapphires. But I reckon y'all know all that, havin' rode in with him and all."

Chapter Twenty-One

Matthew Dunn did not take defeat from his English sapphire mine partners graciously. However, his was behavior that was in his genes. Descendant of irascible Scots forebears, followers of reformist John Knox, a leader of the Protestant Reformation in Scotland, they, along with Knox took refuge in the castle of St. Andrews to escape Catholic persecution and was thus captured by French troops invited in to besiege the castle. Knox and his followers were sentenced as galley slaves where Douglas Dunn distinguished himself by refusing proper reverence when Catholic mass was performed aboard ship, even spitting upon a painting of the Virgin Mary and tossing it over the side.

The recalcitrant Scot survived a subsequent flogging and was ransomed, along with Knox, in February, 1549, after spending a total of 19 months as a galley prisoner.

With the protestant reformation exploding throughout Northern Europe, and Catholicism in retreat, it was another Dunn, Thomas, great-grandson of Douglas, who led a Presbyterian revolution in Scotland against the emerging sympathies of King James and, thus, fled to America in 1636 to join other "Puritan" sympathizers who'd fled English religious persecution. Being something of a "man of means", Thomas fit in well with the ecclesiastical leaders of the Massachusetts Bay Colony, such as John Cotton and Richard Mather, and in fact became a merchant of note, trading into the western Indian country peopled by the five tribes of the Iroquois. And when, inevitably, the aging Thomas Dunn broke with the powerful and influential Mather family over religious differences, he was able

167

to secure privileges in the fledgling Dutch Colony of New Amsterdam, at the mouth of Hudson's River.

From the later English Colony of New York, it was a Dunn (Charles) who alerted wealthy entrepreneur John Jacob Astor to the possibilities of an American fur trade venture in the Far West, offering his many St. Louis (and beyond) trading contacts (and adding not a little of his own financial assets) to establish the American Fur Company. That company, by 1830, had grown to monopolize the fur trade in the United States, and became one of the largest businesses in the country.

Lauchlin Dunn, for all practical purposes, John Jacob Astor's factotum, was Matthew Dunn's grandfather, a powerful influence in New York, St. Louis, and along the Missouri River, into the fledgling Montana Territory.

Matthew Dunn's family was powerful in the East, powerful in the Midwest, and with some influence in Europe and the Orient. Power was an inherent familial trait, as was elements of residual Puritanism, short temper, and an unwillingness to suffer dissent from outsiders, or even from within the family.

Short tempered and ugly of disposition summed up Matthew Dunn. But the man was combative, as well. He had forebears with General Braddock's expedition to the French Fort Duquesne in 1755 (both scalped during the subsequent massacre of Braddock and his command); an aide to General Washington at Brandywine during the American Revolution; a master's mate on a naval sloop under Oliver Hazard Perry's fleet command at the Battle of Put-in-Bay on Lake Erie during the War of 1812 (drowned along with his entire ship's company while under fire from three British warships); a lieutenant at Chapultepec in 1847, during the war with Mexico; and finally, forebears on both sides during the bloody American Civil War, including Matthew

Dunn as a drummer boy in the 4th Brigade of the 6th New York Infantry.

The inheritor of a substantial fortune and equally inherited interest in the Missouri River West, Dunn arrived at the Great Falls of the Missouri only a few months after Paris Gibson, the Maine and Minnesota manufacturing industrialist convinced his friend James Hill to found the city of Great Falls and pledge a railroad to the townsite. Naturally Matthew Dunn acquired many choice building lots; naturally Dunn and Gibson crossed purposes and became antagonistic developers. Unfortunately (in Dunn's view) Gibson had already acquired rights to power generation at the huge Missouri River falls. And Gibson's close friendship with the railroad magnate gave Dunn's competitor a significant advantage. But the ex-Union drummer boy's ruthlessness and take-no-prisoners business dealings leveled the playing field. And when that same drummer boy proved adept at bringing in business partners (particularly banking interests) from throughout the region (including Simeon S. Hobson's bank of Lewistown), Dunn's financial interests began to surge ahead of Gibson's. Until, that is, Jim Hill came to his friend's rescue by holding his railroad to Helena, Butte, and Anaconda as ransom for a new Anaconda Mining Company smelter on Gibson's property near Great Falls.

With Gibson finally ensconced as the recognized patron founder of the city of Great Falls, he and Dunn stepped down their bitter face-off; two bloodied warriors, exhausted and reeling, realizing there was nothing further to be gained by continuing their vendetta.

Enter S.S. Hobson with Jake Hoover's fabulous sapphire find.

Enter Dunn's engineering Hoover's disgusted flight from his discovery.

169

Enter Dunn's bringing in the English gem firm, Johnson, Walker, & Tolhurst, Ltd. as equal partners.

Enter the English gem firm's maneuvering to gain control.

Matthew Dunn had someone else to hate. And all the man's anger and vitriol was focused on the grim recollection that hatred for the English had been a family trait for over three hundred years through Old World religious tyranny, taxation without representation, the Colonial revolt, and the War of 1812.

Matthew Dunn began plotting his revenge.

* * *

That he'd been outmaneuvered by world-class strategists, Matthew Dunn knew quite well. Prior to this point, Dunn had been the shrewd one instead of the pawn, but before, he'd been playing against simpletons. The Britishers were something else, and he should've sensed it going in.

True he'd ridded himself of the ignorant millstone, Jake Hoover. But even that victory failed to achieve the results Dunn wished: he'd planned to acquire Hoover's interest, but the gemstone discoverer had sold his quarter interest in the mine to the interloper George Wells for half what the Great Falls man would've offered. Missing from Matthew Dunn's computation was the fact that Jake Hoover would not have sold to Dunn at any price; such an outcome, more driven by attitude than economy, was unthinkable to the choleric New Yorker with Scottish roots who thought only in terms of power and coin.

Dunn's thoughts turned to the man to whom Hoover had sold his interest, the English rancher who he and Hobson had helped acquire the Utica ranch; the Trojan Horse they'd rolled into their Yogo board meetings and begged to intercede for them with the English gem firm. Dunn cursed: he should've seen that one coming. Hmm, when did George Wells first hit the country?

170

Was it after Hoover's discovery, or before? He made a mental note to consult Hobson. Was Wells a plant from Johnson, Walker, and Tolhurst or an opportunist who saw a chance for himself and took it?

Either way made no difference: Wells belonged to the English. And with him, the English controlled a half-interest in the Yogo find. How could he have been so stupid as to transfer a quarter-share of the mine to the gem firm! The answer was greed, of course. Not his alone, but the other partners, too: Hobson and (at the time) Jake Hoover. Their objective, of course, was to secure the marketing expertise of one of the world's greatest gem firms. Wells had a hand in that, too. True, he didn't exactly recommend contact with Johnson, Walker, and Tolhurst, but his hand was there, pushing the Yogo mine principals in that direction. He should've been more suspicious.

Forget Wells! It's Hobson that he must have for his revenge on the English. Though Dunn thought the banker's turn against him in the board meeting granting effective operational control to the English verged on treachery, he could at least understand Hobson's motive: money. The man very simply feared the collapse of their venture if the Englishmen, Tolhurst and Wells, continued to block the Americans, Hobson and Dunn. That Hobson finally voted with the English to delay mine production for three years while the gem company prepared sufficient market to receive the Yogo's potentially enormous supply would seem logical to a banker was perhaps understandable, it was still treachery to Dunn. And in his present mood he dwelled solely on how the man's desertion could be reversed. Securing Hobson's support in future board decisions should be the ex-Union drummer boy's first order of business.

* * *

The same future board dynamics was also deliberated by

key individuals in Johnson, Walker, and Tolhurst. Of primary concern was whether Jake Hoover, their (at the time) unknown stagecoach companion, disclosed any of Brownstone Tolhurst's, and his professional counsel, Edward Keller's unguarded plans for the Yogo sapphires to Simeon Hobson or Matthew Dunn.

Secondly they wanted to insure Hobson's voting block to their side in future operating decisions.

It was for those twin purposes that, prior to leaving New York, Brownstone Tolhurst telegraphed George Wells, summoning him to a London meeting.

* * *

"Since Jake Hoover left the Judith country at the same time you did, then boarded the Northern Pacific Railroad heading west before you and Mr. Keller boarded it eastbound the next day, I deemed it unlikely that he discussed anything you people might have said about the Yogo mine with either Mr. Hobson or Mr. Dunn, or even with their agents." George Wells, spraddle-legged with his back to the fireplace in Brownstone Tolhurst's study, pulled the tails of his frock coat aside for more warmth. He smiled, shaggy moustache spreading and lifting until the man's prominent teeth were on display.

"Indeed, information that I acquired subsequent to your cable is that early on the morning following the man's Seattle arrival, Hoover boarded the steamer ..." he paused to glance down at a sheaf of papers fanned on a footstool before him "... called the 'Lovely Helen', direct for Ketchikan, Sitka, and Skagway. I could find no evidence that he sent off any wires, or mailed any letters."

Glancing first at the inscrutable Tolhurst who sprawled on a chesterfield directly before him, then at Edward Keller who leaned indolently against the room's entry door. "Questions?"

"How can you be sure Hoover never sent a wire en route

from Montana to the Pacific Coast? Or wrote a letter, which could be mailed anywhere?" the counselor asked.

Wells shrugged, then displayed his oversized, yellowing teeth again to the gargantuan, sprawling, managing partner of Johnson, Walker, and Tolhurst. "Of course I can't. But knowing how much Hoover detested the overbearing Dunn, and how he wound up hardly communicating with his grubstake partner at the end of his association with the mine, I'm hardly suspecting that Hoover would even care, one way or the other, what happened to his discovery or his former partners."

Tolhurst heaved himself to a sitting position. "Are you satisfied, Edward? Regarding that question, I mean?"

"Besides, I casually asked Mr. Hobson if he'd heard from Mr. Hoover after the man left for the Yukon. The circumstances was during a chance meeting at his Glendennan Ranch, do you see? Mr. Hobson replied in the negative. He told me that, 'Given the circumstances of Mr. Hoover's parting, I doubt I shall ever hear from him again'."

"And what were those circumstances?" Keller asked.

A deep breath, the toothy smile. "This is merely my surmise, gentlemen. A guess, do you see? But I think Mr. Hoover abandoned the mine because Mr. Hobson abandoned him in favor of Mr. Dunn."

Brownstone Tolhurst harrumphed. "Which brings us to our second point, Edward."

The barrister moved further into the room, but seemed to stare out the room's bay window into the London fog. "It seems apparent that Simeon Hobson is a man of shallow loyalties; he abandoned Matthew Dunn for our position, did he not?"

George Wells sobered, barely nodded. Staring thoughtfully at Brownstone Tolhurst, he murmured, "The man's flight from Dunn may have been for monetary salvage rather than because he's enamored with Johnson, Walker, and Tolhurst."

"Meaning?"

"Meaning Mr. Hobson may have been unwilling to follow Matthew Dunn to the executioner's block."

Tolhurst broke in: "Share with us your impression of Dunn."

"Opinionated. Arrogant. Without grace. Not nearly as intelligent as he believes himself to be."

"Wealthy?"

"Apparently. Though how wealthy I don't really know."

"Share with us what you know of his background."

Wells moved from the fireplace as a servant shuffled in with more coal, stirred the existing embers, added fuel, stirred again, then departed. Still thinking, Wells drifted into the window bay, then faced his inquisitors. "Prestigious family of dissenters who arrived in America with the first wave of Scottish Puritans. I'm unsure of Matthew Dunn's route from New York up the Missouri. But from what I've heard, he strikes sparks everywhere he lands. Just before crossing swords with Johnson, Walker, and Tolhurst, he lost a gigantic battle with Paris Gibson, the founder of the community of Great Falls, over control of the townsite. During that fight, the man antagonized not only Gibson, but the mining magnates in both Helena and Butte—not an easy task because Clark and Daly are bitter antagonists without Dunn. Naturally, James Hill, the Minnesota railway builder is also scorned by Matthew Dunn. Dunn's scorn is hardly unique to those just mentioned, however. He also scorns equally many—if not most—of the Treasure State politicians. If it were not for Dunn's money, as nearly as I can tell, he would be virtually friendless."

Tolhurst grinned at Keller. "Sounds like Lord Lucien,

174

doesn't it?"

Keller said, "Yet you ingratiated yourself with the man?"

"Only as per your instructions. It was not my favorite duty. He really is an insufferable man."

"How did you manage it?"

George Wells explained how he first arrived in Central Montana posing as an Englishman with an interest in cattle ranching. Naturally his search for ranching possibilities took him up the Judith River where he "learned" of a new sapphire mine discovery. Common barroom gossip told him who the mine owners were, and that Matthew Dunn of Great Falls controlled the lion's share. It was easy to locate Dunn's residence in the burgeoning new townsite, and send in a message that I may have some gem marketing knowledge. "Greed did the rest."

Tolhurst asked, "Didn't the man question how you knew he was interested in gemstone marketing?"

Wells chuckled. "I may have forestalled the question by murmuring that it was common rumor in the Utica bar that the New York gem company had turned the purchase of additional sapphires down."

"And that didn't alert him? Knowledge that no one outside their circle should have known?"

"I assumed Dunn suspected Hoover of spilling it. After all, Hoover often frequented the fleshpots of Utica. Certainly he never suspected your Tiffany's source. And I never apprised him of that fact."

Keller murmured, "Well, Mr. Wells, your infiltration seems bereft of subtleties."

"But," Tolhurst chuckled, "It was effective. Perhaps Edward, you should employ such direct approaches in your service to our firm." The big man pondered their American

175

agent. "George, you performed flawlessly on your first assignment. The firm is quite pleased. But more is needed."

George Wells nodded, but said nothing while waiting.

"Tell us about Simeon Hobson."

Wells again nodded, glancing first at Edward Keller, before returning to the jewelry firm's managing partner. "The man seems well-respected, although common gossip is that he's extremely close with his money; his and that of the bank he manages."

Keller interrupted: "If money was the reason Hobson broke with Dunn, why, then, did he abandon Hoover for Dunn?"

Wells murmured, "Money. What else? They'd just lost their basic financial partner and they needed another source of revenue. Hoover had none, Dunn did."

"And was Dunn the only available source of capital available?" Tolhurst asked.

"Obviously not. I believe I've already mentioned several financiers in what is being mentioned as the 'Treasure State.' Gibson, Clark. Daly; even James Hill, the railroad magnate...."

"So why ..."

"But I think it rather possible that Mr. Hobson already had investments with Mr. Dunn, and Dunn may have used them to lever himself into the sapphire strike."

Another servant arrived bearing a tray of sandwiches and a bottle of wine and three long-stem glasses. After they'd retreated, Tolhurst said, "If your assumption is correct, then what gave Hobson the courage to break with Dunn and join us in the meeting vote?"

Wells waved his wineglass so vigorously some of the liquid slopped out, staining the cuff of his shirt and jacket. "Mr. Tolhurst, Mr. Keller ... doesn't it seem obvious that Hobson believes there's potentially more value in the sapphires than lies

176

in his indebtedness to Dunn."

"Yet Dunn is a vindictive man, I believe you implied?"

"Yes, all my indicators point this to be true."

"Are you aware of any interchange between the two since the meeting?"

"No sir, but since Mr. Hobson is a Montana State Legislator, he's absent from his bank often. It's possible he and Dunn could meet while he's traveling to or from the Capitol. I simply don't know."

Keller carried a half-eaten sandwich and his wineglass to a window seat, seemingly disinterested. Tolhurst pushed to his feet, then backed against the fireplace blaze. The big man's jowls appeared to dance as he wallowed a mouthful of wine. The man stared at the floor, musing, "It would seem vitally important to our position that Mr. Hobson continued to align his interests with ours." Then he stared at Johnson, Walker, and Tolhurst's American agent. "Does Hobson have the courage to withstand Dunn's anger if he was no longer monetarily indebted to the man?"

To Tolhurst's approval, Wells took a long pull from his wineglass swallowing in driblets while gazing steadily at his employer. "Ye-e-s, I would think so." Then, "The man is a rather thoughtful one, not, I believe, given to rum moves. He had time to consider before making a motion to reconsider the marketing agreement with you gentlemen. No doubt, he'd already worked out what might result between him and Mr. Dunn. Wouldn't that seem logical?"

Edward Keller moved from his window seat to also stand at the fireplace. "But that doesn't preclude Dunn's application of other pressures unknown to either us or Hobson. If he pocketed Hobson vote, he could, in essence, throttle future mine operations enough to move the mine's management into a court

177

of law. An American court of law. Should such an eventuality occur, Johnson, Walker and Tolhurst is concerned that a foreign syndicate, no matter how well argued in such a court, might not fare as well as two American 'salt of the earth' investors—especially if one was in on the discovery."

Without bidding, Wells poured himself another glass of wine. Then he asked, "What is it that you wish me to do?"

Chapter Twenty-Two

Matthew Dunn believed in the adage, "waste not, want not". And to Dunn, time was a commodity almost as important as securing loyalties—the reason he sent a summons to Simeon S. Hobson at the same time George Wells was in London conferring with the managers of Johnson, Walker, and Tolhurst about which side of what fence S.S. Hobson presently resided.

Dunn's summons arrived via the mail coach, and was not in the least unexpected by the Lewistown bank president. Hobson folded the imperious letter and used its edge instead of a pencil to tap on his desktop. The summons annoyed the banker much as his imperious summons of Jake Hoover had, years before, annoyed the mountain man; except that Hobson failed to appreciate any connection. With Hoover it had purely been an issue of personal freedom. But Hobson's was much more important: money. The banker tapped faster. He was under no delusion; Dunn's obsession was with power, not money (unless the money brought power). What should he do?

One thing was certain: Dunn's summons was to Great Falls; to his mansion, probably to the man's office. And Hobson was sufficient businessman-banker enough to know that to allow the coming confrontation to take place in the other's lair would place him at a decided disadvantage. Would Dunn threaten him? The banker nodded to himself. Not physically, of course. But the Great Falls investor wouldn't hesitate to utilize their mutual investments as a tool for coercion. Hobson locked his office door and pulled down window shades to insure privacy. Then he took several file folders from a drawer for review, hoping to armor himself by learning what investments Dunn could use against him.

At the end of the day, Hobson sighed, then drafted a carefully worded letter regretting his inability to immediately respond to Dunn's summons, using his Montana legislative responsibilities as reasons, such as the Billings hearing on Federal Imminent Domain procedures for proposed railway and roadway easements. The banker held the letter for a week before mailing, then boardrd a southbound stagecoach to the Yellowstone Valley railroad town.

A week later, Hobson arrived at his legislative office in Helena to find a legal notice from Dunn's attorney recalling a note owed by Hobson and held by Dunn. The note was for an investment in Red Lodge coal, originally for ten thousand dollars, but now reduced through partial repayment to five thousand, two hundred and seventeen dollars and sixty-three cents. The recall was no more than an annoying pinprick to the Lewistown banker, but he recognized it as a warning. He sent a bankdraft for the amount, bereft of any note, conciliatory or otherwise.

Again, Dunn sent his summons. This time, Hobson ignored it. So Dunn sent a foreclosure on a loan enabling Hobson to invest in Idaho silver. It was while the banker was in his Lewistown office, assembling funds to ward off Dunn's power moves that George Wells was ushered in to see him.

The English rancher was no fool. He'd not been in the office for more than a few seconds before his alert eye caught a folder with Matthew Dunn's name on it. Although he warmly grasped Hobson's hand, his response to the banker's greeting was to grin, nod at the folder, and say, "Don't tell me he's giving you a spot of trouble?"

Hobson waved at a chair, picked up the folder and slid it into a drawer. Then he asked, "What can I do for you today, George?"

Wells shrugged, "I'm in town and it's a bit late today for me to journey out to the ranch, so I thought I'd pop in and see if you might join me next door at the American House for a steak?" He thought he detected a flicker of wry humor in the banker's eye. Then it was gone.

"Thank you, George. But no."

Simeon Hobson was slightly taller than average height, with slender, supple physique—for which his high starched collar and dark seersucker suit seemed especially appropriate. He, as had Jake Hoover, arrived in Montana Territory from Maine. Though Hoover's and Hobson's families dwelled but a few miles apart, theirs was an insurmountable economic divide. Hobson's was a lumbering family, with sawmills and fishing fleets along the coast, and timber camps inland. It was the Hoovers—and ones like them—who supplied their labor. Oddly, both young men eschewed their heritage to follow Horace Greeley's advice to "Go West Young Man." Hoover, though still young, already possessed the skills of an advanced wilderness woodsman. But he arrived in Montana equipped only with a certain native intelligence and a willingness to work. Hobson, a few years older and well equipped in the ways of his family's finance, arrived with a sack of gold coins and advice on how to search for proper investments in the raw land. As did the Hobsons of Maine who invested in their robust Hoover neighbors, the Hobson of Montana invested in his own Hoover neighbor's search for precious metals and other valuable discoveries. Now the banker's challenge was in how to retain and profit from Hoover's sapphire discovery; a discovery his Maine contemporary had thrown away to follow yet another will-'o-the-wisp dream in far-off Yukon. Hobson stared disconcertingly at the Englishman, suspecting the man's visit had a reason; even suspected what that reason might be. But

181

heritage and experience told the banker to play his cards close to the vest.

"I've just returned from England," George Wells ventured.

"I knew you were away. It seems obvious that you've returned."

Wells' embarrassment was palpable. Yellowing teeth flashed beneath the handlebar moustache. "Might we talk."

Hobson pointedly swung his swivel chair so he peered through his office glass to the bank lobby where his clerks were pulling the outside shades and locking the front door. Wells murmured, "P'raps another time?"

Hobson turned back to his visitor. "What do they want, George?"

Wells face flamed. "I'm to see if you might consider selling your portion of the New Mine Sapphire Syndicate?"

"And their offer?"

"I say! Are you indeed interested?"

"No." But I am interested in knowing what kind of value your handlers might place on acquiring my portion."

Grandis, the clerk knocked and thrust his face through the door, with a raised eyebrow. "Go ahead home, Kelsay. But dim the lobby lights first. And lock the doors as you leave." The door eased shut. Hobson returned to his visitor.

"What did they authorize you to offer, George?"

"I told Mr. Tolhurst you wouldn't sell. I told both of them ..."

"What did they authorize, George?"

"Jake Hoover sold his quarter share for ..."

Hobson shoved back from his desk and stood. His tone was biting: "You've already insulted my intelligence by asking me to sell. Now you've insulted it further by assuming I'm no smarter than an illiterate grubstake miner."

The Englishman leaped to his feet, blurting, "They paid Dunn forty thousand for twenty-five percent."

Hobson sounded hollow. "So far, George, you've told me nothing I don't already know. Just to remind you, I asked what they authorized you to offer? Answer that, please. Or leave."

The still red-faced Englishman lifted his chin. "They said I could offer you fifty thousand American dollars."

Hobson settled back into his chair, waving George Wells back to his. "Now we're getting somewhere. Is that figure subject to their approval?"

"No. I'm authorized to go that high."

"And how high can you go subject to their approval?"

Wells, who'd only perched on his chair edge, shifted deeper into it, grasping that he was negotiating with a tough adversary. "I'm afraid I can't answer that question, Mr. Hobson. They were closer to their vest than that."

Tap, tap, went the banker's pencil. "You haven't even been to your ranch have you—since your return from England?" The other wagged his head. "And I assume you returned the same way you left, via the stage from Big Timber?"

"An elementary assump ..." was the flippant response Wells started to make, then changed it to a simple "Yes."

"Your ranch is much closer to the Moore stage stop than my bank in Lewistown. So your mission has some urgency, doesn't it?" Again the uplifted moustache and yellow teeth. "And if I refuse, you plan to approach Dunn with an offer?"

The visitor turned sober, shaking his head. "No, Hob. That would, I fear, take more courage than I possess, given the circumstances."

Hobson's two-minute stare was disconcerting to Wells

183

and the man began to fidget.

"Did you really tell them that I wouldn't sell?"

"I did."

"Yet they sent you out anyway to make an offer—an offer, by the way, that you bungled by insulting my intelligence." Wells again flushed, but Hobson seemed not to notice, merely appearing to be intrigued with the oak grain of his desktop, musing almost to himself: "I should think your masters would've sent someone with more talent, more experience...."

The Englishman muttered through clenched teeth: "I told them. I told them the only reason you would've voted against your own business partner was that you saw more value in the sapphire's potential than you saw in pursuing Dunn's self-inflicted destruction."

"... Yet your mission involved great haste. So much so that you never took time even to stop off at your ranch on the way." Hobson lifted his gaze to his visitor. "Don't you think it's time we're honest with each other, George?" Still fixing Wells with that penetrating gaze, he said, "Why, then, are you here?"

George Wells gazed out into the dimly lit bank lobby, then returned to the banker. "All right, Mr. Hobson ... by the way, may I call you Hob? I see your friends do." When the banker failed to respond, the Englishman continued: "To call a spade a spade, old chap, my principals are Johnson, Walker, and Tolhurst...."

Hobson interrupted: "Do they really dominate the gem market, as they claim?"

"Aye, they do. You would be wise to believe that." He waited to see if the other had more questions, then began again: "My principals thought it was in their interest to stem what they believed would be a glut in their lucrative sapphire market coming from you people's discovery...."

184

Hobson concentrated on the desktop, his pencil tap, tap, tapping. "Is their purpose, then, to halt production from the Yogo forever?"

"No, no, no...! Their intentions are ..."

"Because if that's their intent, my own course of action will become quite clear."

"Mr. Hobson ..." (though the banker never glanced up, he was aware of a new note of urgency) "... Brownstone Tolhurst's statement that his firm needed time to prepare markets to absorb additional sapphires is quite true. When those markets are established and ready, my principals will be in a position to work the Yogo mine extensively. That's the truth, so help me."

Again, S. S. Hobson stared at George Wells, stared through him. The small central office's gas light flickered, then brightened. Finally the banker softly asked, "Why are you here, George?"

"I do have a mission, much as you guessed. That mission is to give you any assistance we can should your relationship with Matthew Dunn go awry." Silence fell, then was brushed aside as the Englishman added, "That fact alone should help to assure you that Johnson, Walker, and Tolhurst intentions are parallel with yours."

"I'm interested in profiting from what may be the greatest gemstone discovery of all time."

"As is theirs."

Wells thought the subsequent silence nearly deafening. Though Simeon Hobson stared at him, he doubted he even registered on the banker. He chanced a glance at the bank lobby's drawn window shades. No daylight filtered in. Still Hobson seemed lost in thought. At last, the Englishman cleared his throat and asked, "How much of a financial lever does Dunn

185

have on you?"

"What makes you think he has any?"

Wells nodded. "It's an elemental guess, but if I'm to bare my soul, might it be fair for me to ask you to do the same?"

"You can ask. Whether I respond or not is up to me. After all, I'm not the solicitor here. You are."

"If, old chap, we're really honest with each other, we might question whether there are any solicitors here? Perhaps *supporters* would be a better choice of words."

"Meaning?"

"Meaning that we think Matthew Dunn is a quite vindictive man. One who would not hesitate to use coercion, perhaps even entertain violence to achieve his ends. Suspecting that you might have economic ties to the man ..."

"What makes you think that?"

"Why not? He's the one you first turned to after ..."

"Jim Bouvet was my first choice as an investor."

George Wells nodded. "But upon Bouvet's death, Dunn was the one to whom you turned." Hobson silence appeared to acquiesce. "My information was that you and Dunn had several investments together; has he invested in this bank?"

The question surprised Hobson, but again he took refuge in silence.

"At any rate, it's known that you supported Dunn in his struggle with Gibson over the character of the Great Falls community, and the man came out of that like a whipped puppy, right?" Met by more silence, Wells continued: "When I met him, he still seethed; a hooded snake ready to strike at something. Eh?"

Hobson pulled out a lower desk drawer to draw out a dimpled quart bottle of Haig & Haig and two glasses. "I say!" George Wells murmured.

"Is it good?" the unsmiling banker asked. "Brownstone Tolhurst brought it as a good-will gesture."

The yellow teeth stayed exposed as Wells reached for a glass.

"Now," Hobson said, "please continue."

"Well, old fellow, we think it unlikely you would've abandoned Jake Hoover to side with Matthew Dunn, had there not been a good reason. The only reason my principals could see was financial."

Hobson took a measured sip. "And it seemed equally obvious that the reason you sided with Johnson, Walker, and Tolhurst in the board altercation was also financial. Right?"

"Go on."

"We feel Dunn is a bloody type who, unlike Hoover, might turn on a supporter who might wish to deviate from his directives. Right?"

Both men peered over the top of their tilted glass. Their glasses returned to the desk at the same time. Wells murmured, "Are you in trouble, Hob? And if so, can we help?" As Hobson poured another dash in both glasses, Wells question was little more than a whisper: "How much does Dunn have invested in your bank?"

* * *

It was while the two men polished off their T-bone steaks at the American House that S. S. Hobson learned why George Wells had been dispatched to foster better relations with him.

"'Why should you trust me?' That's what you just asked, isn't it?"

Hobson nodded.

The Englishman chewed thoughtfully. "For one thing, I've not lied to you. I might not have told you everything, Hob,

187

but I've never lied."

"But you would if it was in your best interest."

Wells shrugged. "Let's hope we need not find out."

"What about Jake? You stole his share out from under us."

His table companion guffawed. "He certainly wasn't going to sell to Dunn. And admit it or not, he felt you'd betrayed him. I just happened to be there in the Utica saloon when he decided to give it up."

"Was it your money or theirs?"

It was the Englishman's turn to employ silence.

"Ah well, now tell me why your principals, as you call them, are so interested in me? Why not Dunn?"

"That's easy, old top. Dunn's reputation doesn't travel well. He's vindictive. He's not trustworthy. And he doesn't bring anything of value to my firm."

"Money?"

Wells chuckled. "Let me assure you, Johnson, Walker, and Tolhurst are financially sound. Dunn has nothing that interests them. But you? You're a respected Montana businessman, a state senator, and you are the keeper of the Bank of Fergus County, an institution my principals will certainly wish to utilize for their New Mine Sapphire Syndicate's banking needs. You have assets, Hob. Assets that transcends your one-quarter interest in Yogo sapphires. Believe me, Brownstone Tolhurst is *very* interested in tying your many assets firmly to Johnson, Walker, and Tolhurst. That's why he called me to London, gave me instructions, and sent me back to learn if there's any way we can help you if and when you have problems with Matthew Dunn."

"How much help did he authorized you to extend?"

Wells smiled, pushed his empty plate away and signaled

188

the waiter. "How much do you need?"

"No, George. That's not how it works. Assuming Tolhurst will want my stock in the Yogo as collateral, I want to know how broad a line of credit they'll extend?"

When Wells had ordered coffee, he said, "I'm not sure they'll extend a line of credit. A loan was what I gathered they had in mind."

Hobson smiled for the first time since George Wells loomed in his office. "Well you go back and tell them that what I want is a line of credit to the full extent of value they place on my Yogo interest. You see, my affairs with Matthew Dunn is somewhat tangled and I'm unsure how much I'll actually need to untangle them, but it'd be much to my benefit if I was assured of a sufficient amount to do so."

"It may take some time to get that kind of commitment."

"Take your time, George. You have clear up until I can no longer fend off Matthew Dunn's attempts to blackmail me."

Wells sighed. "I'll take a stage back to Big Timber in the morning and send a cable. P'raps I could have some kind of answer back for you in a couple of days."

Hobson nodded. "That might be soon enough. Dunn is demanding a meeting next week. Otherwise he says he'll foreclose on my bank."

They stood to shake hands despite a certain wariness. As they parted on the American House Hotel steps, S. S. Hobson added, "And George, I'll want something in writing that your outfit will begin mining operations at the Yogo after their three year grace period."

Chapter Twenty-Three

Matthew Dunn was livid! Not only had Simeon Hobson ignored multiple summons to the man to whom he owed considerable money, but by now—three months after the Great Falls financier's first attempt to confront the Lewistown banker—it was obvious Hobson was deliberately avoiding him. Finally he caught the State Senator in his Helena office.

To his credit, the senator affected a reasonably calm front. "All right, Matthew, what can I do for you?"

Dunn waved the two men behind him into the hall, then without shutting the office door, wheeled like a rabid dog. "It's not what you can do for me, you insufferable son-of-a-bitch, it's what you've already done to me!"

Hobson seated himself behind his desk without asking his visitor to take a chair. "If, Matthew, that's the most appropriate language you can use to a Montana State Senator, in his office, while the legislature is in session, then I'll have to ask the Sergeant-of-Arms to have you removed."

"That does it! Carl! Hubert! Do your duty."

The men, one of whom the senator recognized as a process server, stepped into the office. The process server shoved a paper forward and intoned, "Simeon S. Hobson you've been served with this demand warrant for payment of a loan against the Bank of Fergus County."

"And how much is the lien for?"

"I haven't any idea, sir. My role is to serve it. Mr. Draeger, here, is to witness that I've done so."

"It's for the full thirty-thousand," Dunn snarled. "And I'm demanding it!"

Hobson pushed a button on his desk. A chair scraped in

an adjoining room and a young man poked his head through a connecting door. "Henley, would you do a kindness for me and these gentlemen and ask Judge Leeper if he could spare a moment?"

The head disappeared and a couple of minutes later, Judge Adolph Leeper strolled into the room with an eyebrow raised. "Your honor I've just been served a properly executed demand note for a thirty thousand dollar loan I incurred some time ago. And as you are a man of unquestionable authority and impeccable integrity I'd like you to ..." Hobson reached into a drawer at his desk and took out several small buckskin bags that appeared heavy and tinkled as he threw them on the desk ... "witness the payment in response to the demand."

"Just a minute ..." the man referred to as 'Draeger' said. "I haven't added my work on collecting the note yet."

"What work, sir," Hobson said. "I haven't even read the demand yet. But I certainly stand willing to execute my pledge. How could you even think to have any collection role when I pay at the moment of demand?"

Judge Leeper was obviously puzzled, turning from one man to another. But he knew Simeon Hobson and liked him. And he also knew of Matthew Dunn, a man about whom few had anything good to say. The judge reached for the demand note and quickly scanned it. "I'm confused. Why does such a demand note require a process server?"

Dunn said, "I've tried to reach the son-of-a-bitch for three months and I wanted to make damned sure he ..."

Judge Leeper gently laid the paper on the desk. Then he turned to Matthew Dunn and mildly asked: "To which son-of-a-bitch are you referring?"

It was easy to see how this was developing. Dunn snatched up the sacks of double eagles and stalked from the from the room without counting their contents, followed by the process server and the Great Falls man's imported Chicago attorney.

* * *

On the first day of May, Matthew Dunn filed suit in Fergus County, claiming that a foreign national company was practicing restraint of trade on an American mining company and its American citizens. The suit was dismissed out of hand by Fergus County Judge Anthony Joubelier when the other American stockholder filed as a friend of the English defendents.

Within the week, Dunn's attorneys filed the same suit in U.S. District Court in Butte Montana, seeking federal jurisdiction to protect American citizens. That suit, too, was dismissed in the wake of several counter motions filed by the staff of English barristers representing stockholders Simeon S. Hobson and the firm of Johnson, Walker, and Tolhurst. It was noted in the dismissal, that Hobson, also an American citizen, held equal shares with those of Matthew Dunn, and that the total shares held by Hobson and the English firm was three times that held by the plaintiff.

"If merit was recognized in this suit," the deciding judge wrote, "the precedent could negatively affect any international operations, including those with majority ownership by U.S. citizens in other lands. Obviously such precedent is the province of the political and diplomatic processes, not one to be effected judicially."

* * *

Dunn's rout appeared complete. The only thorn he had left to combat Hobson and the hated English was his one-quarter interest in the Yogo sapphire mine. So he retired to his Great Falls enclave to brood. He caused each Hobson investment he'd financed to be recalled, only to have the requested payments

192

made in full every time.

His attempts to slander the Lewistown banker received little traction, especially ones stemming from a man as irascible and disliked as the Great Falls financier.

When 1897 turned the calendar with disappointing value results produced by the one-hundred thousand carats of sapphires accepted by Johnson, Walker and Tolhurst, Matthew Dunn had no witness to his angry private-office tirade as he crumpled the report and stamped on it. He tried to contact the New Mine Sapphire Syndicate Chairman, Simeon Hobson, but received only a terse noncommittal reply to his complaint.

Next was a demand for a board meeting with an equally terse response that the 1898 winter meeting had been rescheduled for late summer.

Again Dunn filed suit. Again it was dismissed.

His payout on the 1897 raw gemstones was six hundred and twelve dollars and six cents, all of which, he was advised, was retained for maintenance costs via an executive decision.

Dunn filed suit. This time he didn't even receive the courtesy of being advised the case would not be considered.

* * *

Matthew Dunn's talent was in simply dismissing his failures as though they never occurred. He began discreet feelers for buyers for his one-quarter sapphire mine interest. He turned down two offers that would return only fifty percent on his investment, one of which he thought might be another undercover agent for Johnson, Walker, and Tolhurst, Ltd. But when the wealthy Pittsburgh steel mill executive turned up with an interest in the Yogo, Dunn was all smiles.

Recollecting, however, his experience with George Wells (the personable Englishman Dunn thought was a remittance man) he was as wary as a thrice-trapped coyote.

193

However, Angus Macallister did everything right. The watermark on the New York law firm's letter of inquiry was traceable, and Dunn had it traced. Then he had an investigator discreetly check with Dashford Wallace, of Harmon, Peters, Lohman and Wallace to see if the man really had sent the query letter. When the investigator's response was affirmative, Dunn replied cautiously, yet encouragingly. Macallister's telegram was brisk and almost insulting, just as Dunn expected from a wealthy steel mill owner. Therefore Dunn issued an invitation. Instead of Macallister, the man's accountant arrived, a bent, middle-age gnome wearing a monocle, a vandyke beard, and a vandyke collar, who insisted only on examining Dunn's Yogo records.

The Macallister accountant, Mr. Leonard Marion, tsk-tsked through the meager records, made a few notes, then prepared for departure. Every attempt Matthew Dunn made to explain the Yogo situation in more cogently favorable terms met a blank stare. Obviously Mr. Marion was more accustomed to dealing with substance than abstracts. But the man did hold out a ray of hope when he said, "Mr. Dunn, I can only promise that my report will contain your request that you talk to Mr. Macallister in person. Whether he invites you to make a presentation is up to him."

Up to Angus Macallister? Matthew Dunn had the patience of a starving horse in the open doorway of a filled grain silo. He first telegraphed Macallister. Then he tried Alexander Bell's newfangled invention at the telegraph exchange's just-installed telephone service, finally giving up in disgust at the tedious wait, scratchy line noise, and incomprehensible voices when he was at last connected to someone somewhere. So he sent a registered letter. And after a month without response, he boarded one of the hated James Hill's Great Northern Pullman cars bound for Pittsburgh.

First, Angus Macallister was out of town. Then he was in a meeting, out of the office until Wednesday, and simply "unavailable". And finally, "Did Mr. Dunn wish to make an appointment?"

His Pittsburgh wait was an intolerable fifteen days, but finally Matthew Dunn was ushered into the august, fifth-floor presence of Angus Macallister. The appointment called only for an insulting ten minutes, but the Great Falls financier was well acquainted with intimidation employed during the process of financial negotiations; that he was granted an audience at all meant the steel baron's interest was intact.

Angus Macallister was tall, broad-shouldered, shaggy-haired, bushy-bearded, and stand-offish. He gestured to a hard ladderback chair on the opposite side of his desk, then raised an eyebrow. No greeting, no welcoming hand, no small talk. Dunn understood the opening was his. "I believe, Mr. Macallister, that you exhibited some interest in my sapphire mine?"

The brown eyes were expressionless, but the black beared exposed a hole enough to say, "That was before my accountant made his report."

"May I ask if that report included a copy of the government geological assessment on the extent of the mine, including its potential?"

Again the hole. "You can ask."

Dunn muttered to himself while the other remained expressionless, even bored. Dunn tried again, "There may be some extenuating circumstances relative to the mine that I was unable to impart to your accountant."

The hole said, "You referred to the mine as 'yours'. It's my understanding that the bulk of the shares belong elsewhere."

Dunn said, "That's what I mean. Half belongs to an

English gem firm who seem bent on withholding production to protect their existing gemstone markets. Unfortunately, my ally—at least I thought was my ally—who controls the remaining shares, abandoned me for the English."

"Why?"

"For, I believe, expediencies sake."

"Explain."

But before Dunn could launch an explanation, a clerk opened a side door and said, "It's time for your inspection tour, Mr. Macallister."

Macallister took a watch from his vest pocket. "Yes, uhm." He glanced up at Dunn and said, "I am scheduled to make an inspection tour of one of my mills. Perhaps you'd like to accompany me?"

Matthew Dunn's heart leaped! He knew then that he had his man!

* * *

Theirs was a 'walking-tour' of an Andrew Carnegie steel mill—Matthew Dunn never understood the connection between Carnegie and Macallister. But he did understand that the white-coated entourage accompanying them on the inspection proved Angus Macallister's importance to the operation; as did the extension top cabriolet waiting at the curbside as they exited Macallister's office building. Dunn was disappointed that he was pointed to sit by the liveried driver, while the steel baron and the accountant, Mr. Marion, had their heads together in the back seat while going over what Matthew Dunn thought were reports. He was disappointed, too, that mill personnel surrounded Macallister so closely, talking and gesticulating throughout their rather rapid walk-through, that he still had no opportunity to talk about gemstones to the host.

But on their return, Angus Macallister seated his

accountant by the driver and invited Matthew Dunn to sit with him. And when they reached Macallister's building, he bade the accountant to leave them and instructed his driver to drive down Duquesne Boulevard and around the old Fort Pitt Park. At last he said to Dunn, "You were saying your ally abandoned you in favor of the English, and I asked why? Please continue."

For the next two hours, Matthew Dunn explained how the English manipulated their shares in an attempt to limit Yogo production to benefit their sapphire gemstone monopoly. He went over the discovery in detail, along with an overview of its dimensions as per an analysis by the United States Geological Survey. He talked of studies conducted by three different mining engineers and how their reports were unanimous about the deposit's apparent endlessness. He discussed the mining operations to-date; about the gravity-feed, five-mile-long water ditch from Yogo Creek, the halfmile tunnel through limestone to penetrate the deposit at a lower level, the mine car rail tracks, lode rock extraction, the weathering pads (with a lengthy digression while he explained how he tried unsuccessfully to develop interest in more progressive extraction and rendering equipment). And finally, he outlined the administrative complex and access roads. Throughout Matthew Dunns two-hour discourse, the steel baron sat silent, listening, apparently absorbing, staring straight ahead. Only once did he move, to tap the driver on the shoulder and ask him to stop at the junction of the Allegheny and the Monongahela.

At the water's edge, the two financiers exited their cabriolet to stroll the shore path, Dunn still talking, Macallister still listening. Finally the steel baron held up a hand and asked more about the discoverers, Hoover and Hobson?

Dunn was terse about Hoover who, he claimed, was an illiterate prospector who lucked into the strike in an unorthodox

197

way. Hobson was merely Hoover's grubstake partner. Macallister asked what 'grubstake partner' meant? So Dunn explained the process widely used throughout the West as more prosperous investors subsidized knowledgeable or lucky prospectors by providing survival funds during their search for 'color' or, in this case, gemstones of high quality.

"So was Hoover knowledgeable, or just 'lucky'?"

Dunn shrugged. "I'd say he was lucky because I'm told the man didn't know a sapphire from a hole in his head."

"Had the man been 'lucky' before?"

Sensing a possible trap, Dunn answered truthfully: "Apparently he discovered two gold strikes earlier." When he sensed Macallister's eyes on him, he added, "So perhaps he wasn't merely lucky with the sapphires."

"Why is he no longer associated with the mine?"

"Frankly I'm glad he's gone. We sruck sparks. When I wanted to expand the operation with modern extraction methods, he opposed it."

"Why?"

Dunn was slow in responding. Finally he said, "I think by then he was adamantly opposed to anything I proposed."

"So did the English side with him?"

"The English weren't in the picture at the time."

"Oh? There were just the three of you?"

"That's right."

"Equal partners?"

"No," Dunn said. When Hobson approached me as an investor, my requirement was that I must have a fifty percent share. Hobson and Hoover both sweetened the deceased investor's one-third."

It was at this point that Macallister suggested a return to

their transport. "So you control fifty percent of the mine?" he asked.

"Non-controlling share. Hoover insisted on that."

The two were silent for perhaps a hundred yards, then Macallister asked, "How and when did the English come in?"

Dunn's laugh was hollow. "They came in by selling us a bill of goods. To explain, I must get into gemstone marketing...."

Their return to the cabriolet amid gathering dusk was used by Matthew Dunn in an attempt to explain the Yogo mine owners' search for a suitable gemstone market. He told how Simeon Hobson had sold their first cigar box filled with sapphires to the prestigious New York jewelry firm of Tiffany and Company for thirty-five hundred dollars and how the easy sale launched Hoover's and Hobson's frantic moves to tie up the gemstone dike. It also sent Hobson on a search for investment capital, resulting in James Bouvet buying a one-third interest for forty thousand dollars in development funds that ultimately disappeared via water ditch construction and the access tunnel to the sapphire-bearing dike.

Bouvet's untimely death, of course, brought Matthew Dunn's story full circle, with only a more comprehensive explanation of the appearance of Johnson, Walker, and Tolhurst, Ltd remaining.

And their sabotage of Yogo sapphire production.

* * *

As the two men climbed into the cabriolet, Macallister instructed his driver to take them to the "River House," a private club of prominent Pittsburgh business, industrial, and investment tycoons. When Matthew Dunn picked up his narrative where it'd been interrupted, the steel baron waved him away, "Later. Right now I'm famished. And I assume you are, too?"

199

Macallester's guest wasn't exactly unacquainted with opulence, but the River House exceeded anything he'd yet seen. The entrance door off a side street was ordinary enough to excite no comment, but once the visitor passed through that door into the hallway beyond, the extraordinary began. First was a huge man behind a stand-up desk. "Good evening, Mr. Macallister," the man rumbled. "Your usual table, sir."

Macallister nodded, and at the gatekeeper's raised eyebrow to Macallister's visitor, the steel baron jerked his thumb and said, "He's with me."

"Very good sir." And the gatekeeper apparently hit a hidden button and a second door swung open to reveal a lounge with several members at leisure, some before a ten-foot fireplace stuffed with eight-foot oak logs. Some members were in close conversation while seated on leather-covered benches lining two walls and equipped with silk-covered pillows and nearby footstools. Two aged members slumbered in deeply cushioned upholstered armchairs, and another was obviously engaged in an attempt to drink himself to oblivion as swiftly as possible.

A maitre d' hurried to the new entrants, saying "Welcome Mr. Macallister. Would you prefer a table right away, or perhaps a drink first? We just acquired a shipment of an excellent Bourdaise vintage from before the Franco-Prussian War—should you wish a bottle delivered to your table."

"The table, Elton, if you please. I'm afraid my guest and I are famished. And bucket the wine and send a bottle of sour mash with ice and a couple of glasses."

"Certainly, sir," the headwaiter said, waving at a white-coated servant hovering in a doorway. "Please escort these two gentlemen to the alcove room, corner table. And should there be no fire in the grate, torch it, then return here for further instructions."

The alcove room seemed to be the club's most remote. On the way, Dunn was struck by the rich mahogany paneling and the huge crystal chandeliers. There were no other members seated at the room's four other tables; no fire either. But tinder and coal were in place and shortly after seating them the servant bent to ignite the blaze. As he did, a second white-coated waiter hurried in with a tray containing a bottle of whiskey, two empty glasses, a small bucket of ice, and a pitcher of water. He laid a menu before each guest, then pulled the cork on the sour mash and asked, "Would you like me to pour, sir?"

Angus Macallister waved him away. The waiter said, "I'll return right away with the wine, Mr. Macallister. We all hope you enjoy your visit." Both servants exited the room together.

Macallister poured each glass half-full, handed one to his guest and said "Cheers" as he downed his in one gulp.

Dunn masked his failure to follow suit by hiding behind the menu. Macallister said, "The venison is superb. But perhaps someone from the wild west grows satiated on venison and would prefer lobster? The club's shipments arrive daily from the coast. Alive in special tanks you know."

Matthew Dunn laid his menu down, sipped from his whiskey and said, "I haven't had lobster since I left the east several years ago."

It was two hours later when at last Angus Macallister and Matthew Dunn rinsed in finger bowls, patted their lips with fresh napkins, threw off the last dregs of the Bourdaise and leaned back in their wing chairs. "Now," the steel baron said, "tell me how the English acquired their interest in your gemstone mine."

Matthew Dunn took a moment to compose his mind. In the interim, his host slid his chair to front the fire and gestured to

201

his guest to do likewise. "It all began," Dunn murmured, with the appearance of George Wells, who passed himself off as an English remittance man looking to acquire ranching property in the American West."

"Was he?" the other interrupted.

Dunn shook his head. "What he was was a spy inserted into our midst, who insinuated that he knew something about gemstone marketing right after we learned we needed more marketing knowledge."

"How did this man—Wells, was that his name?—know that you needed marketing help? He had to get this knowledge from somewhere. Did it come from one of your other partners? Hoover? Or the other one?"

"No. Neither knew Wells until I introduced them." The Montana man stared at his feet, then murmured, "I suppose he got his information from Tiffanys." Then he stared up at Macallister. "That would mean, of course, that the assholes was spying on an American gem retailer."

Macallister chuckled. "My, my, aren't we naïve?"

Dunn's face reddened, and his lips pinched while the larger man poked at the fire and waited. Finally the narrator's color returned and he said, "So I took Wells to a board meeting where he convinced we three shareholders that he could represent us to English markets."

"Just like that? For what in return?"

"Hobson. It was Hobson who said we might assist this Wells in locating suitable ranch property in return for marketing contact assistance across the ocean."

"And did you? Did he?"

"Hobson located the property Wells now owns. Yes."

"And that was in return for what?"

"He claimed he represented us to what we were given to

believe was the world's leading marketer of high quality gems and jewelry."

"Who is?"

"Johnson, Walker, and Tolhurst, Ltd."

"Do you doubt their redoubtability?"

Dunn shook his head.

"Tell me how this Wells represented you to the English firm."

Dunn took a deep breath, then said, "He displayed samples of rough stones, along with what we had in scanty engineering reports and prior investment construction. He said they asked for more samples, which he provided. And he said they decided to make a representation offer."

"And the offer was?"

"They would agree to be our exclusive marketing agent. But they wanted at least a one-quarter share of the mine to seal the offer."

"How did you handle that stipulation?"

Dunn took a deep breath. "I transferred half of my fifty percent share into an escrow account pending closure. They snapped it up as quickly as possible."

"I assume you were amply compensated for doing so."

Dunn recognized the 'fishing' expedition and tersely replied, "Well enough."

More coal was carried in for their fire and Macallister ordered cognac for both.

While waiting for their after-dinner drinks, the steel man asked, "Please explain your thinking behind bringing the English into the ownership."

"We wanted to tie them to our gems. To guarantee their representation. They'd agreed to the same market formula Tiffany had used in their previous purchase: So much for first-

203

and second-class rough stones, and so much for 'industrial grade' sapphires—I have their agreement, along with other relevant papers in the safe at my hotel."

Macallister thought it likely that his partner was growing more morose, a sure indicator that they were closing in on the crux of his English problem. "So the English controlled one-quarter of the mine operation. Yet you and your allies controlled three-quarters. How then are they able to halt the mining operation?"

"It was that goddamned Hoover. And that double-goddamned Wells. Hoover sold his share to Wells. Sold to an agent for the goddamned English! Probably in a drinking bout at the Utica bar. Maybe a gambling debt, for all I know."

"And I take it, Hoover didn't offer to you? Or to his original grubstake partner Hobson—why?"

Dunn tossed off the remains of his cognac, shook his head, and said, "Hoover and I had fallen out over his operation of the mine—he was manager, you know. I begged him to consider more modern rendering and recovery methods, but he flatly refused. Then when Hobson, his original partner supported me, he fell out with him, too."

"Then," Macallister asked, "is it possible Hoover sold to Wells out of a spirit of spite?"

Again Dunn's face reddened and he stared at his square-toed boots.

"So," the steel man said, "In essence, the English controlled half the mine's shares. But how are they halting production?"

"Through the marketing agreement. One of the stipulations for their exclusive was that production was to be limited for a period of three years to allow, so they said, for them to prepare their markets for the huge wave of American sapphires to come. When I discovered how tight they planned to squeeze production, I wouldn't sign the exclusive agreement. But when that other bastard—Hobson—abandoned me, they, in effect, shut mine production down."

"Completely?"

"For three years. It's restraint of trade! In America! By the sons-a-bitchin' English. I tried going to court, both Montana's and to the U.S. District Court. But when Hobson sided with the English, the attempts were dismissed."

"So you've fallen out with your last remaining partner, too?"

Macallister thought the toes on Dunn's boots must be very attractive to the man, but he masked his smile by softly asking, "And that s why you wish to sell your share of the mine?"

When his guest seemed only to sink further into gloom and silence, the steel man slapped him on the shoulder and said, "Come on. You'll spend the night at my estate. Tomorrow we'll send a man to close out your lodging, wherever it is, and bring your effects. From now on, you'll be my guest. That will provide us sufficient time to appraise your support papers and delve into your mine properties in depth."

When a wide-eyed Matthew Dunn's mouth corners turned to a seldom-used upward slant and the man leaped up to grasp his host's hand, Angus Macallister said, "You see I don't like the English either."

Chapter Twenty-Four

When he strolled the grounds in mid-morning, Matthew Dunn thought Angus Macallister's estate fit the man. The two had arrived from the steel baron's club only minutes before midnight. Dunn's room assignment and the following deep slumber meant the visitor shuffled down what he thought must be the grand staircase nearer to noon than breakfast. He was met by the butler who said Mr. Macallister had ordered him to arrange Mr. Dunn's hotel bill and retrieve his belongings.

"And Mr. Macallister?" Dunn asked.

"Oh, sir, he left for his office three hours ago."

The visitor accepted a poached egg, toast, and coffee, then received permission to walk the grounds unattended. The mansion was gabled, with turrets and at least two wings, constructed in a Tudor style. Vines clambered up the weathered shingled exterior. Shade trees abounded: large oaks and elms and maples. A four-foot stone wall surrounded the grounds, broken in three places: the main entry gate, an obvious service gate, and a carriage gate to outbuildings housing horses and carriages. A convenient flagstone footpath meandered through the grounds, accessing trellises, arbors, even a screened gazebo for summer entertaining. Two gardeners were at work in the grounds, one with a reel mower, one with hedge clippers.

Angus Macallister found him admiring the carp and goldfish swimming in a rock-lined pond that edged against one side of a gazebo. Dunn's host gestured inside the gazebo and said, "Shall we continue last night's discussion? Sinclair will be here with martinis in a moment."

Dunn swept an arm around, "You have a splendid residence, Angus. Very impressive." It was the first time he'd ventured toward familiarity and he closely studied his host's reaction. None seemed apparent.

"It's adequate. I tried to re-create the one commanded by the Laird of Dunlitch. But it's only a shell of that noble edifice."

Sinclair arrived with all the ingredients to mix martinis on site. A second servant trailed behind carrying a tray of caviar and crackers. He also carried Matthew Dunn's briefcase.

After the servant had shaken, poured, and retired, Macallister gestured at the case and said, "I presume that contains some documentation of your mine and its surrounding circumstances?"

Dunn nodded. He picked up the briefcase, noted with some satisfaction that it was still locked and idly wondered if the lock had been picked, then fastened again. He wished, as he unlocked the case, that he'd been careful enough to place markers, or bend document corners to reveal tampering, but sighing, he opened the case and withdrew a folder. "Let's start with this one, Angus—the just-issued U.S. Geological Report on the Yogo discovery...."

Macallister swiftly scanned the report, then set it aside. Dunn suspected the man was already privy to the report. But, then, the report was public information and his host could already have a copy of his own. Macallister sipped his martini and said, "I'd like to see your board meeting minutes."

Dunn dipped his head and drew out a file, leafed through it, and handed several sheets clipped together to his host. Macallister carried the minutes and his martini outside the gazebo, to a bench thirty feet away and spent the next fifteen minutes both reading and in thought while Matthew Dunn tried not to fidget or otherwise display nervousness.

Finally, Macallister ambled back to the gazebo, carefully laid his meeting minutes atop the U.S.G.S. report and said, "I

207

presume there are more?"

Dunn nodded, reached into his briefcase and said, "Yes, indeed. I have here copies of engineering re ..."

"No," Macallister interrupted. "I mean board minutes."

"No, sir. That's the only board meeting involving the English."

"Please don't toy with me, Dunn." Macallister waved at a servant who hovered at the far end of their path, and said, "This may be the only minutes with direct English involvement, but it cannot be the only one where they were discussed. I want to see them all."

Chastened, Dunn slipped a folder from his case and silently handed it to his host. The steel man laid it atop the other sheets and said, "They handled you a bit rough, didn't they?"

"I haven't forgotten it," Dunn muttered.

"But you're taking it lying down?"

"I take that as an insult, the smaller man flared, slapping another file folder on the table. "That's the judicial results of three different suits I brought against the English bastards."

That folder joined the others. Angus Macallister watched the butler set fresh martinis on the table. "Thank you, Sinclair. That will be all. Please tell Dalen that we would entertain dinner in the dining room in an hour." The servant bowed and backed away. As he did, the steel man murmured, "Yet both Wells and Hobson abandoned you."

A still hot-collared Dunn spat, "Wells never abandoned me—he was their man from the beginning."

"Yet you didn't discern that until they could use him to considerable effect. What of Hobson?"

"The bastard betrayed me, too."

"Too? Who else betrayed you? Do you mean the English? Or do you refer to Jake Hoover?"

208

"Hoover was an illiterate ..." then recalling what might be called damning evidence contained in the files now lying under Macallister's casual hand, Dunn continued with "... uneducated man without any scientific or engineering background." His host stared so fixedly at him that Dunn felt compelled to explain: "We just couldn't get along."

"So Hoover left. Does that constitute a betrayal?"

"It damn sure does, especially when he sold to that double damned English undercover spy."

"I see. But did he offer to sell to you?"

"I didn't know a damned thing about it until the English spy showed up with Hoover's bill of sale."

"All right. But did you offer to buy Hoover's shares?"

Dunn shook his head.

"Why not?"

"Dammit, sir, I didn't know he wanted to sell!"

Macallister slid a folder from the stack, drummed fingers on its stiff and flattened surface, murmuring, "Perhaps he didn't actually want to." He opened the folder, paused for a few seconds while staring at the top page, then closed the folder and said, "Still, you suspected nothing?"

Dunn jerked his head. "I thought Wells was on our side. I thought his would be a more trustworthy vote than the ignorant, unreliable Hoover. I thought we still controlled the mine operations with the three resident investors."

"Yet Wells was never yours and Hobson betrayed you."

Matthew Dunn leaped to his feet and strode to the edge of the fishpond. He could "feel" Macallister's eyes following him. At last he returned to confront his host. "Is this some kind of inquisition? If so, you're wasting your own time as well as mine. You already know I've lost control of the Yogo sapphire mine; you know I also want to sell my holdings. And you know why! I'm unwilling to have my management dragged through the mud if that's your intention. That's what I wish to know, sir: what is your intention?"

Angus Macallister met Dunn's fiery anger with almost a calm indifference. "My intentions, sir, as you so formally put my salutation, is to explore whether I wish to invest considerable fortune in an unusual proposition. To do so requires that I receive detailed information and that I ask probing questions. The overriding question is whether the English intend to suppress mining operations forever? And we have yet to approach that question, have we not?" When Dunn continued standing—though his ardor obviously began to cool—Macallister said, "Please sit down, Matthew. You haven't touched your second martini and hardly even sipped your first."

As Dunn settled to his chair, Angus Macallister gathered up the folders and said, "I'll carry these up to the library and study them while we wait for dinner. Why don't you relax here for, oh, say forty minutes, then return to the house. Sinclair will show you to the dining room."

* * *

By the time Matthew Dunn downed the two martinis and bemusedly studied carp and goldfish for a half-hour, his pulse rate had slowed to normal and he paced slowly to the house where lights had just begun to flicker.

Again, there were just the two for dinner—the entrée a standing rib roast done to perfection, pink and juicy on the inside, seared almost to charcoal on the outside, served on a table that could easily seat a dozen. Dunn wondered if there was a woman of the house, but could see no way to diplomatically broach the subject. Instead, since his host seem disinclined to further discuss the Yogo sapphire mine at dinner, Matthew said, "You indicated last evening that you had a low opinion of the

English, Angus. May I ask the circumstances?"

The mere fact that each was seated at opposite ends of the table, allowed distance to serve as something of a barrier. Macallister laughed. "You mean more is needed than merely being a Scotchman?"

"I'm Scots, too. So I can say 'yes' to that. But I didn't hate the English until they did me dirt."

Macallister took a swallow of port, patted his lips with a napkin and said, "In the steel business, one competes regularly with the English. Birmingham and Leeds wants to control steel supply worldwide, even to America. That competition is sometimes vicious. Need I say more?"

Dunn shook his head, but Macallister added, "Fortunately, America's railroad system is the envy of the world, and their trackage remains nearly half the world's total. Rail and rolling stock, coupled with ocean- and river-going vessels, along with armament: cannons, mines, light arms; then add in steel for girders and trusses for bridges and metropolitan towers and you'll find it constitutes the bulk of all industrial uses for steel throughout the world. Thus far we've staved off Birmingham's attempts to penetrate our North and South American markets. But the doing leaves me with no good opinion of the English."

"They're bastards!"

"Aye, they're that. And that's one good reason why I'm continuing this discussion with someone as touchy as you've proven to be."

"I'm forthright."

Macallister chuckled. "Yes, you are that. But I'm wondering if you can control your emotions sufficiently to continue our discussions until we can reach your asking price? We've yet to discuss money. And we've both been around long enough to recognize that any transfer of assets is going to hinge

211

on money."

"I wondered when we were going to reach that point?"

The steel man pushed back from the table. "Then should we repair to the library?"

Three of the library's walls were lined floor-to-ceiling with row after row of leatherbound books. The fourth wall was entirely taken up with rough stone and a fireplace. Inside the fireplace a brazier of reddish coals fluttered. The packet of folders Angus Macallister had earlier carried from the gazebo lay neatly stacked on a small, low table before the fireplace. Two deep armchairs perched either end of the table.

As the gentlemen settled into the chairs, the host said, "I do have one or two more background questions, Matthew: Why did Hobson abandon you for the English?"

Calm now, Dunn said, "I believe that question is properly answered in the last board minutes; Hobson is more interested in short-term profits than in considering the long-term possibilities. By ingratiating himself with the lobsterbacks, he hopes to make a tidy profit on his initial investment."

"Have you made no attempts to bring him back to the fold?"

"Certainly I did. We had several mutual investments where his portion was obtained with my backing. I began by calling first one, then another loan in." A pause. "But he made every mortgage recall, including a very substantial one on his bank."

"The English?"

"I'm certain of it. They're bankrolling him. They've got to be. Otherwise word of his new investor, or investors, would've leaked out."

A tiny ridge of coal collapsed in the brazier and both men stared into the sudden flare. Macallister asked, "What about

212

Clark? Or Daly? Or even Gibson? You do have Montana enemies, right?"

Still staring into the fire, Dunn murmured, "Gibson has some residue of distate for me, that's true. But he's already over-extended because of our recent townsite altercation— unless Hill came to his rescue."

Macallister shook his head. "I'm intimately acquainted with Jim Hill; we produce most of the rails for his road. And I doubt he'd become involved in anything not directly affecting his Great Northern Railroad."

"So it has to be the English," Dunn muttered. "They're insidious. They plant spies, plant operatives, buy off principals; they have a veritable espionage network in place. I can't beat them!"

Macallister laughed, then said, "How much do you want for your shares of the sapphire mine?"

"How can you do it?" Dunn asked, ignoring the question.

"Eh? How can I do what?"

"Beat the English in their control of the mine."

Macallister laughed again. Then he gathered up the folders and said, "I believe I'm equipped with all the information I need to make a decision about whether I care to become involved. All I need now is sufficient time to absorb what these files disclose. That's why I'm going to leave you to your own devices: think, read, stare dreamily into the fire, or retire for the evening."

At Dunn's obvious surprise, the steel baron said, "Tomorrow will be soon enough for us to discuss terms."

Chapter Twenty-Five

They met in the garden gazebo again, stared at in wonder from the abuting pond by suface-lipping carp and darting goldfish. The noon air was early summer balmy, with just the refreshing essence of a fitful light breeze. Matthew Dunn's file folders were neatly stacked by Angus Macallister's elbow, with fresh markers scattered throughout the files. "How much?" the steel man asked.

"One hundred and fifty thousand dollars."

There was the briefest of smiles on the host's face, averted now to a fascination with the carp and goldfish. "And what's the least you'll take?"

"One Hundred and fifty thousand dollars," Dunn repeated.

Macallister peered at his guest under beetle-like brows. "Matthew, Matthew," he murmured. "I understand the principle of starting high, then ratcheting down toward an acceptable agreed price. That's all part of the negotiating process." The larger man sighed. "But have you no shame?" He wagged his head. "Surely you're joking. Surely you're trying to inject a little humor into today's meeting, eh?"

Dunn's face was blank. "You asked, I responded"

"No you didn't. If you intend your number to be serious, then there's little advantage in negotiations going forward."

Dunn asked evenly, "What, then, are you willing to pay?"

"Five thousand dollars." But Macallister's figure was obviously banter, wasn't it?

"You're right, sir. This meeting has no future."

"All right, Mr. Dunn." Macallister was grinning now from ear to ear. "We've established endcaps to our negotiations:

One hundred and fifty thousand as the high; five thousand as a low. Now shall we strive to find acceptable numbers between?"

The two men fenced for over an hour, with neither demonstrating any willingness to give. Finally Macallister asked his guest, "Tell me, Dunn, what was your dividend payout last year?"

Matthew Dunn clammed up. "That's privileged information! You know that. I can tell you that whatever it was, it's hardly indicative of the potential and reflects the divisive battle currently going on between stockholders."

Macallister picked up a folder, laid it down. "Let's get real, Mr. Dunn; it was six hundred and twelve dollars and six cents, wasn't it?"

Dunn sank back into his chair. "How could you know that? It wasn't information contained in any of those folders."

Macallister's countenance, formerly smiling, was now stern. "And you were enamored with a goddamned jewel merchant's espionage system! Damn it, man, I represent one of the world's top steel companies. We don't just put pretty rings on dainty maidens' fingers, we sell steel to countries where they make cannons and guns and build warships to humble nations! The people I deal with aren't playing drawing room games. Don't you think I must have accurate reports about my competitors? Getting inside information from Johnson, Walker, and Tolhurst was child's play—including their gemstone payout to the New Mine Sapphire Syndicate stockholders for last year."

Dunn's mouth hung open; if his jaw was hanging from a flagpole it would be at half-mast.

"Now," Macallister whispered, "do you think I'll be able to hold my own against the English?"

Dunn nodded, murmuring, "And repay Simeon Hobson in kind for selling out America?"

"And get even for you with the Lewistown banker."

The host patiently waited for his guest to process what the steel man was saying. Finally Dunn murmured, "I'll take one hundred thousand."

Macallister guffawed. When he ran down, he said, "Jake Hoover sold his one-quarter for five thousand, and you're asking twenty times that for a discovery that produces less than it did when Hoover managed it? Face reality, Dunn."

"Hoover was an illiterate ... he could've got ..."

"Eight times as much? That's what you sold twenty-five percent to Johnson, Walker, and Tolhurst for—forty thousand."

Dunn jumped up, overturning his chair. He trotted around the fishpond, then returned to the gazebo. Beaten, he said, "I'll take my folders back now."

"Certainly," Macallister said, pushing the stack across the table. "But you'd better reconsider walking out of here if you think anyone else will pay as much for your shares as I will."

Dunn tucked the stack of folders under his arm and started away, but stopped. He turned. "Then tell me what you're willing to pay to become a player in the Yogo sapphire game?"

Macallister stroked his chin while again studying the tabletop. At last he looked up and said, "Oh, for Christ's sake, sit down. It's taken a while, but we're getting somewhere now."

Dunn righted the overturned chair and slowly sank to its edge.

"I'll give you twenty-five thousand ..." one look at Dunn's suddenly reddening face changed it to "... no thirty thousand."

Dunn sank back into the chair. "I won't take a penny less than what I already have invested in it—forty thousand. And that's that!"

Macallister pulled two cigars from an inside coat pocket,

216

slid one in front of Dunn, bit an end off his and lit it. Pondering his guest for what seemed to Dunn forever, the steel man at last blew out a big cloud of smoke and said, "I should think you might consider what you'd be getting Mr. Dunn: revenge for one thing, satisfaction in escaping a bad situation for another. Thirty-five thousand."

Dunn pushed his cigar back across the table and said, "How long until martini time?"

Macallister strode into the garden, talked briefly with a gardener that Dunn wasn't aware was near, then returned. The folders were back in the middle of the table.

"Forty thousand," Dunn repeated.

Macallister toyed with the corner of one folder. "No, Matthew. If I paid you forty thousand for this fucked up mine mess, I'd be letting you escape responsibility for your bungling." When Dunn's hackles began to rise, Macallister's voice rose with it. "Come now, these folders disclose how badly you bungled your involvement. You can get pissed off about it, or you can cut your losses without totally losing your investment. I'll compromise for the last time—I'll pay you thirty-eight thousand."

The martinis arrived. After the servant moved away, Dunn picked up the glass and over the rim, said, "Thirty-nine."

Macallister murmured, "Thirty-eight, five."

Dunn swallowed once, twice, three times, then thumped his empty glass down and said, "Done!"

* * *

Three weeks later, Brownstone Tolhurst announced at the annual summer meeting of the New Mine Sapphire Syndicate that Johnson, Walker, and Tolhurst, Ltd. had recently acquired Matthew Dunn's shares in the Yogo operation....

217

Bonus: Chapter 1 of *Sapphires At War*, Book 2 in the *Sapphires of Yogo Series*, next page

Bonus: Sapphires At War
by Roland Cheek
Chapter One: Excerpt

Sapphires At War

Chapter One

They made a striking couple as they emerged from the stage amid the swirling dust of a windy day during Easter Week, year of our Lord, 1903. Only moments before there'd been clattering hoofs on the hard-packed road, and the bounce and jounce of the swaying coach. Then sawing reins and a shouted "WHOA!" from the driver brought the horses to a sudden halt in front of a long log cabin with a sign above its single door: 'Utica Hotel'

"She's near 'bout the sweetest thing," Pete Weatherwax told bartender Hanley Duncan, who sagely nodded. Pete added, "Better lookin' than a bowl full o' turnips after a long winter." The cadaverous man stepped outside the batwings for a better look, then ambled back inside. Both men had gone to the swinging doors to view the town's single predictable social occasion—arrival of the thrice-weekly stage.

"Reckon it's the new mine manager?" Weatherwax asked after he dumped two fingers of whiskey in both the bartender's glass and his own.

Duncan shrugged. The barman picked up Pete's whiskey bottle and swabbed with an almost clean rag at an imaginary spot beneath. "Prob'ly. Don't the fella look like the one what left last fall?"

Weatherwax patiently waited for the whiskey bottle to be repositioned so he could reach it should any emergency arise. "Beats me, he muttered. Lobsterbacks been coming and going out at the Yogo so thick I can't keep track." When all Duncan said or did was shake out his rag, Weatherwax picked up his glass and said, "Here's to you!"

Hanley Duncan return-saluted his lone customer.

Out in the single Utica street—actually the main road up the Judith Valley—the young man assisted the elegantly dressed lady onto the hotel's board sidewalk, then returned to the coach's rear luggage compartment to help the driver struggle with two large trunks bearing shipping tags from the trans-oceanic "White Star Line."

A lounger who'd been whittling while perched on the board sidewalk stood, dusted himself off, tipped his hat to the lady, folded the knife, then helped haul one trunk inside the hotel.

A second man, greasy and bald and wearing the leather apron of a blacksmith, also hurried to help.

As the second trunk was carried inside, a buxom gray-haired lady of indeterminate age came from the kitchen, dusting flour from her hands. "I declare, is this Mr. Gadsden? It surely is! Where is she?"

The man's smile was broad and winsome. "Good afternoon, Mrs. Waite," he said with a clipped British accent. "I shall bring her inside in a moment." He threw arms around the shoulders of the two Utica gentlemen who'd helped with the trunks and, as all three men passed back outside, said, "You, sirs, are scholars and judges of fine whiskey, which, if you'll step next door, I'll buy."

In a few moments, the handsome Charles T. Gadsden

returned to introduce his recent bride to the hotel proprietress. "This Madam Waite, is Maud Margaret Gadsden, recent resident of Birkenhead, County of Cheshire, England, and a threatened old maid until rescued by a"—grinning, he avoided a kick in the shin—"shining white night from across the broad water."

Mrs. Waite said, "Old maid, hmph! She hardly looks out of her teens." The elder woman grasped Maud Margaret by both hands, then murmured, "My, my, you are the lovely one, aren't you?"

The Britishers were indeed a handsome couple. Hers was an unblemished heart-shaped face, framed in the current popular style that permitted no sun ever to burnish the image. The face was inset with a button nose and wide, saucy blue eyes. Rich blonde curls framed the cheeks, falling well below her shoulders. The lips were an unpainted pink. She was clad in a close fitting plum-colored habit with extravagant lapels and buttons of pearl down the front. A high-necked white silk blouse squeezed through the habit's lapels, and brown leather riding boots peeked from beneath the habit's skirt.

For his part, Charles Gadsden seemed tall enough, though close inspection proved his presence was more commanding than overwhelming. His was an open face, angular, browned from exposure and possibly from a 'black-Irish' heredity. The eyes were as drops of chocolate, hair thick and dark and wavy, nose straight, lips—what one could see beneath a drooping shoe-brush moustache—were full and curving upward. Beyond the moustache, dimples winked either side. The man's attire was of forest green corduroy. His trousers were pulled over the tops of coal-black boots that were shined to brilliance. He, too, wore a white silk shirt beneath an unbuttoned jacket. The shirt was open at the throat.

Charles Gadsden held out his hand to the Hotel

proprietress. "Then am I to suppose, Mrs. Waite, that you approve of my choice of a foot-warmer for cold wintry evenings?"

The elderly lady perused the young bride, saw only good-humored pride for a husband she obviously adored. "Well," Mrs. Waite murmured, "if I were you, Mr. Gadsden, I don't think I'd wait for winter."

Charles Gadsden had originally arrived at the Yogo from England during the summer of 1899, in the company of two school chums. The three young men accompanied English mining engineers Lansing McWilliams and Reginald Kensington and were to comprise the labor battalion as the New Mine Sapphire Syndicate prepared to re-open the dormant Yogo Sapphire Mine.

Owned primarily—now that Matthew Dunn had been squeezed out—by the London gem firm of Johnson, Walker, and Tolhurst, Ltd, adjudged their market sufficiently prepared to absorb a modest increase in world sapphire production. Though the lone original discovery holdout—Jake Hoover's grubstake partner, Simeon Hobson— still retained his twenty-five percent block of stock, negotiations were under way to obtain that last vestige of American ownership.

"We'll want to set the mine up to weather the companion rock for three years," Lansing McWilliams told his employers in 1898. "If we begin mining operations next year, it'll be at least 1901 and probably '02 before we can get production into full swing."

"Good!" Brownstone Tolhurst exclaimed. "Two or three more years of but a few pounds return will lay our Mr. Hobson by the heels sufficiently well to transfer that bloody Yogo millstone to our account, what?"

It was mid-July before the English team arrived at the

Yogo mine. The first order of business was for the two engineers to survey and mark out a series of additional holding pads for ore storage, one after the other, stairstepping down the hill toward the Middle Fork of the Judith.

McWilliams hired a lead carpenter and obtained several wagonloads of tongue- and-groove "car decking" for pad construction. Then leaving Kensington, the junior engineer, to design both tramway system and water pipes to each individual pad, McWilliams spent the remainder of that season's mild weather mapping the extent of the sapphire-bearing dike and estimating the number of shoring timbers needed for a full season's work.

The first full-scale winter blizzard blew in during October and blew out Jeremy Waterston, who had little stomach for below-zero Montana when the balmy south of England beckoned. With the pads and trams not yet completed, the remaining carpenter crew shoveled snow and marked time until the second blizzard struck on New Year's Day. Melvyn Lexington jumped the Yogo for England after that second blizzard, and Lansing McWilliams decided to lay off Dolph Galla, the lead carpenter, until Easter.

Reginald Kensington was next to leave, returning to England, so he said, for a fortnight's holiday. When one fortnight stretched into two, three, four, and eight, McWilliams elevated his sole remaining English comrade, twenty year-old Charles Gadsden to the Yogo's second in command—an elevation without any real portfolio when only the two Englishmen and a watchman constituted the Yogo's full winter's crew.

But the following spring ushered in momentous change. First of all, Dolph Galla returned to complete the series of storage pads and tram systems, bringing with him his own crew.

Meanwhile, Lansing McWilliams and Charles Gadsden devoted most of their attention to getting the Yogo into mining condition.

Gadsden, displaying a remarkable and previously unknown mechanical wizardry, busied tuning up the mining equipment while McWilliams devoted his efforts to obtaining a crew of experienced miners. Gadsden also provided oversight for Galla's construction, and welcomed two teamsters and a blacksmith to the crew.

Before April turned into May, one shift of miners began work—two four-man crews, digging both ways along the sapphire-bearing dike at the three hundred-foot level. Ore spilled onto the original leaching pads Jake Hoover had designed and cleared and Galla's carpentry crew went to twelve-hour days to extend the tramway scaffolding as needed.

Lansing McWilliams returned at the end of May with a second-shift mine crew and Charles Gadsden was assigned the duty of overseeing that night shift.

By the end of June, thirty-one men toiled in the New Mine Sapphire Syndicate's Yogo operation, spilling ore-trucks filled with crumbling gray-green host rock onto a stepping-stone series of washing pads. By the end of June, Dolph Galla's carpenters had finished all trestle scaffolding and two blacksmiths toiled to lay tracks and switches and hand brakes and metal-plated spillways along the tramways.

Both teamsters were kept busy hauling sheet iron and dimension lumber and loads of coal to fire boilers and cooking and heating stoves. Barrels of flour and beans and sowbelly and beef were wagon freighted to the hungry mine crew, where feeding the mass was more than two cooks could handle during a twenty-hour operating day. So two helpers and a third cook were thrown into the cookhouse mix.

The now thirty-four member crew, of course, was so

large that armed guards were employed to bring the payroll from the railhead. Meanwhile, cowboys and ranchers and a single banker from Lewistown rode out to watch the beehive of daylight-to-dark activity.

Throughout 1900 and 1901 great heaps of ore was piled on the Yogo's weathering pads, repeatedly soaked and exposed to the elements. But none of the deteriorating ore was washed through the sluices. And when the year 1902 rolled around with additional stockpiling going on while it was still all financial outgo and no income at the Yogo, Simeon S. Hobson threw in the towel and sold his twenty-five percent interest in the mine to Johnson, Walker, and Tolhurst, Ltd. for one hundred and fifty thousand dollars (less the eighty-seven thousand, four hundred and twenty-two dollars he had already borrowed against his hundred thousand letter-of-credit with the English firm).

As soon as the transfer was consummated, a cable to Lansing McWilliams crossed the Atlantic with only two words: BEGIN WASHING.

When the sluicing began, it was carried out by McWilliams and Gadsden, supervisors who could be trusted not to high-grade rough stones of gem quality. But it soon became apparent that the scale of the job was too much for the British supervisors alone. Thus Pete Weatherwax, who already had previous sapphire washing experience back in Jake Hoover's time, was hired. In addition, Pete vouched for Lawless Laulis's integrity, and the second aging Yogo Gulch placer miner was hired to help direct water and crumbling ore into the sluices. Meanwhile Charles Gadsden kept the tramway machinery running and the sluice traps emptied, while Lansing McWilliams maintained oversight.

Sluicing and its consequent recovery of raw gemstones stopped with the onslaught of winter weather, but mining and

225

stockpiling the crumbling gray-green dike rock continued full apace.

Then Charles Gadsden was ordered to accompany the latest shipment of Yogo gemstones to London, with a directive to report to the owners upon arrival.

Until ushered into the display lounge of Johnson, Walker, and Tolhurst, Ltd., Charles Gadsden had never seen such opulent surroundings. The chair to which he was directed was of Roman design, with velours upholstery and richly carved mahogany legs and armrests. The floors were carpeted in deep Persian wool. Silver chimes tinkled at the doors and sunlight was multi-color refracted through stained-glass inserts in high cathedral windows.

Gadsden had paused in New York sufficiently long to purchase a suit of top quality wool cheviot cloth; dark brown and with the occasional twist of gray thread in round cut sack style. Grinning at the recollection, he'd taken it at face value when the clerk told him his new suit "will stand wear, hold its color, and retain its shape."

The suit, coupled with his MacHurdle full dress shirt with changeable collar and silver cuff links (three for $4.85), along with the shiny new satin calf dress shoes, made him feel ridiculously elegant. "But," he whispered to himself as he flicked at an imaginary speck of dust on the Trebor hat perched on his lap, "at least I'm in keeping with the tenor."

Across the lounge, two clerks hovered around an elegantly dressed elderly couple the young Yogo mine foreman took to be Continentals; but what nationality, he couldn't guess. One of the clerks hurried away with what looked to be a golden tiara perched on a satin pillow, then returned moments later with a glass-fronted display case, probably holding an assortment of faceted gemstones.

"Mr. Gadsden?"

His head snapped around. "Yes."

"Would you be so ever kind as to follow me, sir. "He knew he was being ushered into the august presence of Brownstone Tolhurst—the name etched into the frosted glass of the end-of-the-hall double doors told him so. The usher opened both doors at once, paused, and said, "Mr. Gadsden, sir."

The man who leaned back in an upholstered swivel chair was huge. And corpulent. Gadsden wondered if the gold watch chain spanning the opening in his coat and vest actually held a watch, or whether it was anchored on each side to hold together the man's straining middle? He pushed ponderously to his feet, took the half-chewed cigar from his mouth, and waved his young arrival from America nearer. When Gadsden stood across the desk, Tolhurst leaned forward to extend a hand. "You're Gadsden, right? I'm Brownstone Tolhurst."

Tolhurst nodded toward the servant. "Kind enough of you Weystruth. Would you do me the privilege of conveying the news of Mr. Gadsden's arrival to Mr. Walker."

"Right away, sir." The doors clicked quietly as he retreated.Tolhurst gestured to a plush chair. "Um, yes. Do have a seat." The young man had no more than taken the proffered chair when he again leaped to his feet as the firm's second partner, a white-haired, tall, thin, older gentleman tottered into the room from a previously hidden door that swung a section of bookcase aside as it opened. After introductions were made and Charles Gadsden and Brownstone Tolhurst had again taken their seats while Ernest Walker leaned at the window, gazing disinterestedly outside, Tolhurst said, "We wish for your report on the New Mine Sapphire Syndicate's operation in America." He let his words settle for a few seconds, then added, "Tell us what marvelous things we might learn from your experienced

227

observation."

Charles Gadsden twisted uncomfortably, wondering if he was expected to criticize Mr. McWilliams' management? "Lansing McWilliams is a splendid manager, sirs, if that's what you mean. He's impeccable in both his work and personal habits, and his performance is outstanding. Besides that, he's ..."

"That's not what we mean, young man," Tolhurst growled. "Our confidence in McWilliams knows no bounds. It's you in whom we're interested."

Charles' heart leaped. "May I ask in what way, sir?"

"How do you find America?"

"How do I find...." The young man eyed Mr. Walker, but he responded to Mr. Tolhurst's question. "I like it. It's wild, but it's free. It's raw and its people are rough, but there's a certain peace there, too."

"What do you know of the mine's prospects?"

Charles gazed down at his new hat while choosing his words. Then he gazed up at Brownstone Tolhurst's porcine face. "What I *know* and what I *think* may differ, sir. What I know is that we've moved roughly four thousand tons of gemstone-bearing rock from the mine; that we've recovered eighteen hundred tons from which we've taken approximately seven hundred and fifty thousand carats of uncut gemstones, seventeen percent of which is of a size for cutting. What I think is that ..."

Brownstone Tolhurst interrupted. "Mr. Walker and I are given to believe you've brought one stone of nine carats in the last shipment."

"And another of eight carats and three more of seven."

"And what do you think?"

"The mine is absolutely unlimited. Mr. McWilliams and I both concur that we should start a vertical shaft down into the bowels of the discovery with twin purposes, to better examine

228

its dimensions, and to see if there's a chance of extracting larger stones from the discovery's depths."

Ernest Walker turned from the window and tottered over to perch on the edge of Tolhurst's desk, but he continued to avoid looking at the young miner.

Gadsden took a deep breath. "Of course, if you gentlemen wish increased production, a vertical shaft as well as two horizontal ones can employ a much enlarged crew of miners." When neither of the two Yogo owners commented, he added, "I think."

Tolhurst's eyes met those of Walker. Then he said, "What of your compensation? Are you satisfied?"

Charles nodded. "I feel I've earned both opportunity and its financial reward, sir. I've received both."

"If you were in charge of the Yogo mine, Mr. ... ah ..." The big man fumbled for a sheet of paper on his desk and young man wanted to help Tolhurst by reminding him that his name was Charles Gadsden, but he hesitated. Meanwhile his heart was beating a staccato tattoo on his ribcage. "... Yes, here it is—Mr. Gadsden—could you follow the policies of your predecessor while taking direction from the owners? Give guidance to a crew? Maintain desired production levels?"

"Yes! Absolutely, sir!" Then the young man's face colored. "But, sir, I'm not a mining engineer."

Brownstone Tolhurst swiveled his chair to glare at light streaming through the window, then swept back, noting Ernest Walker's brief nod as he did. "Lansing McWilliams wishes to return to England. He recommends you as his successor."

There was a gasp, then silence. At last, Charles Gadsden murmured, "I'm quite young, sir, only twenty-three."

"McWilliams has nothing but praise for your talent, industry, and commitment to the work. I will hazard with some

229

confidence that age has nothing at all to do with those attributes."

Charles again studied his hat. When he looked up, he said, "This will require a dedication to America, won't it sirs? You must be tiring of Englishmen without tenacity, who flee back home at the slightest reverse."

Brownstone Tolhurst murmured, "I trust you're not talking of Lansing McWilliams."

Charles cursed himself, blurting, "Oh no, sir!"

Both owners were peering at him now. He said, "I would be happy to accept, sirs, with one condition—that I'm permitted to take ship from Liverpool and that I'm accorded sufficient leave to visit Birkenhead—which is just across the bight—and take a wife."

Ernest Walker's face appeared as sorrowful as that of a bored bloodhound. For the first time, he spoke to their new mine manager: "An insistence on celibacy is not a requirement for a position at Johnson, Walker and Tolhurst, young man."

This constitutes the end of the first chapter of *Sapphires At War,* book two of the *Sapphires of Yogo* series.

Visit Roland Cheek's "Storefront" page for additional titles by this author:

http://www.rolandcheek.com/RolandsStorefront.html

Nonfiction

Learning To Talk Bear
The Phantom Ghost of Harriet Lou (about elk)
Dance On the Wild Side
My Best Work Is Don At the Office
Chocolate Legs
Montana's Bob Marshall Wilderness

Fiction

Echoes of Vengeance
Bloody Merchants War
Lincoln County Crucible
Gunnar's Mine
Crisis On the Stinkingwater
The Silver Yoke

The Dogged and the Damned

(more)

Unless you're largely devoid of most outdoor graces, or at least outdoor inclinations, you might appreciate exposure to others of Roland Cheek's work. Perhaps the best single location to find a range of his work will be through his website at:

http://www.rolandcheek.com/

* You can visit his bookstore, view each of his dozen or so books, read their first chapters, and, should you wish, order print copies directly from the author at discount prices.

* There are also links to Roland Cheek's page on Amazon's Kindle store where most of his titles can also be downloaded into electronic reading devices at reduced prices.

* While you're on his website, perhaps you'll want to visit Roland's and Jane's audio/visual library where they take you on the 1930's construction of Ptarmigan Tunnel in Glacier National Park, demonstrate the magic of Jane's campfire lobster (and other culinary delights), and lead you on an expedition to track the ancient Anasazi.

* And finally, there're are Roland's blogs:

"Campfire Culture is the long-running weekly outdoor's blog, where Roland brings decades of experience throughout much of the mountain West to your reading pleasure. Posted each Saturday. Click here to follow him vicariously through a lifetime of adventure:

www.rolandcheek.com/Newcampfireculture/index.html

Then there's his sometimes irreverent, sometimes humorous, sometimes introspective "Mountain Musing" blog, most often posted each Tuesday. This blog has, over time, evolved into picturing Roland's love affair with America's best-loved Wilderness: the Bob Marshall. With over 2,500 photos taken over a forty year period, it's unlikely he'll run out in this lifetime.

http://www.rolandcheek.com/Mtn%20Muse/mtnmuse.html

Finally, it's not too hard to find some of Roland's stuff exposed elsewhere. Google "Roland Cheek" and you'll find hundreds of listings where his work may be found.

He's proud of his craft; proud to be have lived and loved in the Mountain West; proud of a wealth of stories acquired during a lifetime of adventure. Nothing will please him more than to see readers seeking out and browsing through pages he's smeared with his own creative blood.

Thanks for being you!